G.A. CHARNOCK

Veil of Secrets

Book One in the 'Secrets of the Veil' series

GAC

First published by GAC Publishing 2020

Copyright © 2020 by G.A. Charnock

This novel is entirely a work of fiction. The names, characters and incidents portrayed in it are the work of the author's imagination. Any resemblance to actual persons, living or dead, events or localities is entirely coincidental.

G.A. Charnock asserts the moral right to be identified as the author of this work.

First edition

ISBN: 978-1-9162399-0-6

This book was professionally typeset on Reedsy.
Find out more at reedsy.com

For Mum & Dad, with love and gratitude

"There's nowhere you can be that isn't where you're meant to be."

JOHN LENNON

Contents

Acknowledgement

Firstly, thanks to my mum and dad for all they do, for their unwavering support and guidance, and for just 'being there'.

And, of course, to Niall, my long-suffering husband who's been forced to listen to me witter and prattle on about the ups and downs of writing my first book - your patience and understanding know no bounds!

I am also grateful to Claire Wingfield, literary consultant extraordinaire, for not only helping me edit the book into a solid second draft, but for giving me the confidence to bite the bullet and publish it. If it hadn't been for your encouragement and inspiring words, I can honestly say, I would never have done this.

Prologue

Genevieve steadied herself against the cold marble of the mantelpiece.

"I'm tired of this, Gabriel. I don't think I can do it anymore."
She closed her eyes, her throat tightening as the words tumbled
freely at last.

"Do what exactly, my dear?" he huffed, looking out onto the
sprawling landscaped gardens of the estate. "A bit of high-society
mingling and some needlepoint? Of course, there's your reading—"
he paused, clasping his hands behind his back, "—and the painting
lessons..."

He turned towards her; the first eye contact they'd made since
she'd entered the room.

"They're becoming a lot more frequent these days, aren't they?"

He shot her a cold, hard stare. She brushed an invisible fleck of
dirt from her dress, trying desperately to conceal the fluster in her
cheeks.

"Yes, it's a passion of mine now – I don't deny it." The quiver in

1

her voice all but negated the conviction. Her heart pounded as her eyes slid to the elaborate carvings on the fortepiano in the corner.

"I don't doubt it for a second." His thick heels clicked sharply on the polished wood as he marched towards her. She flinched as he swooped in, the coarse fibres of his blond wig scratching her ear. "As long as you keep it a secret, Genevieve. I'm afraid I don't do public humiliation very well."

Heat roiled in her belly as she subtly pushed her precious fabric further down inside the drawing bag dangling from her wrist. "Of course," she said smoothly. "Anything to avoid upsetting you, Gabriel."

Their eyes met and locked in silence – conveying more than words ever could. Gabriel dropped his gaze then made for the gilt-edged doors leading to his private chamber. He stopped; his hand resting on the curved gold handle as he glanced over his shoulder. "Just be discreet, that's all I ask."

She smirked at the irony. His less than subtle dalliances with the stable boy were the worst-kept secret in the chateau. She certainly wasn't going to be the one to tell him that his frequent trysts hadn't gone unnoticed.

"You knew the deal before the wedding. So it's a little late for regret now, mmm?" He tugged at the sleeves of his lilac silk jacket as though they were a source of immense irritation. "The sooner you provide me with an heir – maybe even a spare – the better for us both, yes?"

A warm tear spilled down her cheek onto the stiff bodice of her dress; the exact spot where her beloved pendant kissed her skin beneath the blue embroidered silk.

The bedroom doors clicked shut and Genevieve stood alone in the room, thinking about the façade of togetherness they would dutifully re-enact for the invited aristocracy that evening. She'd long perfected the regal smile, polite chit-chat and perfunctory handshakes. But it was the intimacy of the dancing or the moments he would snatch her hand for effect, that made her want to weep; made her heart break just that little bit more.

She stepped out into the dim hallway to the distant echo of familiar footsteps – allowing herself a smile as they came ever closer. Her eyes caught the black key in the lock of the door, just as a firm, warm hand slipped into hers.

As she turned to face Henri and felt the sweet, comforting warmth of his breath on her lips, a bad thought crept into her mind. He nodded towards the door at the bottom of the corridor; leading to the room they had shared many painting sessions in. But the look in his dark brown eyes suggested there would be no art involved when they closed the door behind them this time.

With her pulse racing and every nerve-ending on fire, they hurried down the long, narrow corridor.

But, Genevieve could resist it no longer. Casting one last glance over her shoulder to focus on the black key, she reached inside her bag with trembling fingers.

Holding her breath, she finally heard the sharp turning click she'd been waiting for.

Then, she had another bad thought...

CHAPTER ONE

Alice checked her watch; 10:05pm.

In a few minutes he would gesture for the bill, and the girl would disappear to the ladies', always to emerge as breath-takingly immaculate as before.

This scene played out every Friday evening without fail. And, every Friday, Alice would grow more uneasy; the knot in her stomach tightening just that little bit every time she watched them at their exclusive table by the grand piano.

But something was different this time. Something she just couldn't put her finger on. In the time it had taken her shallow breathing to mist up the round pane of glass in front of her, she was calm enough to re-enter the glorious aromatic bustle of the restaurant.

One lung-deep inhalation and standard 'waitress smile' in place, she was ready to leave the stifling kitchen behind and enjoy the refreshing breeze that always cooled her face as the white double doors whooshed open in front of her.

As if on cue, the man caught Alice's eye. He thrust a hand up, his oversized platinum watch twinkling in the glow from the centrepiece candles. Alice had recognised him for some time. He was Victor Davies: self-made millionaire entrepreneur, esteemed charity fundraiser and all-round good egg in Joe

Public's opinion. She'd encountered him several times in her 'proper' job as a reporter for the local paper; a job that paid so handsomely she had to boost her earnings by waiting tables in Amo Mangiare twice a week.

A brief nod to acknowledge Victor's gesture, then Alice's pumps squeaked their way across the chestnut floorboards towards the cash desk – just as his blonde and much younger companion headed for the ladies'. The heady scent of her perfume lingered in the air as she glided past; an undisputed vision of elegance, ethereal beauty... and hopelessness.

The two women glanced at one another for slightly longer than was necessary; something more than polite acknowledgement passing between them this time. Alice could have sworn she caught the faint curl of a smile on perfectly-sculpted, scarlet lips; a gentle crinkling in the corners of youthful azure eyes – eyes that were the silent voice of a thousand words.

"You know, I can't begin to understand your obsession with that couple." Kate appeared from behind her, arms crossed, standing stiffly. Alice could feel the heat rising in her already flushed cheeks as she nodded towards them.

"Christ, he even orders for her; never utters a word, that girl. Textbook control issues."

Kate flicked her thick fringe from her forehead and turned her attention towards the kitchen where a hectic stream of waiters appeared and disappeared through the constantly swinging doors. She looked back at the couple, then again at Alice: "Speaking from personal experience?"

Alice tutted as Kate leaned in. "Quite the authority on relationships, aren't we? Hasn't stopped you snubbing baby-face when he appears with his tongue hanging out, though, has it?"

Alice swivelled to look at Ben, the new start. "Christ knows why you think *he's* interested. Besides, not into pretty-boy blonds – not my type, way too obvious." She turned back towards Kate with a knowing smile. "Well, in *my* opinion anyway…"

Kate's thin lips had all but disappeared. "Yeah, pretty sure he'll be teacher's pet soon enough. Just like you, eh?"

"For God's sake, get over yourself—" Alice yanked her shoulder away from Kate's hand and headed towards Victor with his bill.

Swallowing hard, her dry tongue sticking to the roof of her mouth, she made for the dimly-lit Art Deco alcove that nestled the couple's table. In the instant that he sensed her presence, Victor's demeanour switched with eerie, calculated ease. The stern, controlling expression vanished; instantly replaced with his down pat, public-persona smile – the same smile Alice had witnessed many times before at countless media events. Yes, this man was master of the facade; of turning on the charm at will. Flashing his perfect teeth whilst running his fingers through a mass of suspiciously thick, dark hair for a man kicking fifty, there was no denying Victor's charisma. And standing at over six foot with a vast array of perfectly-tailored suits, he undoubtedly commanded attention at every turn.

Then, Alice shivered as she noticed something in his eyes, black as midnight. A recognition, perhaps?

Does he know who I am?

No, the chill in her blood was due to something more personal; much closer to home.

Alice couldn't believe she hadn't noticed it before – Victor reminded her of *him*. At least, what she forced herself to remember of him.

He stared at her name plate as he prised a credit card from his leather wallet, sweat glinting above his clean-shaven top lip. Without looking at the bill, he held the card out towards her then watched intently as she slotted it into the machine before offering it back to him. He barely glanced at the tiny keyboard as he punched the four numbers in. The few seconds of awkward silence before the receipt spewed up and out of the machine felt like an eternity. In a fluster, she tore it off as quickly as she could, causing the paper to snag halfway along and rip up the middle. She cursed under her breath as she was forced to hand the crumpled mess over to, not just one of their most valued customers – but to *him*.

"Thank you... *Alice*." The deep emphasis on her name was slow, deliberately so.

"You're welcome, Sir." Her eyes slid to the woman, staring down at the table, lost in thought.

"Ma'am," Alice nodded gently, "I'll get your coats."

Her legs trembled all the way to the cloakroom.

By the time she'd reappeared with their coats draped over her arm, Victor and the girl had already made their way down the steps by the side of the piano. He flashed an awkward smile as he helped the blonde on with her long camel coat. All the while, not a single word passed between them.

"Right then, thanks again." Victor's brusqueness all but negated the polite comment as he checked his watch then made for the door.

Walking a step behind him as they left the restaurant, the young woman looked over her shoulder. Alice couldn't read her expression; it was neither a smile nor a frown but the intensity in the girl's eyes stirred something deeply uncomfortable in Alice as she watched her leave.

Wrapping her trench coat and scarf around her to brave the icy walk home to her apartment, Alice's stomach gave an almighty rumble – in protest, no doubt, at how long it had been since a morsel of food had passed her lips; seven and a half hours since she'd wolfed down that tuna wrap at her desk. No time for lunch breaks with a copy deadline looming.

As if to taunt her more, Ben breezed past with two steaming plates of sizzling steak and pommes frites, leaving the most delectable aroma lingering in the air.

"Alice, just a minute—" He seemed flustered as he headed towards a table of professor types in dinner jackets and bowties. Fumbling in his deep apron pocket, he hurried back towards her, smiling sheepishly. "Sorry, forgot to give you this earlier – that blonde girl handed it to me."

Alice stared at her name, scrawled in red pen on the crisp white envelope. Self-consciousness washing over her, she glanced back up at Ben – his wide blue eyes were searching but she was giving nothing away.

"Cheers. That's me off, then." She left it at that and flashed him the most nonchalant smile she could muster despite the churning in her stomach.

The look of intrigue on Ben's face as she walked out of the restaurant only fuelled her curiosity. There was no way she would make it home before tearing open that envelope. Searching frantically in the shadows of the street for the nearest decent light, she ran as fast as the satchel bashing off her hip would allow towards a deserted bus stop.

Beneath the flickering fluorescence of the timetable, she ripped the envelope open; her heart thumping in her chest as she unfolded the lined paper and her eyes soaked in the words scrawled in scarlet.

Alice, I need your help. I'll be inside Bar Rio on Monday at 8pm. Please be there, Eva.

CHAPTER TWO

Lost in thought, Alice looked out at the dark, threatening clouds heavy with snow – and shivered.

Most of the third-floor workers were long gone and only a fraction of the open-plan office was still lit up. She glanced down at the note in her hands, now slightly dog-eared after countless readings.

Footsteps approached her desk from behind – heavy, ungainly, impatient.

"How's the housing article coming along, Webbie?"

Alice jerked herself upright in her squeaky black recliner; grimacing at his pet name for her.

"Nearly done, Alan – a few tweaks, then it'll be straight on your desk." She reached for the neckline of her blouse, checking the top button was fastened. Ever since the leg-brushing incident in his office, Alice was painfully aware of her boss' penchant for directing conversations towards her chest.

She flinched, then stiffened as he leaned in closer – thankfully she'd closed Eva's note.

"You know, sometimes I think you work too hard, Alice." He was close enough for her to feel the warmth of his stale cigarette breath on the nape of her neck.

"Well, not really—" Her faltering reply was interrupted by a familiar, and much appreciated, voice.

Pete's cheery greeting from above the partition was cut short the moment he clocked Alan behind her. The familiar disdain on his face was all too evident.

Alan bristled and stepped back from her desk. "Just make sure it's with me by nine tomorrow."

"Will do." Alice caught Pete's eye as her editor sloped away. "Thanks," she mouthed. "Great timing. You just back from a shoot?"

He dropped a bulging beige canvas satchel crammed with cameras and lenses at his feet. "Yeah, the new rehab centre that opened in the West End – eventually got the money shot of the mayor cutting the ribbon. Edge-of-the-seat paparazzi shit, eh?" His hazel eyes twinkled mischievously beneath a sweeping chestnut fringe.

One of her closest friends since their university days, Pete never failed to put a smile on her face.

"It's great to see you so enthused about your job after all these years, though."

He folded his arms across his chest. "And you're not Editor-in-Chief already because…"

"…of sexist eejits like him." Alice thumbed behind her. "There's no danger a pair of breasts will ever break the glass ceiling in editorial, Pete – sad but true."

She picked up Eva's note and waved it in front of him. "Anyway, I've more important things to deal with just now."

She studied his face as he slowly absorbed the words.

"So, that'll be Victor Davies' glamorous young companion. Always knew there was some weird shit going on there."

He looked up. "Ever the Samaritan, eh? You want company?"

"Thanks, but I'm not sure she'd appreciate it if she knew I'd already blabbed to someone else."

He raised an eyebrow and smiled, just as she caught sight of the clock on the far wall. "Shit, it can't be that time—" She sprang to her feet, snatched her coat and bag then reached over to switch her computer off; flashing Pete one last smile before she left.

Passing the half-open door of Alan's office, she caught him hunched over his desk, mobile phone clutched in both hands; the harsh glare reflecting onto his sweaty furrowed brow. Just when she thought he hadn't noticed her, his eyes darted towards her in the doorway.

"Hey," he barked from his pristine leather recliner.

She drew in a slow, deep breath.

"Check this over for a second, would you?" He ordered her in with a flick of his wrist.

She exhaled slowly and nudged the door open.

"I'm actually in kind of a hurry, so—"

"Forgot to run this past you earlier," he cut in, sliding a double-page proof across the desk towards her.

"This is good, Alice – really good. Fracking's a really contentious issue but you've got the tone just right. Starting to see real potential in you, I must admit."

She narrowed her eyes at the disingenuous grin that followed his out-of-character compliment.

"Ok—" It was all her mouth could produce as he barrelled on.

"Good selection of pics, too. Though she's a creepy-looking one." He poked a nicotine-stained finger at the photo of the oldest protestor she'd interviewed a couple of days before.

A bitingly cold wind had howled around them on Leyton Moor that morning, yet 80-year-old Betty Jackson barely shivered as her thin black blouse and cotton trousers flapped frantically in the icy breeze.

It was only after sleeping on it, that Alice had realised the old woman was the only local whose main concern hadn't been the environmental ramifications or the fact that the proposed fracking site was a treasured local beauty spot.

"We're needing a photo caption for her, by the way."

But Alan's words didn't register as Alice became lost in the pull of the wide green eyes staring out, almost scrutinising her from the shiny proof paper.

It was that same unblinking intensity that had stayed with Alice long after she'd left that day. That, and the all-consuming, inexplicable energy of the moorland that seemed to buzz through her like a post-sugar rush; coursing through every nerve and vein to make her feel more alive than she'd ever felt before.

She reached inside her coat pocket to check her crystal was still there. She'd been carrying it around ever since she'd got her *news.* In times of stress, it always made her galloping heartbeat instantly slow if she stroked the perfect smoothness of the rose quartz.

Still, the woman's words needled away in her brain.

"The ground here is sacred. Nothing – and I mean nothing – can disturb it. It must be left alone."

Despite being side by side on an exposed moor, wild winds whipping around them, Betty's husky voice was as pure and clear as if they'd been standing alone in an empty room.

"You understand that... don't you, my dear?" Alice guessed she was referring to it being an ancient site for practising witchcraft centuries ago. She always did her homework before a story.

"Certain things shouldn't be disturbed." Alice was whispering the old woman's last words under her breath when a hand on her back made her jump.

"I thought you said you were in a hurry?" Alan was standing right beside her.

Alice edged away as the hand began to gently rub her shoulder.

"Shit, yes." She shook her head to get herself back into the moment, then hurried out of her editor's office – still wriggling her shoulder away from the memory of his hand.

CHAPTER THREE

Alice stopped at the antique mirror on the wall, tucked a stray curl behind her ear then made for the front door. The somersaults in her stomach were now impossible to ignore.

God, this is worse than first-date nerves.

The high-pitched trill of her landline in the dark hallway made her jump as she reached for the door handle.

Alice knew who it would be as she tutted and hurried to answer it.

"Hiya, Mum. Just on my way out – I'll call you back later, yeah?"

"Sweetheart, how did you know it was me?"

"Oh, you know – lucky guess." Her mother was the only reason she still *had* a landline.

"Sad news, I'm afraid. Your Aunt Emily passed away this morning."

"Oh, Jesus. Oh, no…" Hot tears pricked her eyes as she pictured her uncle's raw grief.

Her mum sniffed. "I'm going to see Jack now, actually. You know, in a way, it's probably a relief that she's gone. The cancer took everything out of her – she had nothing left…" Her voice tailed off.

Alice felt a rush of guilt at her initial irritation. "I'm sorry,

Mum. Look, if you need me to come with you..."

"I'll be fine, sweetheart. The funeral's a week today, same cemetery as—"

Alice cut in with some empty platitudes; she couldn't allow her to finish the sentence.

"I'd better let you go, sweetheart. I'll call you later."

Alice wiped the tears from her face then ran a tentative finger over the scar above her eyebrow; faded now but still there if you looked closely enough. And she did, often.

Maybe some scars never heal.

Outside, the temperature had plummeted to freezing. The pavement glinted in the moonlight and car windscreens were clouded with frost. The air was dense with the threat of impending snow. With a heavy heart, Alice remembered her aunt and uncle in happier times. She'd never known a couple so besotted with one another – even after forty years of marriage. Alice doubted she'd ever experience such deep, unconditional love and trust in her lifetime.

The echoing chimes of the Square's church bell signalled eight o' clock.

"Shit." With another few streets to go until she reached her destination, Alice picked up speed; each shallow breath forming a ghostly cloud in front of her eyes as she pounded the straights and bends of the twinkling pavements.

Her heart was hammering in her chest when she finally placed a freezing palm on the tarnished brass panel of the swinging door.

What if I can't find her?

The potent stench of alcohol invaded her nostrils as she jostled herself through the crowded bar area. Conscious of being on her own, she gathered her trench coat tightly around her collarbone – moving as swiftly as she could past the lewd, drunken stares. Alice had always been oblivious to the effect she had on men. Her flowing red waves were a constant burden; it was only in recent years that the carrot tinge she'd so detested in childhood had faded to a rich auburn hue.

Nudging her way towards the seated area, she peered through the dim light for Eva. A shadowy figure in a secluded booth at the back caught her eye. Edging closer across the sticky wooden floor, she could see a young woman staring at a picture on the wall beside her.

Alice didn't recognise her at first; she looked even younger than she remembered. Her golden hair was scraped back into a high ponytail, accentuating her razor-sharp cheekbones even more. In the near darkness she appeared make-up free – a natural beauty in her white t-shirt and faded denim jacket. At the last second, she turned to face her.

Alice slid herself along the velvet bench and held her hand out.

"Pleased to meet you – *properly* this time." She took a deep, juddering breath and let out a nervous laugh; relief sweeping through her.

Eva smiled, cautiously extending a slender manicured hand. "You, too. Look, thanks for coming – I wasn't sure you'd turn up." Her eyes flitted nervously behind Alice towards the crowded bar. "I *really* shouldn't be here. If he finds out I've spoken to anyone, God help—"

"You mean Victor?" Alice moved closer on the bench.

Eva looked down at the glass cupped in her hands.

"He's really generous – actually, ridiculously generous – but I can't take it anymore. I don't know what's going to happen..." Her voice faded to a faltering whisper.

17

Alice reached out to hold her hand. She recognised the signs. "Is he hurting you?"

Bowing her head, Eva began to sob. "I'm so scared, Alice. I've nobody to turn to but I felt I could talk to you. Thought maybe... you wouldn't mind."

She reached inside her jacket pocket to produce a long chain with a pentangle symbol dangling from it. The silver pendant glinted in the glow of the wall light as she cradled it in her palms.

Alice leaned in to look at it more closely. "Unusual but pretty. A gift from Victor?"

"You could say that. All I know is that I have to wear it soon." She paused. "Some sort of ceremony he talks about."

Alice narrowed her eyes as she stroked the italic letters inside the symbol. "What does *obv* stand for?"

"That's just it, I have no idea. He meets with a group of guys every Friday after our meal at the restaurant. He doesn't tell me much, and I'm afraid to ask – in case he's in one of his moods..."

The knot tightened in Alice's stomach. "Has he been hurting you for a while, Eva?"

"He started off sweet and charming in the beginning, but—"

"—But now that he's got you where he wants you, it's the *real* Victor – not the smiley, media-friendly one?"

Eva nodded. "You seem to have him all figured out."

"Let's just say, I've some experience on the subject." Alice raised an eyebrow. "How'd you hook up with him, anyway?"

"I was working as a chambermaid in the Carlton with barely enough money to live then this suave, successful businessman wants to pamper me, have me on his arm at dinner parties, move me into his luxury penthouse apartment – what girl's going to refuse that?" Her face softened. "I suppose I was flattered – even grateful that he was interested in me at all. When you've been in and out of care most of your life, attention's the one thing you crave."

Alice couldn't argue with her sentiments. "But the luxury lifestyle comes at a price?"

"I'm trapped. He controls pretty much everything I do and I'm too scared to do anything about it."

"So where does he think you are now, then?" Alice asked.

"I have a Pilates class every Monday at eight; it's the one freedom he allows me." She pointed to the sports bag concealed under the table before checking her watch. "Look, I'll have to leave shortly if I'm to get home at the usual time."

Alice flinched as a familiar figure trudged past their booth. The cumbersome silhouette and lingering waft of stale sweat confirmed her suspicions. "Shit."

"What's wrong?" Eva asked.

"My boss at the *Gazette* – he's just walked past."

"You're a journalist?" Her eyes widened.

"Yeah, for my sins. Look, I don't want him seeing me so I'm going to split. I'll check out the pendant letters for you, okay?" She slid herself along to the end of the bench then stopped, resting her hand on the table. "Look, don't worry. You're not on your own, I'm here to help, ok?"

Eva smiled and placed a hand on top of hers. "Thanks for coming – it means a lot. More than you know."

Alice stood up and headed for the secluded side door of the bar. "Let's meet next Monday at the same time, yeah?" Eva nodded. "Take care."

Out of the corner of her eye, she saw Alan reappearing through the swinging door. As quickly as she could, she slipped out into the bitterly cold night – not knowing whether he'd seen her or not.

* * *

When sleep finally came to Alice that night, she would wish it had not.

A bolt of adrenalin shoots through her veins as a door slams shut in the hallway. Peering over the top of her freezing duvet, she flinches at the harsh icy breeze from the curtains, billowing furiously in front of the open window; flapping like evil winged beasts in time with the hellish pounding of the heartbeat thrashing inside her head.

A switch clicks outside her room; a sliver of light appears under the door. She hears slow, heavy footsteps – then she doesn't. A shadow freezes outside, breaking the light before slithering through the gap onto the floor in her room. She holds her breath, her hands trembling – every hair on her body prickling with fear as the handle moves slowly down and the door creaks open inch by torturous inch.

A towering figure, veiled in shadows sweeps into the room. The fiendish silhouette looms over her bed – faceless, voiceless – screaming with deafening malevolence. The sickening stench of evil invades her senses as the shadow stoops closer to her face. Petrified, she is desperate to cry out with each shallow, icy breath but he will not allow it...

"No, stop. Oh God, please don't..."

Alice sat bolt upright, drenched in sweat.

Her nightmare was back.

CHAPTER FOUR

Rubbing her tired, dry eyes, Alice stifled a yawn as she pressed the call button for the lift. A nudge on her back jostled her forwards.

"Morning, lady—" Pete's grin faded as he took in her dishevelled appearance.

"Think somebody's had a heavy night," he said with a wink.

Alice huffed as she released the clip that was snagging her hair, allowing her unkempt waves to tumble to her shoulders. "Christ, I wish. No, just the worst night's sleep you could possibly imagine."

The doors opened and they squeezed in together amongst the huddle of chatting workers. Pete's eyes softened as he glanced down at her. "You okay?" he whispered.

"Yeah – nothing a double espresso won't fix," she muttered, stifling another yawn.

Pete rummaged in his satchel as they made to go their separate ways out of the lift. "Hey, look at this." He waved an official-looking letter under her nose. "They gave me the job – can you believe it?"

"What, the one in London? The mega-bucks one?" Alice said just a little too loudly. Pete put a hushing finger against his lips.

"The very one," he whispered, grinning.

"No shit." Alice slapped him on the back. "Well done, bud – so pleased for you. When d'you start?"

"Just a month's notice here then it's *adios*. Feels a bit weird, actually." He took a slow, deep breath. "Hey, almost forgot – how'd it go with restaurant girl last night?"

"Catch up with you later, maybe?" This was neither the time nor the place to be discussing Eva.

"Cool, yeah." He flashed his token lop-sided grin then turned to disappear through the fire door leading to the Art Department. As Alice watched the door click shut behind him, a feeling of heaviness cloaked around her shoulders. She walked towards her desk, forcing herself to breathe deeply and slowly as her lungs suddenly cried out for air.

Trying desperately not to think about what Pete had just told her, she bumped down onto her chair and flipped her notebook open; a rough pencil sketch of the pendant was staring her in the face.

Her every waking moment since meeting Eva had been consumed by the curious symbol. Internet searches had revealed nothing; although there was one route she was yet to venture down.

The nagging doubt in her head had become too insistent to ignore; she held her breath as she pressed the search button on her mobile.

Did you mean: religious cults? Her finger hovered over the question that had just pinged onto the screen.

I can't believe I'm doing this.

As she frantically scrolled through the list of options, her phone rang. The caller display instantly replaced the results on the screen.

"Great timing, Mum," she muttered, pressing 'accept'.

"Sorry to bother you at work, sweetheart. Just to say I'll be away for a few days at your Aunt Anne's. She's coming back with me on Monday for the funeral." She paused. "Didn't want you worrying, in case you couldn't get me."

Alice rolled her eyes. "It's fine. Maybe just keep your mobile switched on so I can get you anytime, though," she said pointedly. "Oh, and I've asked for the time off, by the way." She knew the little white lie would appease her and she'd speak to Alan about it soon.

"Great. We'll pick you up at midday then."

"Say hi to Aunt Anne for me." An abrupt knock on her partition wall cut short the conversation – it was Lynn; the features' department trainee, with a comically-serious look on her spotty face.

"Alan wants to see you in his office – soon as." The rookie journo was clearly relishing the kudos of summoning a senior member of staff to the editor's office.

Bless her, the novelty will soon wear off.

Realising her mum had already hung up, Alice stood to brace herself for the encounter with her boss. At the very least, it would give her the chance to request time off for the funeral.

In a moment of panic, she reached back to snatch the phone off her desk. Pausing outside his office, she could make out two shadowy figures behind the opaque glass. Two male voices instantly stopped talking.

"In you come, Alice."

Taken aback that he knew it was her, she pushed the door open. The first thing she saw was the back of a man's head – it looked strangely familiar.

23

"You wanted to see me?" She couldn't control the quiver in her voice.

The man didn't acknowledge her.

Alan pulled a spare seat towards to the desk. "Sit down… please."

Crossing her legs as she sat on the leather chair, she glanced at Alan's guest – just as he turned to speak.

"Nice to see you again, Alice." Victor held a hand out. "So this is what you do when you're not serving me every Friday?" He smiled, but it didn't reach his dark-as-midnight eyes.

Caught off-guard and conscious of what was on the phone in her pocket, Alice struggled to keep her composure as she shook his hand. "You, too," she said quietly, realising that her response made no sense whatsoever after his question.

Victor only dropped his grip as he continued to speak.

"Look, I'll cut to the chase, Alice. My company's set to launch a high-profile media campaign for a new building project – my latest business venture." His jet-black eyes twinkled with excitement.

Alan rested both elbows on the paper-strewn desk in front of him. "This is potentially a really big deal. Victor's promised us exclusivity on the launch." He clasped his hands in front of him and took in a slow, deep breath. "Which is why I'd like to offer you the chance to cover it for the paper; to showcase your talents, Alice." He stroked the grey-flecked goatee designed to conceal his double chin and turned to Victor. "Really good of you to give us the tip-off on this."

"Let's just call it payback for all your help in the past." The two men smiled at one other. There was clearly a bond between them.

"You know, Alice," he continued, nodding towards Alan.

"I'm told this could potentially be a swift move up the career ladder for you."

Her boss cut in. "Yep, specially with the features' ed job up for grabs soon." He raised an eyebrow at her; she swallowed hard. "You know I've always thought you have great potential, Alice." He sank back into his chair, clasping his hands behind his head. "You've proved there's more to you than fillers and readers' letters with that fracking piece. Onwards and upwards, eh?"

Alice shifted in her seat as she studied his relaxed yet dominant pose. He was clearly in awe of the businessman and looking to impress him.

She swivelled towards Victor. "Any chance of a heads-up on the new venture, then?"

"Embargoed for now, I'm afraid – at least until the finer details are finalised. My PA will email the info the day before our interview. I look forward to working with you, Alice." He extended his hand again, revealing the familiar platinum Rolex.

"Who knows, with your new pay rise you could even give up the waitressing?" His deep, authoritative tone made the remark sound more like an order.

Alice laughed politely. "Actually, I really enjoy working in Amo Mangiare. Always a pleasure serving you – and your lovely companion, of course."

Victor looked up. "We thoroughly enjoy it, too." His smile was tight, pulling on his eyes.

As she uncrossed her legs, Alice felt the phone slip closer to the edge of her skirt pocket. "Alan, before I forget," she paused, adjusting it as casually as she could, "I'll need to take the day off on Monday, if that's all right? It's my aunt's funeral—"

"Quite sure we can accommodate that." He laughed nervously – no doubt to distract from the awkward atmosphere the mention of Eva had created.

Victor budged his chair back and stood up. "Let me know the arrangements at your end as soon as, Alan." His voice was curt as he adjusted the gold cufflinks on his crisp white sleeves.

"Actually, there's one more thing, Alan—" He nodded towards Alice, implying that the meeting was over.

Her boss gestured to her that it was time to leave his office and closed the door behind her.

* * *

As she swallowed the first heavenly mouthful of crisp, chilled Pinot Grigio, Alice felt the day's tension slowly melting away. Pushing away the unappetising plate of lukewarm mushroom pasta, she slugged another generous mouthful of wine; then another.

Maybe alcohol isn't the best way to forget about this futile pendant search?

The clock was ticking towards her next meeting with Eva and she still hadn't found a single crumb of evidence or unearthed any potential leads in connection with Victor's group.

A sudden, intense hopelessness overcame her and she shivered in the cool air of her usually cosy living room. Drawing the curtains, she watched small, occasional flakes of snow dancing in the evening's gentle breeze; floating like tiny embers in the hazy amber glow of the lampposts. A chink of light escaped through a gap in the curtains, softly illuminating the gilt-edged frame on the mantelpiece; the one surrounding her favourite photograph.

She smiled to herself as she remembered the story behind the picture. It was the day after graduation; she and a group of university pals had climbed to the top of a nearby hill, in a bid to clear their heads after a hectic night's partying. She and Pete had somehow become separated from the rest and, as they sat huddled together on the windswept hillside, he put his arm around her; not saying a word. It was the most relaxed and truly happy Alice had ever felt in her life.

The familiar warm fuzziness bubbled up again inside her as she gazed at the photo.

Alice never knew if he'd meant it or not; she'd shrugged off his peck on the cheek and 'we'd make a great couple' comment that night as nothing – a meaningless gesture, fuelled by alcohol in the heady atmosphere of the party.

Despite the fact neither of them had mentioned it since, Alice had never forgotten it. Now they were too far down the road to go back there again. She pulled her cardie tightly around her chest; it would only be a matter of time before he broke her heart anyway. She reached for the glass of wine but stopped before picking it up.

Logic reminded her what a great opportunity this was for Pete; one that he fully deserved. God knows, his talents were wasted at the newspaper. Besides, it wasn't as if he was going to the other end of the world. They'd still see each other – occasionally.

So why does it hurt so much?

Clutching her favourite photograph to her chest, Alice drifted off to sleep on the living-room sofa.

CHAPTER FIVE

Choking back tears as her aunt's coffin was lowered into the grave, Alice looked up to see her uncle kissing a single red rose before placing it gently onto the gleaming mahogany lid.

Glancing at the sea of umbrellas surrounding the grave, she couldn't have pictured a more fitting tribute to a woman so adored and respected by so many. Indeed, she knew that her uncle's grief would be tinged with great pride at the number of people who'd gathered to pay their respects.

Alice's mum reached for her hand as the respectful skirl of the bagpipes signified her aunt finally being laid to rest. Her mum had been in tears ever since his heart-rending eulogy in the church. It was rare to see her so emotional; Alice couldn't remember when she'd last seen her cry.

It certainly wasn't at the last funeral – that much she did remember.

The crowd began to drift towards the cemetery gates.

"I'll just be a minute, sweetheart." She watched her mum walk slowly up the gravelled path of the hill towards a cluster of bare, spindly trees silhouetting the horizon.

Alice knew exactly where she was headed.

Stopping at the first grave in the top row, she knelt to place a small posy of flowers at the base, before bowing her head and kissing the crucifix she always wore around her neck.

Clenching her fists, Alice mustered every fibre of self-control to stay rooted to the spot. She didn't know if she was ready to deal with this again; maybe she never would be. Yet, her legs overruled her heart and carried her begrudgingly to the top of the hill; to *his* grave.

Side by side, they stood in silence; each waiting for the other to say the first difficult word.

Her mum took a deep breath and placed an arm around her.

"He had his demons, Alice – God knows, we all do – but there's not a day goes by when I don't think about him…"

Alice stared at the epitaph, engraved in gold on the mottled marble:

Here lies David Webster, beloved husband of June and father of Alice—

Unable to suffer it anymore, she tilted her head back to absorb the infinite bleakness of the slate grey sky. A gossamer veil of drizzle fell onto her face.

"You still defend him – even after what he did to us? You have to believe this is where he belongs."

"Good God, Alice – he's stone cold in his grave. Can't you let go of this anger, this bitterness?" Her mum's voice was stern yet pleading.

"My apologies for not being as in control of my emotions as you." She wriggled free from the arm around her shoulder. "Christ, you never talked about any of it." Tears of frustration burned behind her eyes. "You've no idea, do you? Not a clue about what *that man* did to me, not just physically, but up here as well." She poked the side of her head repeatedly. "He wasn't my father – a father's the kind of man that doesn't beat the crap out of you whenever he feels like it, or come home drunk more times than sober." Her face flushed with rage as she turned towards her mum, eyeballing her. "Or am I just being mean?" All the hurt and resentment that had been repressed for so long was threatening to erupt into something beyond Alice's control.

"This is neither the time nor the place for this sort of talk, Alice. Today's about your Aunt Emily."

"Yeah, God bless her. The good ones don't deserve to die."

After a few moments of strained silence, mum and daughter turned to look at one other; silently acknowledging the emotional deadlock between them.

Alice's mum reached for her hand. "Come on, your Aunt Anne's waiting for us at the car."

* * *

Picking up the tray of drinks off the hotel bar, Alice made her way slowly towards her uncle's table in the bay window. Following the refreshments he'd laid on for family and friends after the funeral, she'd noticed that much of the tension had disappeared from his face.

"Great buffet, Uncle Jack – I'm stuffed." She playfully rubbed her stomach then leant in to kiss him on the cheek. "You're gonna be okay, you know," she whispered in his ear.

He held her at arm's length, admiringly, "And you're going to make some lucky bloke a fantastic wife one of these days, Pumpkin."

Alice chuckled at his affectionate childhood nickname for her. "Not ready for those shenanigans yet, I'm afraid – though you and Aunt Em were a great advert for it."

"Thanks for your support – it means a lot." He smiled wistfully. "Hey, forgot to say there's a blast from the past over there wants to talk to you." He winked and gestured behind him. "I'll leave you to it."

Alice looked over her shoulder to see a familiar figure downing a glass of whisky at the bar. She smiled to herself; slightly less hair and maybe a bit thinner than a couple of years ago, but still the same grizzled, cantankerous Gordon.

She snuck up behind him as he signalled to the barman for a refill. "So this is what retired journos do all day."

He turned to greet her beaming face peering over his shoulder. "Kiddo – you've got to be careful with a man as old and frail as me, you know."

"Old? Hell, yeah. Frail, though? You must be joking." She plonked herself down onto the bar stool next to him. "Good to see you again, Gordon. Where've you been hiding?"

He took a generous swig of freshly poured whisky and smacked his lips together. "Just trying to stay out of trouble, kid." He half smiled, staring down into the amber liquid. "Shame we have to meet again in these circumstances – your aunt was a lovely woman. My Liz and her were great friends. The pair of them are probably up there putting the world to rights as we speak."

"Oh, Gordon – I'm so sorry, I didn't know you'd lost Liz—"

"Hey, why would you? She lost her battle with the Big C just after I left the paper. Timing could've been better." He sighed, turning towards her. "Anyway, how's my reporting protégé coming along under my successor's watchful eye?"

"Hasn't been the same since you retired – salary's doubled, holidays have tripled, job satisfaction increased ten-fold, you know—"

The corners of his mouth lifted and the faintest smirk appeared on his stubbly, melancholy face. The wall lights seemed to accentuate his unshaven, sallow complexion and Alice couldn't help but notice the dirty, ragged fingernails and unkempt hair.

"Truth be told, everyone was pissed you left without any fuss. We all wanted a massive knees-up with lots of free drink on tap, you miserly bugger." Alice bit her lip as it became obvious that she'd hit a raw nerve.

"Seriously, how's it all going with Alan at the helm?" Gordon's tone changed; his directness took her aback.

"Well, he's putting his faith in me to cover a big up-and-coming launch soon."

He raised his eyebrows.

"Yeah, that megalomaniac businessman, Victor Davies has promised Alan we've got the exclusive—"

"Victor Davies?" Gordon butted in. The little colour there had been in his face instantly drained away.

"Those two still in cahoots, eh?" He shifted on the squeaky bar stool.

"What do you mean? Do they go way back?" Alice leaned in closer. "They looked like good pals to me, anyway."

Gordon huffed as he swirled the whisky and ice around in the glass; he seemed agitated. "Let's just say, Alan would do *anything* to be involved with Victor."

Alice nodded. "Let's got for a wander, eh?" As they made for the door, her mum looked up: her eyes narrowing as she watched them leave.

Alice shivered as they headed out into the bitterly cold night air. Gordon rubbed his hands as he perched on the edge of a metal bench overlooking the hotel gardens.

"What do you know about Victor, Gordon? I know you, you're holding something back." Alice pulled her coat tightly around her collar as an icy breeze whipped a curl across her cheek.

Gordon hung his head; the wounded look on his face made her stomach flip.

"Alice, do you know why I left the paper the way I did?"

"Why, what do you mean?" She shook her head. "You took early retirement because your wife wasn't well and you wanted to be with her. There's no shame in leaving quietly, Gordon. Christ, you did the right thing – absolutely."

He laughed dryly. "Yeah, that was the official line anyway."

"Gordon, I don't get—"

"Walk with me." He stood up; Alice's heart began to pound with fear.

"I have to warn you, kid. Be very careful when it comes to Alan and Victor. These are people you do *not* want to mess with."

"Shit, Gordon, cut to the chase. In a few hours, I'm meeting a young woman who needs my help – Victor's girlfriend. The bastard is obviously abusing her and trying to get her involved in some sort of ceremony—"

Gordon stopped in his tracks. "The *obv* symbol?"

"How the hell do you know that?"

"That's what I'm trying to tell you. I knew too much, Alice – that's why I left the way I did." Taking a deep breath, he went on. "Remember the girl who went missing a couple of years ago?"

Alice shook her head. "Vaguely. I don't remember much about it, to be honest."

"Kelly Stevens. She was the daughter of Bill, a good friend

33

of mine. She was an art student, still living at home. He was always going on about some older guy she was seeing but she'd never say who it was or where she was meeting him – ever."

Alice fiddled with her earring; curiosity burning through her.

"One night he noticed a new tattoo on her arm. She said she'd had it done for her boyfriend and left it at that. Bill told me it had the initials *obv* on it – I knew straight away what they stood for."

"And?" Alice's eyes widened in frustration.

"It's a cult, Alice. They worship the devil. It's called Order of the Black Veil. It's so secretive that nobody outwith it knows anything about it. Don't bother with internet searches, either – this is a unique sub-division of a clandestine cult – strictly by invite only. That's how I know about it."

"You were asked to join?"

Gordon stroked the white stubble on his chin. "Most of the members are really successful, influential men and it was made clear that it'd be a shrewd, even lucrative, move in terms of my career. You scratch my back and so on."

"So Victor's in charge then?"

"Your editor's in it as well, Alice. Alan was Kelly's older boyfriend. I've got evidence of them together the night she disappeared."

Alice's jaw dropped. "Shit, Gordon – did you show it to the police?"

"What, you think the boys in blue aren't involved as well?" He humphed. "Nah, the photo was dismissed out of hand. Circumstantial – no point pursuing it, apparently."

He shifted towards her. "When I confronted Alan about

his relationship with Kelly, his awkwardness was evidence enough that they were involved. When I told him I'd taken a photo of them together because I thought it looked suspicious, I thought he was going to have a coronary. The next day, images of—" his voice began to crack "—of children were planted on my PC and conveniently found by Alan. I was told to go quietly or it'd be made public what was found."

He ran gnarled, agitated fingers through his thin hair.

"Christ, they even ransacked my house to find the bloody camera. Didn't find the prints I'd made as a back-up, though." He shook his head.

"You've no idea how deep this goes, Alice. I know the cult had something to do with Kelly going missing but I can't prove it."

All the shocking revelations were like an assault on Alice's brain. "Gordon, we have to do something about this. It's not right – Christ, none of it's right. I can't believe they did that to you when Liz was ill, the sick bastards."

He placed a hand on her shoulder. "Alice, please don't get involved in this."

"You don't understand, Gordon – I can't *not* get involved now. Look, I have to leave soon to meet Eva. The girl's in trouble and maybe only I can help her?"

He sighed. "Yeah, that's very admirable and everything else but why are you doing this? I mean *really...*"

She caught his searching look. "Because it's not like you know the girl that well or you owe her anything."

Alice swallowed hard as the lump in her throat began to swell.

"You can't really see that scar now, you know." Gordon ran a tender finger above her eyebrow. His hand was trembling in the freezing air.

"What..?"

"Oh, come on, Alice – you think I didn't know what was going on at home?"

She looked up at the endless constellations in the clear night sky, desperately trying to stop the hot tears pooling in her eyes.

"But I never said—"

"You didn't have to say a word. I just hoped you knew I was always there for you?"

His kind words triggered the tears to flow.

"My God, you couldn't have been a more kind, considerate boss. Though I did always wonder why you kept asking me how I was all the time." She gave a wry smile and wiped her cheek with the back of her hand. "Nothing gets past you, does it?"

A gentle flurry of snow drifted in the breeze as they made their way back inside the hotel. Before they walked into the bar, Gordon placed a hand on her arm. She looked down.

"Jesus, you must be freezing – your hand's still shaking." She rubbed hers over the top of his to warm it up but he quickly snatched it away.

"Listen, I will help you in any way I can, kiddo. But please, don't let your past be the only reason for doing this." He blew short, warm breaths into his cupped hands. "Vengeance doesn't suit you."

Her wide, brown eyes gleamed with determination. "I never got the chance to confront what happened to me – at least maybe now I can make it right for someone else?"

She leaned in. "Anyway, it's not about vengeance. It's about retribution."

CHAPTER SIX

Worry seeped into Alice's brain. It had just gone 8:30pm; a full half-hour after they'd agreed to meet again and Eva still hadn't appeared.

Ever since Gordon had insisted on walking her to Bar Rio, she'd had a feeling of dread in the pit of her stomach; a premonition that perhaps the night wouldn't go as planned.

She glanced behind her towards the crowded bar and felt instantly vulnerable. Once again, not many single young women in the pub on a Monday night. She tried not to look awkward as she fiddled continuously with her watch strap.

How long do I give her to show?

A few seconds later, a sturdy figure bumped down next to her, blocking her exit in the booth. Not content with invading her space, the drunken forty-something had the most offensive breath she'd ever had the misfortune to smell. His bleary eyes focused firmly on her chest.

"Saw you in here last week." He leered towards her, brimming with inebriated confidence. "So, where's your little pony-tailed friend then? You're a right couple of stunners, you know that?"

Alice recoiled in a mixture of fear and disgust. "Well, she isn't here – as you can clearly see," she said crisply, hoping he'd get the hint.

"Bit silly for a pretty young thing like you to be in a bar on her own, though, eh?"

In spite of his slurred words, the comment had a threatening undertone to it. She gripped the edge of the velvet seat with her fingernails.

"What's wrong? Cat got your tongue, sweet cheeks?" He shifted awkwardly up the bench towards her; slooshing some of his beer over the top of his pint glass as his thigh bumped up against hers.

Despite her unease, Alice couldn't help but notice how smartly dressed he was in his dark trousers and crisp white shirt. An office worker stopping off at his local before heading home to the wife and kids? Certainly not your typical drunk out to try his luck.

"Excuse me, I need to go to the ladies—" She prepared herself for some resistance as she shoved her bag onto her shoulder and stood up but, surprisingly, he made room for her to pass. She was too on edge to confront the wandering hand as she sidled past him; simply relieved to be free again.

"See you soon, Ginger," he hollered as she disappeared into the toilets.

Staring at her unusually pallid complexion in the smeared mirror, Alice's thoughts turned to Gordon; what the hell was going on with his shaking hand? He seemed oblivious to the concern on her face as she watched him down whisky after whisky at her mum's table; she even thought she overheard him change his last order from a single to a double. Trying to cast all judgement aside, she couldn't help but feel concerned for the former teetotaller.

She rubbed her temples; another tension headache was

building behind her eyes and the muscles in her neck and shoulders were so taut she felt they might snap in two. After tugging a brush through her damp, tangled hair, she glanced at her watch. Eva's window of opportunity for meeting had probably closed – no point hanging around now.

Walking back into the bar, Alice noticed that her uninvited guest was gone. In her rush to escape, she hadn't noticed if he'd been alone or not.

The thought of being watched so closely the week before made every hair on her body prickle with fear. She hated feeling so exposed; so vulnerable. Pushing open the side door leading out onto the main road, her flushed face was met with a welcoming blast of cool air. She pulled her trench coat tightly around her neck and caught sight of what looked like the forty-something getting into a long, dark car sitting just around the corner.

In the time it had taken her to scour the length of the deserted street for any sign of Eva, the car still hadn't moved; a few seconds later, the headlights went off. Hands trembling, Alice reached for her mobile. Pete's apartment block was only a few hundred yards away.

Please be in.

Four long, tense rings later, he answered – still finishing a sentence. "—yeah, I know. Hello."

A voice then some high-pitched laughter echoed in the background.

"Hey, Pete—"

"Alice?" His tone changed.

"Sorry to bother you… just wondering if I could pop up in a few minutes?"

Awkward silence.

"Of course, you're probably busy—"

"—No… no. Don't be silly. Where are you?"

"Just a couple of blocks away. Outside Bar Rio."

"Look, you're not walking on your own in the dark. Just stay by the door and I'll come get you in five minutes."

Alice stepped back under the glaring canopy lights of the main door, not taking her eyes off the parked car for a second.

* * *

"Jesus, Alice. Can't say your life's boring." Pete swept his fringe from his eyes as he rested against the work surface.

"I was going to tell you about it before now, but—"

But how could I possibly mention it after your exciting job news?

"—just never seemed like a good moment."

"So, Gordon's said he'll help you, then? You guys better be careful. That Victor guy sounds like a force to be reckoned with." He raised an eyebrow. "Maybe a bit too powerful and influential to be messing with?"

Alice winced as she stretched her stiff neck. The tension headache was now a dull persistent throb.

"You know what, I'm tired and emotional and I don't want to think about this shit again – at least until I've downed that coffee." She forced a smile.

"I think you deserve something a bit stronger after the day you've had."

The boiling kettle drowned out her sarcastic huff, as she pointed at the two empty wine glasses by the sink.

For a second, Alice thought Pete looked sheepish, as if he'd been caught unawares.

"Good job I'd only had the one else you'd have been stuck,

40

lady."

Alice's curiosity was at bursting point.

"Cosy night in, then?"

The burbling kettle gave a timely click; he turned his back to pour her coffee.

"Just black, yeah?"

His avoidance of an answer irked her; she crossed her legs in frustration.

"Sorry if I interrupted something."

Please tell me what that something was.

"Nah, just a little nightcap with one of the neighbours two doors down."

"Oh, who's that then?" Alice hoped she sounded nonchalant.

"Don't think you'd know her – she's not long moved in."

Another vague response.

"Look, Pete – you don't have to hide the fact that you're seeing someone from me."

He turned towards her again. "I'm not *seeing* someone, as you put it. Can't a guy have a drink with a neighbour without it being a date, for Christ's sake?"

For a second, Alice was lost for words. She tensed as he placed the steaming mug on the table in front of her.

"It's just that I thought we were good friends – I don't know why you wouldn't tell me." She forced herself to look up at him.

"Oh, and you tell me about all your boyfriends, do you?"

She bristled at the sarcasm. "That's not fair, Pete," she challenged, twirling her earring. "You know the whole relationship thing isn't on my radar at the moment."

"But why the hell not? You've got everything going for you – brains, personality, stunning looks… but, Jesus, your

41

defensiveness really irritates me, Alice."

"Well, sorry if I piss you off so much. Maybe it's just as well you're moving away, eh?"

She jerked herself up off the kitchen seat and stomped towards the door. Pete caught her arm; she turned defiantly to meet his soulful gaze. For what seemed like forever, they just stared at one another.

"I… I should probably go. Sorry I ruined your night."

As she reached for the door handle, she could feel Pete standing right behind her.

"Don't go, Alice. Please—"

Her heart was pumping so hard in her chest it echoed in her ears. She slowly turned to face him. There was something in his eyes that she'd never seen – never felt – before. He reached for her hand and began to gently stroke her wrist, all the while his eyes locked on hers.

"How can you not know how I feel about you, Alice – how I've *felt* about you for so long now?"

In a moment of panic, she snatched her hand away.

"But you never let me in – the barrier's always there. It's like you can't bear to trust me." He shoved a hand through his hair then bumped down hopelessly onto the wooden chair.

She stood behind him, her hand hovering above his shoulder; desperate to touch him but terrified as to what it might lead to.

He dropped his head into his hands. "I never told you how I felt because I was too embarrassed, too worried that you'd laugh it off." He raised his head again to look at her; the intensity in his eyes made her heart race faster still.

"But it's never been a joke to me, Alice. God, why's it taken me leaving to tell you this?"

Three hard knocks on the front door jolted them out of the moment.

"You'd better get that," she said, snatching a quick glance in the hallway mirror.

As Pete made to open the door, a familiar voice made her turn around.

"Hey, Pete... sorry... must've left my mobile here earlier—"

Alice stared in disbelief at the girl standing confidently in the doorway. Dressed to impress with a full face of make-up and an immaculate flowing mane of glossy ebony hair, was Kate.

CHAPTER SEVEN

As she sat in the marble-covered foyer of Davies' Enterprises, Alice mindlessly ran the palm of her hand across the oversized couch. She couldn't resist taking a deep breath to fully inhale the delicious aroma of the sumptuously soft brown leather.

To say Victor's head office was impressive would be a serious understatement. Every spacious glass side offered an equally impressive vista of the surrounding upmarket quay area – undoubtedly the most sought-after postcode of the county – and she knew that Victor had paid seriously over-the-odds for it.

The unnervingly pretty receptionist looked over with a blank stare; not even a cursory smile. Her unfeasibly shiny chestnut hair was scraped back into an impossibly tight bun, accentuating her bambi-like lashes to full effect. Alice gave her outfit a quick once-over and sighed; her High Street chain single-breasted jacket and pencil skirt combo wasn't a patch on the designer suit sitting behind the desk but it would have to do. She would just have to make an impression with her journalism instead.

She knew the impending interview should be uppermost in her mind but, no matter how hard she tried, she couldn't erase the image of Kate standing on Pete's doorstep – even worse was imagining them sharing an intimate evening together. Just thinking about all that had happened recently with Eva, Gordon and Pete, made her head hurt. And that was never good.

Jesus, how can so much shit suddenly occur in one person's life?

She frantically scanned her notes on Victor's biography in a bid to re-enter something resembling a professional mindset.

There was no denying that her research had cast up some intriguing revelations. One particular detail stood out from all the rest, concerning his childhood.

She was just about to scribble down a few amendments when a shrill ping made her look up. Victor was striding out of the lift towards her; head-to-toe in an immaculate navy suit. Flashing his trademark perfect smile, he held his hand out towards her.

"Alice – lovely to see you again. Please, let's go up to my office."

Standing side by side as they glided up to the penthouse level, Alice inwardly marvelled at the view from the exterior glass lift.

Sensing her appreciation, he turned towards her. "I don't think I'll ever tire of this, you know."

She kept looking straight ahead. "I'm pretty sure most people would jump at the chance to be able to grow tired of it, Victor."

He laughed under his breath then all was silent except for the gentle whirring of the lift's mechanics.

Alice could feel him studying her as she watched the surrounding buildings shrink into the distance.

Just as the height from the ground was starting to unnerve her, the glass doors slid open in a single fluid movement and he gestured her forwards into the most impressive office she'd ever seen. Once again, the rich leather aroma was all-consuming amidst a sea of light oak and cream furnishings – bright, airy and, she had to admit, very welcoming. If Victor hadn't enlisted the help of a top interior designer, he certainly had excellent taste and a keen eye for aesthetics.

"Please." He gestured for her to take a seat on the huge off-white chaise longue. "A small refreshment before we begin? What can I tempt you with?"

Despite her misgivings about him, Alice felt strangely at ease in Victor's territory – she certainly hadn't anticipated such a warm, relaxed environment.

"Just a black coffee, thanks."

"One double espresso coming up." He smiled at her; she thought it reached his eyes this time but she couldn't be sure.

"So, this new hospice building project sounds very impressive – what prompted such a venture?" She paused for a beat. "Your own childhood, perhaps?"

After a few seconds, his deadpan expression gave way to a subtle but knowing grin. "You *have* been doing your homework, haven't you?"

"It's quite common for very successful people to have had traumatic or difficult childhoods – it's a huge motivation to succeed. Yours is a great rags-to-riches story, Victor: orphaned at six; raised by waste of space, unemployed uncle in one of the poorest postcodes in the country but destined to become one of the wealthiest, most successful businessmen in the country." She leaned in. "Great timing with your 50th coming up as well."

"You know, Alice, I have to say I'm pleasantly surprised by you." He raised an eyebrow as he carefully placed the espresso on the marble table in front of her. "We've never really spoken before yet I feel we're quite at ease with one another."

Alice let his half statement, half question hang in the air for a few seconds. "Well, you're pretty damn intimidating but I think I can probably handle you—"

"Well, thank you for your candour – I'll certainly remember that." He half-laughed as he removed his suit jacket, placing it neatly on the curved chair arm beside him. The soft leather squeaked beneath him as he shifted to face her full on; she remained in expressionless profile.

"So, Alice, going back to your research on my childhood then…" He paused. "I believe you, too, have had your fair share of trauma." Victor's eyes felt like they were boring a hole through her skin.

She turned to meet his penetrating gaze.

"I really don't think my past has any relevance in all of this. In fact, I resent Alan's disclosure of my history at all, if I'm honest—"

"Who said anything about Alan?" His stare was unrelenting. "I was referring to your father's untimely death, nothing more."

Alice swallowed hard, her tongue was stuck fast to the roof of her mouth. "Look, can we just get on with what I'm here to do, please?" The familiar unease washed over her again.

"I apologise, Alice. I was merely trying to point out that you and I are – in certain respects – not so different." For a fleeting moment, she thought she detected an empathy in his unusually dulcet voice. He took a deep breath and leaned in closer. "Cards on the table now, Alice. Interview and hospice aside, I am genuinely interested in getting you on board in one of my flagship companies – in a public relations, press officer sort of capacity."

Alice cut her eyes upwards to meet his. Although intrigued, she couldn't fathom why on earth he'd be interested in employing her.

"What can I possibly offer a successful, established business-man like you, Victor? I'm a part-time waitress, for Christ's sake – sorry…"

"No need to apologise. I admire a feisty, no-nonsense attitude. You strike me as a very intelligent, single-minded young woman – qualities I insist upon in my employees."

She reached for the espresso as he loosened his tie. For a few seconds, his Rolex dazzled in the winter sun streaming in through the windows.

As her lips met the velvety crema layer of the coffee and she savoured the first delectable mouthful, he stood up and walked towards his vast but perfectly organised desk. Not an item out of place; everything neatly aligned to the point of obsession. She swallowed the most heavenly espresso she had ever tasted and quickly scanned the rest of his office – this was obviously a man with tidiness and cleanliness issues, bordering on OCD, perhaps?

He made his way back over with a few pages of headed A4 in his hand, sitting down closer to her this time; just enough for her to get a hint of his spicy aftershave. This close up, he appeared much younger – unless he was indulging in a session or two of Botox, she had to concede that he looked remarkably good for his age. She nervously flicked a wandering curl from her face as it dawned on her how long she'd been watching him for.

"Some documentation for you to cast your eye over. Peruse it at your leisure, Alice – no pressure. Just let me know if this is the direction you could see your career taking…" He paused, waiting for her to respond. After a few moments of awkward silence, he continued. "Did I mention the first-class private healthcare package, a major benefit to all employees – and extending to next of kin?"

The slow and deliberate emphasis on the latter part of his statement piqued her interest; she shifted in her seat. It was a harsh fact that her mum's ongoing physiotherapy didn't come cheap. The direct result of one of her dad's abusive episodes, it had left her with the inevitable need for an expensive operation, as well as treatment into the foreseeable future. This was undoubtedly a tempting perk of her potential new job – surely one that she couldn't pass by? It certainly gave her lots to consider – not least the fact that he'd be poaching her from Alan, an apparent friend and fellow cult member.

He ran pinched fingers up and down the razor-sharp crease of his trouser leg. "There's nothing more important than looking after loved ones, don't you think?"

He turned to look at her. Just as she took a breath to reply, he continued.

"You never know when they might not be around anymore. It can all disappear in an instant."

The sudden raw emotion in his voice took her by surprise.

"Absolutely," she said with a nod. But the conviction in her voice couldn't stop the heartache as her thoughts turned to her dad. She stood up and walked towards the window, trying to quell the sudden burning behind her eyes. She could feel him watching her as she squinted through the sunlight to soak in the varying peaks of the vast urban skyline. Rhythmic footsteps on wood grew louder through the low hum of the air conditioning. She blinked hard as he stood beside her.

"You know, there's no pressure—"

"Sure." She smiled politely, not taking her eyes off the sun-soaked turrets of the cathedral in the distance. His shirt sleeve brushed her arm as he adjusted a cuff. Alice stiffened at the closeness just as he turned and headed back to his desk.

"I only wanted to plant the seed. You don't ask, you don't get, I suppose…" His voice tailed off as she turned towards him with a look that was understanding but also suggested the subject was now closed.

Her eyes caught a selection of framed photographs displayed on the far wall.

"You keep all that very quiet." She nodded to the pictures of him shaking hands with the MDs of the various charities he'd donated to. All selflessly done without a hint of publicity or press acknowledgment. It struck a chord with her that the organisations were primarily child protection or abuse charities – and all had been granted at least seven-figure sums.

He looked down at his hands. "Never needed public thanks. I think it's the least someone in my position can do. There's so many bad things happen to good people. I'd fix it all if I could."

Alice smiled to herself. "Too much money and not enough time to use it, eh, Victor? Maybe in the next life?"

As his eyes met hers, Alice saw a smile tug at the corner of his mouth. "Yes, maybe…"

She let his reply hang in the air for a few seconds before resuming the interview – the real reason she was there in the first place.

Two hours later, just as he was about to pour her third espresso, she glanced down at her watch. "Well, I think that pretty much wraps it up. I'll email you the finished layout for approval before we go to press."

As she entered the lift, something made her reach for the 'doors open' button.

"By the way, how's it going with Eva? Haven't seen you two in 'Amo' for a couple of weeks." She wasn't sure if the question was inappropriate in the circumstances.

He looked down, adjusting the same cuff on his pristine white sleeve. "She's away just now." He raised his eyes to meet hers.

"Oh, ok—" Alice said, waiting for him to elaborate. Nothing.

"Maybe she's found herself a richer, older man?" Despite the tension in the air, she couldn't help but smile at the irony – as did he.

"She's gone to stay with a relative in the country for a bit," he eventually offered with finality.

Alice nodded in spite of herself. Despite the plausible and seemingly genuine explanation, something didn't feel right.

Where is she – really?

"Well, thanks for your time, Victor."

As she released the lift button and the doors closed slowly in front of them, his last words sent a shiver down her spine.

"The pleasure was all mine, Alice."

CHAPTER EIGHT

In the stifling heat of the kitchen, Alice repeatedly fiddled with her black apron ties before heading out for service.

In the run-up to her shift that evening, she'd felt unusually flustered and apprehensive about seeing Kate again. It had been four long days since the shock of discovering her on Pete's doorstep and she knew that this first encounter was going to be tense, if not confrontational.

She tentatively pushed the swinging doors open and immediately caught sight of her at a nearby table of middle-aged men; clearly relishing their high-spirited, flirtatious banter. As if sensing she was being watched, Kate spun around – her eyes instantly locking on hers. She strolled confidently towards her, balancing a few dirty plates in her elbow; the same smug expression on her face as when she'd sauntered past her at Pete's door.

Alice felt her hackles rising as she watched her strut into the kitchen full of obnoxious cheerfulness; a ploy, no doubt, designed to frustrate her even more.

A few minutes later, they came face-to-face by the swinging doors; communication was now unavoidable.

"Hey, Alice – want to know where I'm going later?"

Alice knew that Kate's armful of Denby dinnerware was in

danger of crashing onto the floor unless she reined in some self-control.

"Dunno, why don't you humour me?"

Kate breezed past her, then turned at the last second. "He's never mentioned you, you know."

Alice couldn't ignore the mocking tone as Kate looked down her nose at her.

"There's no reason he should have. We're good friends – that's as far as it goes, I'm afraid." Despite her self-satisfied retort, Alice couldn't stop trembling with rage – and doubt.

"Yeah, whatever." Kate sauntered back towards the inebriated male diners, looking like the cat that got the cream – or, at least, the waitress that got the great tip.

Unable to face another spat, Alice pulled on her coat, smiled at Ben then left the restaurant to head to her mum's. She'd picked up her prescription earlier that day but had forgotten to drop it off before her shift started. The least she could do was get her pills to her before breakfast.

Turning the corner into her mum's street, a gust of icy wind jolted her from her reverie. Perhaps this was the wrong time to be worrying about matters of the heart when there was a young woman in a potential heap of trouble with a rich, influential businessman?

So, where the hell was Eva?

Walking up the dark path to the front door, Alice sensed something different about the house; something wasn't quite right. As soon as she realised it was odd for her mum to have both front porch and hallway lights on, she glimpsed two shadowy figures behind the frosted glass panels of the door. It had just gone 10.30pm – unusually late for her mum to be entertaining. She paused, her finger hovering over the brass doorbell as she desperately tried to make out the other muffled voice. She panicked when she realised someone was heading towards the door and, with a single, abrupt knock, walked straight inside. Embarrassed that her eavesdropping might have been obvious, she swept into the hallway, eyes to the floor.

"Hey, Mum—"

She stumbled as she lifted her head and saw the identity of the late-night guest.

"Gordon? Hi…"

Aware that she'd been staring open-mouthed at him for a bit too long, Alice slid her eyes towards her mum.

"Hi, sweetheart. Why on earth are you here at this time of night?"

Trance-like, she held out the small chemist's bag. "I… I thought you… might need…"

Gordon stood in silence, shifting from one foot to the other.

"We were just having a chat about the good old days and some of the friends we've had in common over the years." She turned to Gordon, smiling coyly as she tucked a stray hair back into her otherwise immaculate chignon. "It's been the most fun I've had in a long time, truth be told."

As they grinned at one other, Alice began to feel like she was interrupting something.

This is the best mum's looked in a long time.

"Thank you, sweetheart – but you didn't have to rush around with them tonight. It could easily have waited for tomorrow."

Alice was lost for words, still reeling from the shock of discovering her mum and ex-boss together late at night – Gordon instinctively picked up on it.

"Time I was heading anyway, June." He held his hand out, just as Alice's mum reached in for an exuberant goodbye hug. Alice was well aware that her mum had had a drink or two; she only ever 'hugged' under the influence.

Gordon slipped awkwardly into his brown cord blazer. As he reached for the door handle, he turned to face them both.

"Thanks for the lovely meal, June. Not sure I could ever repay the favour on such a professional and delicious scale, though." His face lit up as he spoke.

"Oh, it was nothing." She flicked her hand and smiled coquettishly.

Still struggling to absorb the surreal scenario, Alice made her way up the carpeted staircase. As she slid her hand up the oak bannister, she turned towards them.

"Just heading to the loo, Mum. Oh, Gordon – remember that thing we talked about?"

Gordon's expression changed as soon as he realised what, *and who*, she was referring to. "The… newspaper… thing, you mean?"

"Yeah, I might have to give you a call about it – if that's ok?" Alice felt a renewed confidence sweep through her as she stood, mid-staircase, looking down at him.

"Any time, Alice, you know that." His warm smile returned, along with a wink.

"Thanks." Alice continued up the staircase before stopping on the landing. She shivered as she recalled the image that had haunted most of her childhood. Now that she was out of sight of her mum and Gordon, she couldn't forget the real reason she'd come to the house that evening – the plethora of pills for her mum's ailments; both mental and physical.

She gazed down from the landing to the bottom of the

55

stairs – quite a distance to be shoved by a strong man in a drunken rage. She winced as she recalled the horrific noise her mum's head had made as it smashed against the chunky, unforgiving wooden table by the front door. Then came the heart-stopping realisation that she wasn't moving; Alice's trembling legs whisking her down the stairs towards her mum's limp body at the bottom. Alice could again feel the sickening sensation in her stomach as she leaned over to check if her mum was still breathing. All the while, her dad hovered over them, occasionally losing his balance as he swigged from the half-empty bottle of brandy. He looked down at her with such contempt that Alice didn't know what had upset her more – her mum lying unconscious on the floor or her dad's blatant hatred of her.

As she gazed up at the picture of the Virgin Mary beside the gleaming crucifix on the wall, Alice knew that she would never comprehend her mum's insufferable forgiveness of her dad's abuse – especially as she was now on endless medication as a result. It had long been accepted that she and her mum were polar opposites in most respects – the way that they each dealt with the attacks only exacerbated their emotional impasse.

Alice had always suspected it was no coincidence that her mum developed an obsession with Christianity and God as the abuse became more prevalent, more sinister. In hindsight, maybe that was her mum's coping mechanism; her crutch – that 'He' could somehow make it bearable; that she might be exalted and redeemed for all eternity if she dutifully fulfilled her role as martyr in *this* life.

Or did she somehow feel that she deserved to be punished?

* * *

"Alice – you still up there, sweetheart?" Her mum's voice startled her, just as she was drifting off.

"Just coming—"

Her mum frowned as she sat waiting for her on the bottom step. "It was just two old fogeys having a little chat over dinner..."

"Mum, it's alright – honest. It's just—" Alice bumped down next to her on the last step, with a wearied sigh. "Just a bit weird... the two of you – you know."

Her mum nodded. "You know we also got talking about the time you went to California before you joined the newspaper. You should never have gone there, should you, Alice? You weren't the same when you came home..."

Alice rubbed her tired eyes then looked up to watch her mum floating to the top of the staircase, before vanishing into thin air – like an ethereal spirit.

In the half-light, she peered up to the very top of the darkened staircase – with an overwhelming desire to climb it. Effortlessly, she began to glide upwards, her toes barely brushing the red velvet beneath her; lured helplessly towards a force beyond her control.

In the near-darkness at the corridor's end, she could make out a door, shrouded in shadows, waiting patiently; ajar just enough to entice her to push it open that little bit further. She gasped as she entered the room, widening her disbelieving eyes to fully absorb the infinite beauty in front of her. Blood-red church candles stood as proud as small pillars to border the room; their mesmerising flames gently flickering and undulating, as if dancing in unison.

A soft balmy breeze kissed Alice's face and arms; wafting the smoothest of satins against her thighs. As she gazed down at the floaty, scarlet negligee that seemed to caress every curve, she noticed the pendant that hung to her navel glinting in the soft yet all-consuming candlelight. Transfixed by its beauty, her fingertips slowly traced along the letters inside the glinting platinum symbol, just as the most intense and sensual feeling enveloped her bare neck and shoulders. A tingling warmth, so comforting yet so seductive spread through her body, rousing every nerve as her glistening skin grew ever more sensitive. Alice could feel the blood surging through her veins, mercilessly invading every inch of her. Instinctively, she arched her back and tilted her head to the side; a low moan escaped from her lips as a firm hand slid beneath the satin to caress her breast.

"I knew you would come, Alice." The seductive voice and warm breath in her ear sent the most delicious shiver down her spine.

"Why are you doing this to me, Victor?" Alice could barely manage a whisper as her mind and body succumbed to each heightened sensation.

"I want to own you, Alice."

As though she were as light as a feather, he took her in his arms and gently laid her down onto the sumptuously soft velvet spread that draped across the grand wrought-iron bed. He stood looking down at her; taking his time to adore every inch of her; devouring her with hungry eyes, on fire with lust. As she arched her back and their desperate bodies became one, she closed her eyes, losing herself in the heightened intensity. Her nails dug into his broad, taut shoulders as she could no longer absorb any more pleasure. Alice threw her head back as wave after wave of ecstasy flooded her body. When she finally opened her eyes again she found herself staring at writing on the ceiling directly above her.

The hardened red wax had dripped and smudged in places but the message was heart-stoppingly clear:

Owned **B**y **V**ictor

58

CHAPTER NINE

It was 10.30am and Alice still hadn't produced a single word.

She stared hopelessly at the glaring computer screen, willing the feature to magically appear as her writer's block fought tooth-and-nail against the looming copy deadline.

Bumping her head back onto the office chair, she tugged at a strand of hair that was caught on an eyelash – a lash that had been coated with hastily-applied mascara in the mad rush of the morning, as she realised that she'd slept through her alarm – again.

Gazing at the sleet-spattered window out towards the bleak, gloomy skyline, Alice felt a chill building deep in her bones. There was only one structure barely visible in the distance where the dense, threatening clouds juxtaposed the sea, belittling all others around it; its impressive triangular peak rising majestically to dominate the surrounding vista. Alice knew only too well what that apex housed within it – the ludicrously elegant office of one of the wealthiest businessmen in the country; a man about whom she'd had a wholly inappropriate dream only the night before.

As she recalled one of the most vivid fantasies she had ever experienced, Alice could feel her cheeks flushing with… with what, though – embarrassment, desire, self-consciousness?

She wasn't sure what she *should* be feeling. Yet, the emotion overriding all others, the one that dominated everything, mind and body; heart and soul – was carnal.

Despite every misgiving, every doubt, every pessimistic thought she'd ever had about Victor Davies, that dream had instantly obliterated them all. She remembered waking in a state of sheer unbridled lust – the likes of which she'd never experienced before.

She trailed her fingertips along the thick, embossed envelope that had lain unopened on her desk for over an hour – the letters D. E. imprinted in the scarlet wax seal meant it could only have been sent by one person.

Slowly and carefully, she teased the wax apart. Peeling it open, she could see a decorative gold emblem at the top of the enclosed card. Just as she was about to pull it out, a brusque voice came from nowhere.

"Got a minute, Alice?"

She spun around but Alan didn't wait for a reply as he dragged a spare chair next to hers. "I have to say, another impressive piece of writing. Just as good as the fracking piece, actually."

He stroked his goatee in the affected way that always irritated her.

She slid the envelope under some paperwork on her desk as surreptitiously as she could.

He leaned in closer. "Exactly the right balance of facts, back story – and, dare I say, nepotism." He winked and touched his nose as he openly admired her crossed legs.

Alice bristled – he really *was* in awe of Victor. Ever since Gordon's shocking revelation about Alan's involvement with the missing girl, she hadn't been able to look at him without feeling sick to her stomach.

"We must keep Victor on our side, Alice. He's too powerful and influential to piss off." Despite the light-hearted joke, there was an anxiety in his forced smile. He seemed preoccupied as he stood to leave. "I hope you're remembering about the up-and-coming features' ed post, by the way. Be a shame if you didn't try out for it, at least – I can see you going far, you know."

"Thanks. That's good to—"

He disappeared behind the partition as abruptly as he'd arrived.

A brief check behind her, she retrieved the hidden envelope and hastily pulled the card out; the faintest hint of lilac wafted under her nose. She took a sniff of the thick scented card then soaked in the gold scripted calligraphy:

Davies Enterprises' Annual Masquerade Ball – Saturday 26th February, 7.30pm

You are cordially invited to Westgrove Estate for an evening of fine wine, canapes & opera. As a thank you to friends and colleagues for their continued hard work and support, Victor Davies requests your company to share in this evening of music & celebration.

P.S. Don't forget your Venetian mask!

Christ, where do I get one of those?

Mindlessly, she picked up the ringing phone on her desk.

"Hello, Alice Webster speaking."

"I trust you've opened your mail?" The deep, authoritative voice in her ear catapulted her straight back into last night's dream. She struggled to speak as her pulse began to race.

"Victor?" She swallowed hard. "Yes… I got your invite, thank you—"

"Perfect," he sighed, his voice softer than before. "So, firstly, I love the article – I've made a few amendments, nothing important, though. Secondly, I'm hoping you'll accept my invitation." He paused for a beat but not enough to let her reply. "I can have a car on standby to pick you up—"

Her mind panicked at the sudden pressure for an answer. She never liked being put on the spot. "I… yeah, well, I don't have a car so a lift would be good." She tutted, her mind still racing. "But I'll have to check what I have on that night." She rolled her eyes at the irony – after all, she was hardly a social butterfly with an enviably hectic schedule.

"Of course." Victor paused, before taking a deep breath. She visualised him reclining in his oversized leather chair behind his vast, insanely tidy desk. "I don't doubt that you're very much in demand, Alice."

His next statement came at her like a curve-ball. "You know that the invite extends to a plus one? Not compulsory, though – I'm more than happy for you to come alone. I'm sure you'll find it a most entertaining evening."

The gentle vibration of her mobile on the desk was a welcome distraction. It was another text from Pete – his third in two days. She'd ignored them all so far; unwilling to confront their relationship via impersonal typed messages. No, the least he could do was have the guts to talk to her, face to face.

She tossed her hair back with renewed confidence.

"You know what, Victor, count me in for the Ball. I'm pretty sure I've nothing on."

"Excellent, Alice. Shall I mark you down for one or two

attending?"

Glancing at the text again, she didn't hesitate to reply. "Let's say, it'll just be me."

"Perfect. I'll take very good care of you – I promise."

After a few seconds of silence, he continued. "By the way, any more thoughts on my job offer?"

Alice's mind began to race with all the research she'd done on his business portfolios. Not only was Victor the main property magnate in the city, he was evidently a shrewd and opportunistic investor with companies catering for every demographic out there. Her interest had been piqued by a few – particularly the charity-related ones – but she knew that, at this point, she had the upper hand. She wasn't rushing headlong into anything – at least, not yet.

"I'd like a bit more time to consider it – and my options – if you don't mind."

"Take all the time you need, Alice. I'm sure we could allot some time to discuss it more in-depth at the Ball." He took a deep breath. "Maybe after a few glasses of Moët and Chandon you might be more susceptible to my powers of persuasion?"

Her eyes slid to look across at his office in the distance. "And you may find, Victor, that I'm not that easy to win over." In spite of her self-assured reply, Alice couldn't hide the waver in her voice.

She tried hard to remind herself of her initial doubts and fears about Victor, and she knew there was still a long way to go before her suspicions were satisfied concerning Eva. Yet, there was an inexplicable pull towards him; an intangible connection that resonated deep within her – so intense, so all-consuming that she just couldn't dismiss it. The fearful intrigue and allure of Eva's story combined with Victor's dark and powerful charisma, was too enticing to ignore.

She knew that she had to keep the Masquerade Ball a secret from Gordon – *and* from Pete. Both knew that she'd had serious misgivings about Victor and would no doubt think her reckless for willingly putting herself in such a situation.

But hadn't she spent most of her life being the victim; conforming to everyone else's rules and ideals? Maybe now she wanted to break free from the constraints of her everyday, mundane existence and live on the edge a little? Do something reckless for a change; something that gave her a rush. After all, who knows what tomorrow might bring?

A flush of guilt teased her conscience and she hastily typed a non-committal 'Let's talk soon' reply to Pete. Without re-reading it, she pressed 'send'.

No, she wasn't going to tell anyone – this was going to be Alice's little secret…

CHAPTER TEN

Ten minutes late for her meeting with Gordon, Alice rushed into the Carlton Hotel – almost tripping over the last polished step as she swept into the lobby.

Dishevelled and out of puff, she smoothed her hair and loosened the belt on her coat in front of a stunning arrangement of lilies displayed on a circular table in the middle of the marble floor.

As she scanned the luxurious, bustling reception, a tall, slim porter dressed head-to-toe in burgundy and black, wheeled an overflowing luggage trolley right in front of her. As soon as he'd disappeared from view, Alice caught sight of Gordon through the glass of the swinging doors leading to the bar.

The clicking echo of her approaching heels on the tiled floor made him look up. Her heart sank – it had just gone eleven on a Saturday morning and he was already cupping what resembled a large whisky on the rocks.

"Just a little pick-me-up," he shrugged, raising the nearly-empty crystal tumbler towards her. "Forgotten how nice this place is."

Alice caught the barman's eye. "Just an espresso, thanks."

She bumped down onto the bar stool beside him. "Bit early for that, isn't it?" she said quietly, raising an eyebrow at the glass he was lifting to his lips. She fiddled with her left earring as Gordon shifted on the bar stool to face her.

"This, Alice," he said, clutching the tumbler on the mahogany counter, "is kind of medicinal. Helps to numb the pain a bit." He raised his weary, slightly bloodshot eyes to meet hers.

"I'm just a bit worried, that's all," she sighed. "The Gordon I always knew was a confirmed teetotaller. What's happened? What pain?" She narrowed her eyes as it hit home that he was looking more frail than ever.

He hung his head and huffed into the collar of his jacket. "Never been the best at talking about things – *feelings* aren't really my forte." His defeated half-smile broke her heart a little. "You know, you remind me so much of Sally." His craggy face softened at the mention of his daughter and Alice sensed he was about to open up to her.

"Where is she now? Are you close?"

"We used to be… not anymore, though." He blew out a rush of air. "Completely my fault, of course. Suppose that's a big part of the pain…" His voice tailed off as his eyes glistened with tears.

Alice placed a gentle hand on top of his – the one she'd noticed had been trembling ever since she'd sat down. "You know, sometimes it helps to talk – and I'm a really good listener."

He took a last generous swig of whisky then pushed it to the side. "Sally and I were always close. Not as close as she was to her mum but still pretty damn close. I suppose it all started to go wrong after Liz died. She kind of withdrew from me a little – she'd just got engaged and her whole world pretty much revolved around *him*." His expression was that of a man resigned to number two position in his little girl's life. "Of course, it didn't help that I'd never liked him from the off. Too domineering and controlling for my liking, yet she'd do anything to please him – no matter how inconvenient or unacceptable it was."

He turned to look at her. "I just couldn't understand what she saw in him. I'd have given Sally the world – and she knew it."

Alice's heart sank as she compared Gordon's unconditional fatherly love with the desperate fear and hopelessness she'd known.

"Anyway," he went on, "it all came to a head at their engagement party when, after one drink too many, I said some things I probably shouldn't have – after all, it *was* meant to be a celebration."

"So she doesn't speak to you now?"

"I'm hoping she'll return one of my calls soon." He pointed to the calendar on the screen of his mobile. "It's only four weeks til the wedding. All I want is to be able to walk her down the aisle—"

Loud voices startled them from behind as a trio of women bounded raucously into the bar. It was enough to make Gordon sit upright and regain his composure.

"Anyway, enough about me, kiddo." He gave her arm an affectionate rub. "I want to know what the hell's been going on with you."

Resigned to the fact that his emotional disclosures had come to a grinding halt for now, Alice took a much-needed sip of the steaming espresso that had just been placed on the bar in front of her. With a smiling thank you to the barman, she brought Gordon up to speed on all that had transpired since they'd spoken at the funeral: Eva not showing at Bar Rio, the sinister and slightly implausible smartly-dressed drunk, and Victor's job offer. All the while, insisting that Gordon not breathe a word about any of it to her mum – she'd only worry incessantly and that would, in turn, drive Alice to distraction or, more likely, to insanity.

Gordon was a captive audience as she confessed that, only yesterday, she'd investigated a niggling doubt she'd always had about Eva's story. Her gut feeling had proved to be correct as it transpired that there were no Pilates classes locally, or indeed in the surrounding area, at eight o' clock on a Monday evening. Not exactly cast-iron, foolproof evidence that she'd been lying, but still enough for sufficient doubt to linger in the back of her mind.

Alice felt a flutter of relief as Gordon signalled to the barman that he'd join her in an espresso.

"Judging by the way Eva was speaking, I'd say she must've left her job here about – mmm, maybe six months ago, certainly under a year. Someone here *has* to remember her – especially the guys. She's a real looker, you know."

Alice seized her chance as the barman served up Gordon's coffee. "Hey, probably a bit of a long shot but you don't know if a girl called Eva still works here, do you?"

She caught a glimpse of his name badge as he slowly rested his forearms on the wooden counter in front of her. 'Brett' smiled broadly, revealing a set of perfect, pearly-white teeth.

American, surely?

"Eva, you say? Where'd she work in here, then?" he asked in a lilting Texan drawl.

"She was a chambermaid – at least that's what she was doing the last time we spoke. Haven't seen her for about a year now

68

– just thought I'd pop in while I was in town."

"Your best bet's Head of Housekeeping." He nodded towards the bustling reception area beyond the bar doors. "But I like to think I know pretty much all the folks that work here and that name don't ring a bell with me."

"I'm pretty sure you'd remember her – blonde, slim, quite tall, *very* pretty," Alice raised her eyebrows.

"Well, I guess I'd remember her if she were *that* pretty – got a good memory for a pretty face, you see." He gave her a wink as the excitable trio of women approached the bar, demanding his immediate attention.

"Look, gotta go just now – some shameless ladies over there need serving." His green eyes twinkled mischievously. "Give me a few minutes and I'll check with Housekeeping for you, okay?"

"Great, thanks." Alice watched him sashay confidently towards the expectant females. She smiled to herself as the brunette leaned provocatively over the bar, shamelessly displaying an overflowing cleavage.

Gordon tutted under his breath. "Seems to me, kiddo, you could charm the birds out of the trees. Another minute or two and he'd be eating out of your hand."

Alice could feel the brunette brazenly eyeing her up and down as she sipped her freshly-poured Martini and Brett returned to her end of the bar. He gestured 'one minute' with his finger as he picked up the phone beside the cash register.

Alice's eyes were once again drawn to Gordon's shaking hand. At this point, though, she didn't have the nerve to confront him about it.

"Not at all?" Brett turned towards Alice, cradling the phone between his shoulder and ear. "Hey, of course you should know. I know how long you've been working here, you dinosaur." He let out a wicked laugh as he replaced the receiver. "Sorry, nothing to report. I've known George a few years now and if he says nobody of that name, description or nothin's worked in Housekeeping, it's gonna be true." He shrugged his shoulders. "Says they haven't employed a new person for a few years now. Must be a bunch of stubborn job lovers those chambermaids, eh?"

Alice forced a laugh through her disappointment. "Yeah, I must've got the wrong hotel. Thanks, anyway… Brett."

"Hey, happy to help." He flashed another dazzling smile. "Be more than happy to serve you again – anytime."

She smiled back then took a last gulp of espresso as Gordon rummaged in his leather wallet.

"My treat. Let's just head, yeah?"

In awkward silence, they made their way back into the hotel lobby. Alice had never felt so helpless.

"So, what now?" She bit her lip in frustration. "I mean, I can't understand why she'd lie about this – what'd be the point?"

Gordon shook his head. "Any other leads as to where she could be?"

Alice shrugged. "Victor told me she'd gone to stay with a relative but I didn't really believe it. Jesus, who do I believe *now*?"

She shoved her handbag onto her shoulder, and turned towards Gordon. "Look, thanks for coming. Your support means a lot."

He placed a gentle hand on her arm. "Maybe this is a sign that you should just let this go now, kiddo. I've a bad feeling about this – I think you should leave well alone." His frown left Alice in no doubt that he was genuinely worried for her. "And I can't say I'm happy about keeping all of this from your mum, either. It doesn't feel right – we talk a lot these days, me and her, you know. Especially after church." He was struggling to do up the zip of his jacket. "I care for her, Alice, and it just feels a bit – well – deceitful."

Alice sighed. "I know, Gordon but can't you just keep it a secret for a little bit longer? I promise I won't do anything stupid." She widened her eyes. "Please?"

"Don't think you can wind me round your little finger by batting your lashes, either." He leaned in to hug her. "Okay, I'll say nothing – *for now.*" He wagged a finger at her. "Stay in touch, yeah?"

She squeezed his hand. "Of course."

Alice watched Gordon disappear through the revolving doors then made for the ladies'. Maybe a splash or two of cold water on her face might help her come to grips with the revelation that had hit her for six?

As she passed the reception desk, a shiny gold plaque beside a tall archway caught her eye. Her heart pounded as she stared at the engraved lettering heralding the entrance to *The Victor Davies' Conference Suite*.

It was then that Alice knew, in the very depths of her soul, there was simply no escaping him...

CHAPTER ELEVEN

The clock directly above Alice's head gave an abrupt click – signalling that yet another minute had passed – forty now, to be precise – since her mum had disappeared into the Physiotherapy Suite.

She flung an unread leaflet on 'how to spot the signs for diabetes' onto the table in front of her, and sighed.

Not exactly how I was hoping to spend the last day of my week off.

She tried not to think about the lunch she'd cancelled with some girlfriends because her mum had 'wondered' if she'd come to the appointment with her.

Alice did accept, however, that the guilt she would have experienced if she *hadn't* come, would far outweigh the disappointment and resentment she was feeling now.

Despite their strained and often complicated relationship, there were still some duties that, in all good conscience, Alice couldn't ignore.

Her mobile beeped as she rummaged for a bottle of water amidst the chaos of her handbag. As she read the email confirming that her Venetian mask would be delivered in a couple of days' time, she felt a frisson of excitement – followed by a momentary pang of guilt. Yes, she would enjoy the Ball for the evening of entertainment it would undoubtedly be, but she also had to use the opportunity wisely – after all, being on Victor's home territory could be very productive; maybe even enlightening?

Alice massaged her temples as the urge for her first espresso of the day grew stronger – though she knew that it was going to take significantly more than caffeine if she was ever to solve the enigma that was Eva.

Maybe Gordon was right, maybe it *was* time to call it quits? After all, she had no evidence as to where Eva could be; it was almost as if this young woman with supposedly no history or family to speak of, had simply vanished. Victor was surely her only lead now?

She looked up to see her mum being escorted down the corridor by a jovial-looking redhead dressed in a lilac tunic and matching trousers.

"Now, you're going to have to take it easy for a day or two, June, okay?" The physio looked towards Alice as she spoke. "Make sure she doesn't do anything too strenuous, will you? I know she can be pretty stubborn sometimes."

Alice smiled, and watched as she helped her mum slip into her grey woollen coat. Her mum drew a sharp breath and flinched as she tried to manoeuvre the first arm into a sleeve.

"I was pretty vigorous with the manipulation in today's session. Hopefully, these new injections, along with your pills, will help to ease most of the discomfort – at least, until the operation. Probably best if your daughter drives today, though?"

Alice nodded. "Yeah, of course." Thankfully, her mum had had the foresight to add her onto the car insurance.

"This getting old's terrible, you know," her mum joked, but

Alice knew that she was putting a brave face on her pain.

The physio's expression turned sombre. "You know, I think that fall you had all those years ago did more damage than you think—"

Alice looked knowingly at her mum, who continued to stare at the floor as she fastened her coat.

The physio continued. "If they're not dealt with properly at the time, serious injuries or traumas from years ago can end up having a huge impact in later life."

Yeah, mentally as well as physically.

The innocent but pertinent comment was compounded by the abuse poster Alice had clocked on the wall above her mum's head. With the atmosphere taking an awkward turn, her mum turned towards the physio. "Thanks again, Linda."

"Always a pleasure, June. Enjoy lunch with your daughter."

Alice turned to her mum in surprise.

"Thought we might head to that new bistro on the Square? Heard they do a fantastic veggie lasagne. Only if you've got time, though—"

"Of course I've got time, Mum." She swung her bag onto her shoulder. "Bet it's not as tasty as mine, though."

Without saying a word, Alice and her mum smiled at each other, linked arms and made their way out to the car park.

* * *

"This has been really nice – just the two of us having lunch, eh?" Her mum reached over the table to clasp Alice's hand. "We should do this more often – I mean, if you'd like to—"

Here we go again, the blatant insecurity and submissiveness.

"Yeah, I'd like that." Alice leaned back slightly as the waiter placed a generous triangle of lemon cheesecake in front of her. "Mmm, looks good." She gestured for her mum to tuck in.

"So, have you seen Gordon recently?"

Her mum raised a rounded spoonful slowly to her mouth, then rolled her eyes in mock ecstasy as she swallowed the lemony delight. "We see each other every Sunday at church. Occasionally, we meet for coffee or a bite to eat during the week—" Her mum played with the crucifix around her neck. "I know it's probably still a bit weird for you, but we're just enjoying each other's company, that's all." She let out a sigh. "Hopefully, I'm helping to keep his spirits up a bit, what with his daughter not speaking to him and the Parkinson's—"

"The what?" Alice almost choked on her cheesecake.

"You didn't know he had Parkinson's?"

"Shit, no."

"I thought he might've told you when you were chatting after the funeral."

I knew she'd remember that.

"No, that was just boring office stuff—" Alice stared at passing cars in the street outside; she was never comfortable with lying.

"Anyway," her mum went on, "it seems to be at a fairly manageable level just now. Just a matter of time to see how it goes, I suppose."

"I did wonder what the shaking was all about." Alice was eager to find out how much he drank in her mum's company or, at least, how much he'd confessed to drinking. She took a deep breath. "Thought maybe it was alcohol-related?"

Her mum's eyes were wide as she dabbed her mouth with a napkin. "What on earth would give you that idea?"

"Nothing really, just a thought—"

He's obviously watching his step in front of her, then?

Her mum signalled for the bill as she ran a brush through her hair. "It's just so sad that he's not able to share it with his daughter. They used to be really close – apparently, she was a real Daddy's girl—"

Whenever her mum mentioned a father figure in conversation, it was like a trigger for Alice. The devil would instantly appear on her shoulder; urging her to be confrontational, antagonistic; to push her mum's buttons with the same emotional blackmail she'd been rolling out for years.

The waiter appeared at their table before Alice had the chance to say anything. Her mum waved a dismissive hand at her. "Put the purse away, it's my treat."

Alice could see black ominous clouds rolling in from the distance. "Come on, we'd better get back to the car before the downpour."

Seconds after clicking their seat belts in, giant drops of sleety rain splattered the windscreen. As she wrestled with the stiff gear stick, straining desperately to yank it into reverse, her self-control abruptly vanished.

"Christ! See, even when he's dead he's still hurting you. One day you're not able to drive anymore and the next – well, who knows how much he might've crippled you. You need an operation just because 'he couldn't help himself'?" She banged the steering wheel so hard it made her palms sting. "How in the hell do you still forgive him? I mean, try to make me understand." She threw her hands up, desperate to confess about the brain aneurysm her dad's violence had left her with; to prove to her mum just how much he really had hurt her that day all those years ago. The three-second head injury that had hung over her ever since – the unruptured ticking time bomb; silently threatening her all day, every day. But she couldn't do it – deep down she knew she could never share it; never burden her mum with that. Alice took a deep breath and turned to face her.

"Please, just give me something…" she whispered.

Immediately, her mum bowed her head. "He was the man I chose to marry – in God's eyes, I had to stand by that decision. We all have the capacity to forgive if we want to, Alice."

"How nauseating," Alice muttered under her breath as she stared into space beyond the misty windscreen.

Her mum ignored the remark. "Your dad had a lot of pressure after he became Chief Constable – drinking was his way of forgetting about all the hassles, targets, internal politics—" She turned towards her daughter. "He wasn't a bad man, Alice. He just didn't know how to rein in his anger sometimes."

"Jesus, are you even listening to yourself, Mum?" Alice yanked on the handbrake as they screeched to a halt at a red light. "You know the saddest part about all of this? When Gordon was my boss, he was like the father I wished I'd had." She turned towards her mum. "Kind of ironic, huh?"

As the car manouevred the last junction and pulled up outside her mum's house, the heavens opened and the car reverberated to the tinny echo of rain pummelling the roof.

Slipping her hands into black leather gloves, her mum turned to face her full on. "Look, I don't want to part on bad terms today." Her voice was low and gentle and her eyes were misty. "There's something I never told you about your dad." Alice watched as her mum fidgeted continuously with her gloved hands. She couldn't remember ever seeing her this agitated before.

"Since he died, I've been living with something that haunts me, every hour of every day." Alice's blood ran cold as her mum's eyes welled with tears. "I know you've never understood my forgiveness of what he did – to both of us. But believe me when I say that he hated himself for it." The chilly air inside the car was turning each breath into a ghostly cloud.

"Oh, come on. He was hardly the remorseful type now, was he?"

Her mum stared straight ahead. "Wasn't he, Alice?"

She eyed her mum warily before the words she was frightened to utter flowed from her mouth. "What are you saying?"

Despite the bitterness and frustration she'd struggled with for as long as she could remember, Alice sensed that what her mum was about to say, was going to make her feel vulnerable; make her crumble – just a little bit.

"Your dad left me a note before he went out that night—"

Alice could only nod her head as her throat began to close up; she could barely take a breath, let alone make a sound. Her terror was making any interaction between her brain and her vocal cords an impossibility. The feeling of dread was suffocating.

"I knew he wouldn't be coming home that night – or ever. I never showed you the note because I didn't want to burden you with the awful truth."

"What was in the note? Just tell me – I can handle it."

Her mum took a deep breath, just as the deafening sound of the rain on the roof began to fade. "It was a letter of repentance. He said he was sorry to the depths of his soul for what he'd put us through but he couldn't handle the guilt, the self-loathing any longer. The last words he wrote were 'you'd both be better off without me'."

She removed her gloves finger by finger then leaned over to grab Alice's hands.

"You see, that's why I *have* to forgive him. It wasn't an accident that he drowned, Alice – your dad killed himself."

CHAPTER TWELVE

Alice woke up on her twenty-fifth birthday, desperate to cry.

Ever since her mum's bombshell confession about her dad, it took just a second or two of consciousness each morning before the barrage of emotions would launch their brutal attack.

Happy bloody birthday, Alice.

She kicked the duvet off and threw her legs over the edge of the bed. Slipping into her sumptuously soft furry slippers felt like bliss after last night's hectic shift at the restaurant.

As she made her way down the dim staircase towards the kitchen, she pulled her dressing gown around her more tightly than normal and shuffled towards the front door to pick up the mail. A handful of birthday cards lay strewn amongst some bills and circulars. She scooped them up, deciding to open them over some toast and extra strong coffee.

Yawning, she flicked the switch on the espresso maker and bumped down onto the kitchen chair. The gentle gurgling of the machine would usually lift her spirits on a chilly working morning – but not today. Alice was beginning to feel a dark and oppressive mist descending upon her; as if she was drowning, little by little, in a sea of frustration and hopelessness. And it worried her – it worried her a lot.

Maybe now's a good time to try some 'happy pills'? God knows, the therapy was useless last time around.

She picked up the first envelope in the pile, instantly recognising Pete's illegible handwriting. Her heart sank as she remembered that it was only a fortnight now until he moved away. A lump grew in her throat as she read his words.

To Alice – a very special friend. No matter where I go or how far apart we are, I will always think the world of you. Pete x

Threatening tears burned the back of her eyes. She knew in her heart that *she* was to blame for all of this; from the start of their relationship right up until now. If only she could have let him in, let her defences down – just a bit – maybe, just maybe it could have worked between them?

Pouring her freshly-brewed coffee, she promised herself that she'd speak to him later at the press conference. There'd be ample time to corner him before the photo call and the whole media frenzy kicked off.

Her mobile pinged as she reached for the steaming mug of coffee. Her eyes slid from the golden triangle of perfectly-buttered toast to the iPhone on the table. It was a BBC News alert: a photo of a tall building up in flames filled the screen.

She clicked the link below the heading then lifted the phone for a closer look. Her jaw froze mid-chew as she fell back into the chair; her weary eyes widening at the wild, rampant flames engulfing every charred storey of a tower block in the city. The background hysteria of wailing sirens and frantic voices only magnified the horror of the shaky handheld footage. Yet Alice couldn't take her eyes off it. It was both horrifying and morbidly fascinating as she let the terrifying burning image slowly sear into her brain. She finally swallowed the warm, soggy mound of toast she'd held in her cheeks for the last few minutes; its claggy stickiness lodging itself in the back of her throat. She covered her mouth, preparing for a coughing fit, but nothing – nothing… except hot, unexpected tears spilling down both cheeks.

The thought of all those innocent unsuspecting people, potentially trapped; burning alive, made her stomach heave and her heart tear in two. It was as though she was imagining what it was like to be there…

She blew out a long, slow breath and wrapped her hands around the mug of coffee in front of her. The instant blast of warmth against her palms was welcome comfort in the cool half-light of the kitchen.

Wiping the tears away, her eyes were drawn to a large red envelope in the pile of mail. Although she didn't recognise the writing, she felt she already knew who had sent it. Tentatively, she pulled the card out; gradually revealing an image that took her breath away. Two ornate cups of black coffee sat in the middle of a wooden floor, bordered by a mass of towering, flaming blood-red candles; their soft, atmospheric glow almost tangible.

Whether it was the similarity between the picture and the image in her dream, Alice couldn't be sure. All she knew was that the illusion of gentle flickering movement in the flames was uncanny. Either that or she was starting to lose her mind.

Before she'd even counted them, she instinctively knew there would be twenty-five candles. Sheer coincidence or a card designed specifically for her? She turned it over to check the company logo on the back – it was completely blank. In a fluster, she flicked it open to reveal the elegant handwritten message inside:

Happy 25th Birthday, Alice.

I look forward to seeing you on Saturday.

Victor x

A chill crept slowly up her spine.

How the hell does he know it's my birthday?

* * *

Alice picked up speed; she was dangerously close to being late for the press conference she'd had in her diary for the last two weeks. This one was going to be a biggie.

The leisurely birthday lunch with the girls from the office had passed in a flash. Now she had just five minutes to find a space, park the company car and get her ass inside the hotel before the boy-band sensation of the decade made their big announcement.

Alice jostled herself through the mass of journalists and cameramen towards a spot near the door of the swarming hotel foyer. Seconds later, a stocky, official-looking suit with an earpiece gave them a ten-minute heads-up on the famous quartet's arrival.

Pete caught her eye from the other side of the room and pointed towards a secluded table and chairs just off the main reception area. She gave him a thumbs up and jostled her way through the crowd towards him. Beyond the huge window beside him was an endless sea of hysterical teenage girls.

Pete smiled at her as she sat down beside him on the double sofa.

"Good to see you." She patted his knee. "Thanks for the card, by the way."

"I wasn't sure if I'd see you today so thought I'd post it, just in case." He leaned in for a kiss and a hug. "Happy birthday, lady."

"Cheers, bud." She nodded towards the manic gathering outside. "Mad, isn't it? What's the bets they're announcing they're splitting up?"

"About bloody time, too," he said, rolling his eyes.

Alice smiled, not just at his remark but in relief; after the recent tension between them, it was starting to feel okay again.

"So, I was wondering if you fancied catching up over some pizza and drinks tonight? You know, to celebrate your birthday—"

"That sounds great but mum's invited me round to hers tonight – can't really say no."

"Sure. How about Saturday, then? We could have a few more drinks at the weekend anyway."

She could feel herself tense. "Shit, no – can't do Saturday, either, I'm afraid."

Pete studied her for a second or two; silently waiting for an explanation. Alice couldn't look at him as she visualised where she knew she'd be that night.

Out of the corner of her eye, she saw the mass of media squeezing through the conference room doors at the opposite side of the room. "Look, how about a night next week?"

He bent over to scoop up a canvas satchel bursting with equipment, before hoisting it onto his shoulder. With his muscular frame, tousled, shiny locks and dark eyes, he was a great catch – by anyone's standards.

"It's my last week at work next week." He pouted his lips. "You're not getting out of this pizza, you know. Don't let me down, Alice—" His pleading, soulful eyes were the last straw for her.

"Oh, bloody hell – enough with the puppy-dog face already." She playfully jabbed his arm. "Let's say Tuesday, then. Come on, mustn't keep the heartthrobs waiting."

Fifteen minutes later than expected, the four band members took their seats on the raised platform. Alice smiled politely at the harassed female who bumped down next to her, slightly out of breath, at the end of the row. Straight ahead, she could see Pete, standing his ground amidst the crowd of jostling, paparazzi and TV cameramen; all desperately trying to manoeuvre their way towards the prime spot.

It took just a few minutes before the lead singer and poster boy of every teenage girl in the country made the announcement they'd been anticipating. After their split was confirmed, there was a brief mention about the next world tour being their last before Simon, the youngest and typically quietest member of the group, leaned in towards his microphone. What came next, blindsided everyone.

"I'd like to say one more thing before everybody leaves… please." He cleared his throat with two nervous coughs. "One of my dearest friends, Kelly Stevens, has been missing for two years this coming weekend. Please, if anybody knows anything – anything at all – about where she could be, or Kelly, if you're listening – please just get in touch and let us know you're okay." He hung his head, emotion overcoming him. "We've not forgotten about you, babe."

The heartfelt plea received a warm round of applause from the media audience, as well as a few empathetic looks between some of the female contingent.

Then something clicked inside Alice's head – it suddenly dawned on her why the day was so significant. This Saturday, which also happened to be the day of Victor's Ball, would also mark the second anniversary of her dad's death. Despite the two traumatic events sharing the same date, Alice had never really connected them in any way before. Now, though, something was starting to fester within her; something ominous in the deepest, darkest recesses of her mind – thriving on her unease, stoking her insecurities.

Her gut instinct had never let her down before, yet she desperately wanted to dismiss it as sheer coincidence; two completely separate events that just happened to occur on the same day, in the same year. Against her better judgement, was she now over-analysing every detail; blowing everything out of proportion?

Yet, no matter how hard she tried to suppress it, a feeling of foreboding was starting to dominate; a feeling so inevitable; so relentless, that it stayed with her, for the rest of her waking hours, until her mind and body finally succumbed to a deep and disturbing sleep.

CHAPTER THIRTEEN

Peering over her shoulder into the narrow, full-length mirror, Alice gave her strapless emerald dress one last check then choked back the lukewarm Pinot that had been sitting on her bedside table for over an hour.

With the dulcet tones of Ella Fitzgerald blaring from her iPod speakers, she tutted before impatiently redoing what she deemed a below-standard chignon for so prestigious an event as a masquerade ball.

She quickly spritzed her favourite musky perfume onto her neck and wrists, slicked her lips with a generous dollop of clear gloss, then held the Venetian mask up to her face. Yes, the iridescent sheen of the sparkling jewel colours complemented her long gown perfectly.

With the harsh glare of the ceiling light beaming down onto her forehead, Alice realised how obvious the scar above her eyebrow still was. Eight years on and she was still dabbing concealer on it to make it 'go away'. But the memory of how she got that scar and what it had left her with could not be so easily erased; nor the emotional scars that had endured ever since.

She shook her head as it all came crashing back. She'd only been five minutes late returning home from her first-ever date, but that was all the excuse her dad needed. More often than not, it was the verbal abuse – so hatefully and venomously spat at her – that hurt the most. But not this time; when his open hand had struck her with such an almighty force that she was thrust sideways, only to fall face-down onto the sharp corner of her bedside table – the impact just missing her eye by centimetres. She thought she'd heard him slur 'stupid slut' as he stumbled out of the room, but that didn't bother her. She was too numb with the pain from her throbbing, bleeding head for anything else to matter. Little did she know then that she'd be living with the consequences for the rest of her life.

Shortly after that, she developed what the therapist nonchalantly called a 'defensive coping mechanism'. Essentially, she'd begun to associate any romantic liaison or relationship with negativity and getting hurt. Alice conceded that, in psychiatric terms, it was a fairly convincing stock phrase – those mind doctors always liked to attach a professional-sounding label to things they could ultimately do nothing about.

But Alice sure as hell didn't fall into the 'I've been diagnosed, so let's have a chat and I should hopefully feel much better' category. Besides, it hadn't been her idea to go to therapy, anyway. Her student-exchange friend in California had cajoled her into it after she'd confessed about the abuse one evening, over one bottle of wine too many. After that initial disheartening experience, Alice swore that she'd never attend therapy again.

Two rings of the doorbell made her quickly fasten her flowing velvet cape; just below the tear-drop diamond necklace that was only granted removal from its velvet box on special occasions.

She scurried in her kitten heels towards the front door, snatching her satin clutch off the phone consol as she passed. A quick peek inside to check for her crystal then she opened the door to greet Victor's driver, standing in full chauffeur regalia on the frosty doorstep.

"Miss Webster. Pleased to meet you." He tipped his cap and extended a gloved hand. "My name's Edward. I'll be your driver to Westgrove tonight."

Alice shivered as she stepped out into the chilly but perfectly still evening air. "Thank you." She smiled at him as he opened the car door for her.

God, this is the size of my living room.

Edward closed the door behind her as she admired the stunning interior of Victor's limo. It appeared to have most of the comforts of a small apartment: the cream leather seat was the size of a large single bed, and there was a ludicrous amount of space between her and the front of the car. A state-of-the-art sound system and integrated bar took up most of the left-hand side below an ultra-thin plasma screen in the top corner, whilst a sprawling leather seat adorned with over-sized cushions in a variety of sumptuous fabrics filled the opposite side. Pale blue, low-level lighting and subtle, tiny spotlights in the roof created a calming and intimate atmosphere.

Alice picked up what was clearly a freshly-poured flute of champagne from the illuminated glass counter beside her, just as the blacked-out screen behind Edward's head slowly lowered.

"I'll have you there in about fifteen minutes, Miss Webster."

"Great. Thank you, Edward." Alice sipped the perfectly-chilled fizzy as she gazed out of the window at the passing urban scenery. Minutes later, the limo accelerated smoothly and quietly out of the city, into the oncoming darkness of the countryside. As the last lamppost disappeared out of view, Alice noticed how beautifully crisp and clear the night sky looked; not a breath of wind or a brooding cloud in sight – just the glorious flawlessness of the full moon amidst infinite twinkling constellations.

She sighed, savouring the tingling sensation of the sparkling bubbles on her tongue before swallowing another delicious mouthful. Her eyes were drawn to rolling footage of the splitting boyband on the plasma screen and her thoughts instantly turned to Pete. Maybe a bit of distance between them would be no bad thing; might even help to put a fresh perspective on things?

Alice turned to look at the deserted road behind her – not a vehicle or cat's eye in sight; just the faultless reflection of the moon on a still lake as they sped past. In her mind's eye, she couldn't picture where this piece of water was. She started to feel disorientated as the limo weaved this way and that around a tree-lined hairpin bend; so densely wooded that no moonlight could penetrate it. For a moment, Alice wondered why she'd even accepted Victor's invitation; put her trust in this uniformed stranger to drive her in the dark of night to somewhere she'd never been before.

Then, a smooth ninety-degree turn later – as the car stopped dead in front of a pair of towering gates – her doubts vanished. Alice gasped as the limo continued on to crunch softly up a sweeping gravelled driveway towards the most imposing house she'd ever seen. Straight ahead, on the brow of a hill, stood half a dozen proud marble columns heralding the entrance above a set of elegant steps; each row narrowing more gradually as it neared the top.

As Edward drew the limo to a gentle halt, Alice could see several rows of expensive cars parked to the side; where the grounds of the house met the flickering lanterns that bordered the vast garden.

Seconds later, the door opened and Edward held a gloved hand out. Alice slid herself along the leather seat towards him; clutch bag and mask in hand.

"If I may say, Miss Webster, you look utterly radiant," he said, helping her gently out of the car.

"You're too kind." She fiddled with a diamante earring as the heat rose in her cheeks. "And thank you for the lift, Edward."

"My pleasure." He tipped his cap again and, with a sweeping hand, gestured her forwards.

Alice smiled nervously, suddenly feeling vulnerable as she stood alone in front of the grand building. She raised the hem of her dress slightly off the ground then carefully made her way up the steps towards a small gathering of guests outside the entrance. As she got closer to them, the masks turned in unison to look at her. It occurred to Alice how unnerving it was not being able to see their faces; after all, wasn't it human nature to want to judge how people might be feeling; gauge what they might be thinking?

Standing in the still but biting air next to one of the marble pillars, Alice appreciated the heat emanating from the flames in the wrought-iron baskets flanking either side of the top step.

She looked beyond the small crowd, into the entrance of the house. Beneath a magnificent glittering chandelier, she could see the back of a tall, dark-haired man in a black suit in conversation with a female in a harlequin mask.

Alice positioned her own mask over her face, tied it gently at the back then edged towards the front door, where she was warmly greeted by a butler offering to take her cape. As she shifted slightly to allow him to remove it from her shoulders, the dark-haired man turned around – permitting Alice a perfect view of his profile. From his scarlet mask protruded a long, slightly curved nose which tapered sharply at the end just above his top lip, giving it a hook-like quality. The woman in the harlequin mask bent over in laughter to touch his forearm then proceeded to inch closer towards him. Despite the mask covering most of his face, it was the mannerisms, the posture, the undeniable presence, that gave Victor's identity away.

No sooner had the butler ushered her forwards into the resplendent hallway, than Alice felt his eyes upon her.

Does he know it's me?

The knowing half-smile playing around Victor's lips as he strode towards her, was all the answer she needed. He stopped, standing directly before her, not saying a word. Although his mask didn't move an inch, he was close enough for her to see his dark eyes slowly and deliberately examining her from head to toe.

And then he spoke. "Simply breathtaking, Alice." He bent forward to place a gentle kiss on the back of her hand. She was thankful for the mask concealing the blush of her cheeks.

"I didn't mean to pull you away." Alice nodded to the female behind him, now standing alone rather awkwardly.

"More than happy to escape – sorry… I mean, leave." She smirked at the intentional Freudian slip, as Victor whisked two flutes of champagne from a passing waiter's tray.

"Please." He offered one to Alice then proceeded to chink them both together.

"To your health and, hopefully, a most entertaining evening."

Four shrill rings halted all conversation as a butler waving a hand-held bell announced that guests were to make their way through to the Grand Hall for the evening's entertainment.

Two elaborate mahogany doors were instantly swept open and, as if on cue, the sweetest concerto music echoed throughout the room. As the crowd bustled into the stately hall, Alice could see a full orchestra positioned in front of an impressive, panoramic bay window. Seconds later, a soprano accompanied the musicians and everyone turned to gaze in awe at the buxom brunette with the harmonious, pitch-perfect voice.

Shortly after, as the heart-wrenching strain of the violins reached a dramatic and spine-tingling crescendo, Victor appeared by the soprano's side, smiling broadly. Applause erupted around the room as he gestured with both hands towards singer and orchestra. With the frantic clapping and appreciative nods slowly waning, Victor took his place behind the microphone stand. He raised both hands towards the ceiling, letting out a theatrical sigh.

"How the hell do I follow that?" He cleared his throat in a half-laugh as the captive audience delighted in his mock despair.

"I'd like to take this opportunity to welcome you all to my annual masquerade ball. Don't worry, folks, the wonderful music and singing will continue throughout the night – as will the flowing of copious amounts of Moët & Chandon, I'm sure. First things first, though." He extended a hand towards a few middle-aged men seated at the nearest table. "I'd like to express my heartfelt gratitude and thanks to these guys sitting here."

Cue a nearby waiter passing him a crystal flute full to the brim with sparkling bubbles.

"Without you, the fracking proposal would have been a dead cert and we'd be looking at yet *another* environmental crisis in the area. So, without further ado, I ask you to raise your glass to my modest but thoroughly-deserving colleagues from the Davies' Conservation Trust." Some champagne slopped onto the wooden floor below as he raised his glass in front of him. "Billy Campbell, Tom Stevens and Matt Jones, I couldn't have done it without you – and you bloody well know it."

Alice's surprised gaze switched to the three men now standing to rapturous laughter and applause.

So, Victor had a hand in the fracking being rejected – she certainly hadn't seen that coming. The man certainly kept a lot under his 'business' hat, that was for sure.

But it was only as he continued his speech that Alice became aware of the effect Victor was having on his audience. His charisma was undeniable – here was a man who could, quite literally, charm the birds out of the proverbial trees. Various sources could also attest to his unparalleled powers of persuasion, his irrefutable influence in the boardroom and other negotiation scenarios. He hadn't accumulated wealth and success of this magnitude by sheer luck.

Alice scanned the sea of masks that filled the room: a truly captivated audience; none more so than the women who all appeared to be completely bewitched by him. In this relaxed environment, it was hard to ignore the flirting that bordered on shameless; the coquettish, surreptitious looks in his direction from the few females who'd already removed their masks.

Perhaps it was the flowing champagne that had loosened their inhibitions; bolstered their confidence? Whatever it was, though, Alice couldn't help but notice the extent to which Victor was being so eagerly and wantonly pursued. Surely he could not be blind to such attention, such blatant adoration? The sycophancy from the men was perfectly understandable – after all, Victor was the epitome of rags to riches, self-made success. But the female reaction wasn't so easy to explain. Alice wondered how many of them had experienced the same intense, inexplicable pull towards him; the almost spiritual magnetism; the burgeoning heat in the very core of their soul. Those emotions surely weren't felt solely by her?

She took another sip of the exquisitely crisp champagne as Victor said his last words and stepped away from the microphone. Alice was lost in the surreal grandeur of the moment when a sudden cool touch on her bare shoulder startled her enough to spill some champagne down her dress. She spun around to confront a tall, lanky figure in a tuxedo and bow tie wearing a mask that could only be described as hideous. Alice recoiled slightly, unable to stop herself from grimacing.

"Pretty gross, isn't it?" The soft, almost adolescent voice was in stark contrast to the gruesome, zombie-like monstrosity she was staring at. "I've had a few not too complimentary remarks about it already." His tone was more immature bragging than remorseful.

Alice was unsure how to respond to the young man's comment and found herself scanning the hall for Victor. "I'm quite sure you have," she offered, finally catching sight of him in the far corner beside the orchestra. He'd removed his mask and looked deep in conversation with a silver-haired, bearded professor type. His expression was solemn and business-like; a far cry from his carefree demeanour only minutes before. As though sensing her, Victor looked over; his expression instantly switching from sombre to curious when he clocked the man standing beside her.

"I just wanted to introduce myself to the gorgeous girl standing all alone."

Alice smiled politely, curbing the desire to roll her eyes at his cringeworthy banter. She could see Victor approaching out of the corner of her eye.

He thrust a hand out. "Philip Thomson – Mr Davies' successor in, oh, hopefully ten to fifteen years—" Although he laughed off the ludicrously ambitious projection of his future employment, Alice sensed an innate confidence bordering on arrogance. Before she'd uttered her name in reply, Victor was standing by her side.

"I see you've already introduced yourself to Alice, Philip." The questioning cadence in his voice made the simple statement accusatory.

"So it's Alice, is it?" Philip removed his mask then bent down to kiss her hand. The reek of his pungent aftershave caught the back of her throat as he lowered then lifted his head again.

Late teens, early twenties, at a push?

"Philip, it's fair to say, is a genius I persuaded to work for me a couple of years ago." Victor smirked at Alice then lent in conspiratorially. "A pain in the ass, but an I.T. genius, nonetheless."

"Hey, he knows a good thing when he sees it." Philip winked

suggestively at her, as the bearded man appeared once again by Victor's side and whispered something in his ear. The two men proceeded to enter into another conversation.

"So, how do *you* know Victor, then?" Judging by the mischievous expression on his face, Philip was keenly anticipating some juicy gossip.

Alice felt a flutter of panic as the question of why she was at the party, coupled with all the recent revelations and events, suddenly became very blurred. "I interviewed him for a feature in the *Gazette* a short while ago—" She didn't know if what she'd just blurted out deemed her worthy of an invite to a mega-businessman's party or not.

Victor turned towards them again. "Alice, I'd like to introduce you to my good friend – and even better lawyer – Charles."

Sensing that he might now be surplus to requirement, Philip excused himself, just as Victor gestured that he'd return in a couple of minutes.

"A pleasure to meet you, Alice." Charles stepped forward to shake her hand. Despite his stiff, scholarly demeanour, Alice noticed how kind and soft his eyes were when he smiled. "Victor's told me all about you." He leaned in conspiratorially. "You know, I can't say I ever recall him speaking quite so openly and enthusiastically about a young lady before—" His twinkling pale grey eyes were intense and searching; imploring her to respond. "I don't mean to embarrass you, Alice," Charles continued, "But you must know that he really is *quite* taken with you."

Alice laughed nervously. "I'm sure a man like Victor gets on perfectly well with most people."

Charles smiled wryly as he gestured to the hordes surrounding them. "My dear, you must appreciate there are very few people in this world who Victor feels he can genuinely trust." He adjusted his bow tie in the manner of an authoritative figure well accustomed to being listened to; whose judgements and opinions were held in the highest of regard by virtue of his wisdom and experience. "I've known Victor since he was a young man. To say he's a complex character would be a gross understatement. Cross him and a grudge will more than likely remain for life. However—" He wagged his finger and peered over his glasses with wide, imploring eyes. "The flip side of the hard-nosed businessman is a deeply passionate, caring person."

Alice couldn't pinpoint Charles' soft, cut-glass accent – his otherwise faultless Queen's English had the faintest continental lilt to it. Nevertheless, the compassion and conviction in it was proof enough that the old man obviously had a lot of time for Victor.

"Surely he trusted Eva, though?" The words were out before Alice had time to think about what she was saying.

No sooner had her name been uttered, than Charles' previously unfaltering stare vanished and his eyes slid to the sea of gowns and tuxedos in the room.

"Eva? Well, I…" He whisked a glass from a passing waiter's tray and proceeded to down its contents in two swift, loud gulps. Alice noticed the tiny droplets of sweat that had gathered in the wrinkles of his forehead dripping slowly into his bushy silver eyebrows.

"Aah, the man himself returns." Relief spread over his flushed face as he caught sight of Victor walking back towards them. "I'm sorry but there's someone I must speak to now," he said, patting a cursory palm on the side of her arm. "I'm sure we'll speak again soon, Alice." He smiled with polite detachment then turned on his heel, just as Victor appeared by her side again and the orchestra struck up the introduction to the Viennese Waltz.

"Right, Miss Webster. Enough of the serious face," he ordered, linking his arm into hers. "Isn't it time we had our first dance of the evening?"

No sooner had he finished speaking, than Alice was being whisked into the centre of the gleaming floor. Victor cut a figure of perfect composure as they stood facing each other directly below the centrepiece chandelier. In stark contrast, Alice felt terrifyingly exposed.

Was it paranoia conjuring the sneers of derision, the intolerant tuts under the breath, the judgemental eyes narrowed in contempt?

"So, how did you know it was my birthday a couple of weeks ago?" she asked, huffing in frustration at herself. Try as she might, Alice could never resist the temptation to fill even the briefest of awkward silences. Victor smiled as he reassuringly cupped her waist; guiding her like a professional across the deserted dance floor. Alice caught a mischievous glint in his eye.

"And you kept the whole fracking thing quiet as well. You do like your secrets, don't you?"

A smug grin was playing around his lips.

"Isn't it nice to have a bit of intrigue in life, leave a little to the imagination sometimes?" He winked before sweeping her off her feet into a spin that left her gliding in mid-air, incapable of speech.

Ironically, his domineering movements didn't offend or rile her; never having been au fait with formal dance of any kind, she permitted herself to revel in his competence. A few couples joined them on the dance floor as the music picked up apace; Alice took a deep breath to relax her shoulders. Confident that it would now not be obvious if she left the room, she whispered to Victor that she needed to get some air.

As she approached the mahogany door, a waiting butler graciously swept it open for her – wafting the most blissful, refreshing breeze across her glistening face and neck. Standing alone in the welcome coolness of the entrance hall, she bent down to adjust the shoe strap that had been digging into the front of her foot for the last hour or so. As she stood upright and removed her mask, her eyes were drawn towards a willowy figure in a black halter-neck dress and sparkling silver mask leaning over the balustrade at the top of the staircase. Alice held her breath as she watched her carefully absorb the party scene below. Although the mask concealed most of her face, there was an air of longing and wonder flowing from her, as though this was the first time she'd witnessed the spectacle that night.

Alice stood transfixed, unable to tear her gaze away – even when the silver mask turned and stopped, setting its sights firmly upon her. Alice was sure she hadn't seen this guest until now, yet the escalating pounding of her heart in her chest, was proof enough that she knew exactly who she was looking at.

Aghast, she watched the masked figure turn abruptly and disappear through a doorway on the first floor. With adrenalin coursing through her, Alice's instinct was to rush after her; the girl she believed in her gut was Eva. For a brief second, she struggled with the dilemma of what she should do. But with every fibre of her being urging her to follow in hot pursuit, she quickly accepted that she'd be damned if she was going to pass this opportunity by.

Snatching a couple of looks about her, Alice attempted her best nonchalant walk up a staircase; silently praying that she didn't look at all suspicious disappearing upstairs on her own in a multi-millionaire's mansion. She glanced back briefly at the top, sighing in relief that her ascent had gone largely unnoticed.

The door that Eva had slipped through now stood directly in front of her and was fully closed. Alice steeled herself and took a deep breath before gently lowering the brass handle. As she crept through the doorway, the background noise from the ground floor faded into the distance. She flinched as the fire door closed with an abrupt click behind her. Clutch bag and mask still in hand, she stood looking up the unfeasibly long corridor towards the right-angled turn at the top.

As her eyes adjusted to the subdued wall lighting, she could feel her heels sinking slowly into the lush pile of the sage green carpet underfoot. Taking her first tentative steps towards the enormous landscape painting on the far wall, she thought she could make out a gently flickering shadow underneath it and slightly to the right; the movements so subtle that Alice couldn't be sure if her eyes were playing tricks on her or not. When the shadow disappeared in one fleet movement, she picked up speed, confident that when she turned the corner, she would come face to face with Eva.

A combined swell of panic and exasperation forced her to fracture the silence.

"Hello?" The word was barely audible.

She peered around the corner to catch the floaty train of

a black dress disappearing around yet another bend in the corridor.

What is she playing at?

Beside her was a ceiling-high window perfectly framing a full moon partially hidden behind the ghostly silhouette of frost-tipped tree branches. In the far-reaching, ethereal moonlight, Victor's vast estate appeared stunningly beautiful.

Fearful of venturing any further into the house, Alice took her frustration out on some hairpins that had come loose during her waltz with Victor. She yanked them impatiently from the now bedraggled chignon and shook her head from side to side, allowing her bouffant, slightly hairspray-stiffened locks to fall behind her bare shoulders.

But as she turned to make her way back along the corridor, her legs refused to move. Something was keeping her rooted to the spot and dragging her gaze helplessly up towards the huge framed picture hanging on an otherwise empty wall beside her. Alice craned her neck to stare up at the portrait, firstly in awe at the sheer size of it, then in sadness. As she studied the expression on the young woman's face, tears began to burn behind her eyes and an overwhelming ache of loss and grief spread through her. With frantic eyes, she consumed every inch of the aristocratic-looking woman; from her melancholy, warm brown eyes to the rich, lustrous auburn hair, scooped neatly into a half bun at the nape of her long, elegant neck. A beam of moonlight from the window opposite highlighted her rose-tinted lips, which, although loosely closed in formality, seemed to scream in mournful desperation. Her porcelain skin was flawless and radiant, as though bathed in the diffused glow of the softest candlelight.

Alice's legs trembled as she stood transfixed; unable to

tear her gaze away, despite the pain and upset it was causing her. There was a palpable empathy; an innate understanding flowing between herself and the portrait that, in her heart and soul, Alice could accept but which logic wanted to dismiss. Had she been lured to this very spot on purpose or had it all been in the hands of fate? Wiping away the persistent tears that flowed down her cheeks, she shuddered as the temperature in the corridor plummeted and each outward breath now became a vaporous cloud in front of her.

In that instant, relief surged through her and, as though an oppressive weight had been lifted, Alice ran as fast as she could back down the corridor and through the door. She stopped dead at the top of the hallway staircase, with no consideration as to how suspicious she might look standing all alone, teary-eyed and out of breath.

She placed a trembling hand onto the bevelled mahogany bannister in an effort to steady both her balance and her nerves. From the middle of the staircase, she looked down towards a gathering of guests under the chandelier and saw Victor among them. He was staring straight at her; his face disconcertingly blank; devoid of all expression. Alice's heart sank as she realised she'd been well and truly caught. Bracing herself for the inevitable interrogation, she stared steadfastly at her feet as she walked towards him, only raising her eyes to meet his at the last second as she stood before him.

He tutted and slowly shook his head.

"You know, Alice," he sighed, his lips hinting at a smile, "if you'd wanted a tour of the house, all you had to do was ask. I hope you didn't get lost when you were upstairs? It's like a rabbit warren, isn't it?"

She tensed as he quietly took in her dishevelled hair and

teary eyes.

"I thought I saw somebody I knew, that's all." She mindlessly shook her head.

He nodded in polite understanding as she nervously smoothed her hair. Her eyes were still nipping from the tears but she couldn't bring herself to touch them.

"Look, it's time I was going—" She looked past him into the jovial, slightly inebriated crowd.

As if to draw a line under their tense exchange, he offered his hand. "It's been my pleasure, Alice."

She held hers out in courtesy and was taken aback when he turned it over to place a gentle second kiss upon it. She could see Charles standing behind Victor, chatting and laughing with a middle-aged masked couple whilst maintaining a keen eye on them both. As if out of nowhere, a butler appeared by Victor's side with her cape.

"Please." Victor gestured towards the front entrance after she'd fastened it. "I'll see you to the car."

Alice nodded and they walked out into the bitterly cold night. Not a word was spoken as they slowly made their way down the regal steps that twinkled with a delicate layer of frost. Alice hoisted her cape up to her chin, as gust after icy gust of wind whipped up and around her, chilling her to the bone. Victor's hand cupped her lower back as Edward drew the limousine to a halt at the bottom of the steps.

She couldn't look at him as she ducked her head into the car then shuffled along the seat.

"Take care, Alice." The howling gale drowned out his voice as he closed the door behind her.

She suddenly felt horribly alone as the car pulled away from the entrance. Alice threw her head back onto the leather seat;

her head throbbing with the painful barrage of conflicting emotions. With a sudden overwhelming urge to look back, she twisted herself around and noticed a softly-lit round window in the apex of the house.

Then, with the car gently trundling its way back down the winding driveway and the house disappearing into the distance, a silhouette appeared behind the glass. The ghostly apparition stood motionless, except to press a solitary palm up against the window.

Edward's voice jolted her back into the moment.

"I trust you had an enjoyable evening, ma'am."

Alice snatched a last backwards glance at Victor's house. "Yes, very enjoyable thanks," she said, just as the light in the round window went out.

CHAPTER FOURTEEN

Alice smiled as she read the text from Gordon that had just flashed up on her phone. She could only imagine how happy and relieved he must be to get, not just a response from his daughter, but an invite to dinner as well. Leaning back in her office chair, she typed a quick congratulatory reply, thankful that his message had distracted her from dwelling on the wretched nightmare that had plagued her for most of the night.

They'd been coming more sporadically of late – and were nowhere near as terrifying – but last night's was a completely different dream to any she'd had before. It was the tears streaming down her face that had woken her this time; quickly followed by an ache so deep inside her, it felt like her heart was slowly breaking, piece by piece. She recalled trying desperately to prop herself up onto her elbows but the sobs – each a gut-wrenching, lung-bursting gulp of air – left her so hopelessly feeble that all she could do was let her body fall like a limp rag onto the duvet. Then, after what seemed like minutes, having fallen into the deepest, most restful slumber she'd enjoyed since God knows when, her alarm *had* to go off.

It was only after stumbling bleary-eyed into the bathroom and looking in the mirror that she noticed the red, scratch-like marks around her neck. Alice hazily recalled clutching at her throat as she'd woken; then came the dull stinging sensation as the tears that had dripped down her hand soaked into a patch of raw, broken skin. As her mind subconsciously fused together the seemingly random, unrelated threads of the dream, she could feel something sinister seeping into her soul.

"Hey, Alice," an urgent voice whispered from behind.

She spun her chair around to catch Matt from the Sports Desk with his eyes and nose peering cartoon-like over the partition.

"When you hearing about the promotion, then?" He proceeded to flit his wide eyes in short darting bursts towards Alan's office.

Alice shrugged, irritated by his melodrama.

"Pretty big deal, though, eh?" he continued, sneaking his way around the partition towards her desk.

Lynn, the unofficial office dogsbody, appeared behind Matt a few seconds later, clutching a scarlet ringbinder to her chest as though her life depended on it. She sighed, pushing her rectangular, rimless glasses to the top of her nose with her index finger one too many times.

"Alan wants you in his office now," she announced with her usual monotony.

"Cheers, Lynn." Alice ignored Matt's persistent gaze, knowing that if she so much as glanced at him, she'd end up biting his head off.

Great, soon everyone on the floor will know my bloody fate.

She smiled politely as she brushed past them both, her stomach somersaulting as she knocked tentatively on the glass panel of Alan's door. Seconds later, an abrupt, muffled voice ordered her to enter. She closed the door behind her with an inconspicuous click, fully expecting to come face to face with her boss and Mr Chalmers, the company's Editor-in-Chief. Instead, she was confronted with the unashamedly beaming, dimpled smile of an unfamiliar twenty-something male sitting next to Alan.

Although no words had been spoken, Alice could feel a sickening dread creeping up through her chest towards her tightening throat. She swallowed hard to relieve the aridness, painfully aware how obvious her discomfort must be to the two men staring at her.

Alan prised himself noisily out of his leather chair. "Alice, I'd like to introduce you to Graham Robertson."

As the sandy-haired young man stood to greet her, she couldn't take her eyes off Alan's perfunctory smile.

"Good to meet you, Alice." She shook Graham's unfeasibly soft, limp hand and scanned his immaculate, charcoal-grey suit and matching tie. She had to concede, he looked every inch the impressive young professional; too dapper to be a freelancer, though; too fresh-faced for an advertising rep.

"Please, take a seat—" Alan said with uncharacteristic professionalism.

As the harsh reality of what was about to be announced struck her, Alice could taste the bitter bile of the Americano she'd guzzled earlier, rising in the back of her throat.

"Alice, I thought you should be the first to know that Graham will be our new Features' Editor." Alan smiled towards Graham as he spoke, then glanced fleetingly at Alice. As she struggled to digest what had just been said, she found herself unable to avert her eyes from the young man: her soon-to-be new superior.

"I see—" Although her own words were clearly audible, Alice had no recollection of uttering them as they'd flowed, automaton-like, from her lips.

Graham leaned forward in his seat, casually resting his hands on his knees. "I'm really looking forward to getting started here next month—"

Alice wasn't sure if she'd imagined the patronising tone in his voice or not. Either way, she felt disinclined to respond to his polite yet pointless statement. Instead, she redirected her stare towards Alan, watching as he struggled to loosen his tie.

Conscious of her judgemental eyes, he duly launched into a timely and word-perfect spiel about Graham's background; naively believing that, in the circumstances, Alice would be remotely interested.

"… and, on top of that, he's also a graduate from Harvard." Alan's voice tailed off; his customary baritone fading to a subdued hush.

Eyes to the floor, Alice took a long, slow deep breath and flicked an invisible speck of dust from her skirt. "No need to justify your decision, Alan." She slowly raised her eyes to meet his reluctant gaze then shot them back towards Graham. "Textbook credentials, without a doubt. I have to say, anybody else who'd applied certainly wouldn't have stood a chance."

Her fingers fumbled for the crystal in her pocket as her pulse began to race.

Graham shifted in his seat as Alan locked his hands behind his head and let out an awkward half-laugh.

A futile attempt to look superior.

Desperate now to goad Alan into a war of words, Alice decided the time was right to play her Ace card. "You know, I've always wondered what Gordon would've done in certain situations—" She paused, summoning the courage to continue. "Of course, that's if he was still here…" She narrowed her eyes.

How would he react to the mention of his former boss; the man he'd so cruelly and deviously forced into early retirement?

Alan didn't respond immediately. Instead, he took a deep breath, exhaling with the faintest trace of a despondent sigh. Alice couldn't help but notice the beads of sweat pooling above his scowling brow. He lowered his arms from behind his head then slowly and methodically rested first one elbow, then the other, onto the desk in front of him. The sombre expression on his face made her catch her breath. Although his body language conveyed a more relaxed attitude, there was an unsettling intensity in his eyes; that of a man who'd just discovered something that somehow threatened him; made him feel exposed, vulnerable and less in control than he'd been only moments before.

As the low winter sun squeezed in through the half-closed Venetian blinds directly onto Alan's receding hairline, a wave of nauseous regret swept over Alice. Her inability to engage her brain before she opened her mouth was never more prevalent than when she felt let down or betrayed.

"Gordon, I'm sure, would—" Alan's cursory response was interrupted by a curt knock followed by the whirlwind entrance of Mr Chalmers into the office.

"Graham—" The stocky, bald Editor-in-Chief, greeted the young man with an exuberant handshake and an overly-familiar pat on the shoulder. "Not long now, eh? A few people I'd like you to meet before we get down to signing the contract and so on."

He glanced at Alice as though she were an afterthought.

"Oh, hello there. Better luck next time, eh?" He smiled with polite detachment as he customarily shook her hand then swiftly returned his attention to Graham. "Anyway, as I was saying, let's pop down to Marketing and H.R. first, then a quick run through all the legalities—"

With an arm around his shoulder, Mr Chalmers ushered Graham through the doorway and out into the hectic swarm of third-floor journalists; leaving Alice and Alan alone in his office.

"Can I just say, by no means did I expect it handed to me on a plate—" She glared at Alan as he sank back into his chair. "But you more or less implied that the job was mine."

"My hands were tied, Alice." He didn't look up as he mindlessly rummaged through a pile of paperwork in front of him.

"Bullshit." She slammed the palm of her hand onto the desk so hard it stung. "So, let me get this straight – what you're saying is the internal interviews were just a fucking formality to tick a few boxes and Mr Chalmers knew all along who *he* wanted for the job?" She glowered at him, her eyes burning with rage. "Christ, did the guy even get interviewed, Alan?" Her heart was thumping so hard it was making her head throb.

The look on his face said it all. After a few seconds, it was more than she could bear. "Gordon's gonna love this, by the way," she said, walking out and slamming the door behind her.

* * *

Conscious of Pete's eyes upon her, Alice looked up from her pizza to catch him staring at her plate as she sawed manically on a stubborn length of stringy Mozzarella.

"And you know the worst part?" she garbled through a mouthful of doughy cheese and tomato, "it was the only reason I put up with the sleazy, backstabbing git for so long." As she swallowed another huge slug of tangy, freshly-squeezed orange juice, she could feel some of the day's tension start to melt away. She was just about to raise another forkful to her lips when she stopped, carefully placing the cutlery down onto the half-empty plate in front of her.

"Look, I'm sorry," she sighed, wiping the grease from her lips with a napkin. "Here's me moaning about not getting the promotion on our—"

"Hey, stop with the apologising, will you?" He effortlessly swept half a dough ball around his plate to soak up every last bit of the tomato residue. "I'm more than happy to let you get it off your chest." He reached over the checked, vinyl tablecloth to grab her hand. "Isn't that what friends are for?"

"Still a bit weird you're moving so soon, though, eh? What time you heading on Saturday, anyway?"

He shrugged. "Dunno, probably just after lunch or thereabouts."

Alice was suddenly aware that his narrowed, quizzical eyes were focused on her neck.

"What's with the marks, lady? I think you might have a bit of a rash going on there." He nodded towards the top of her v-neck jumper before leaning in. "Or maybe it's a hicky from Saturday night?" He winked knowingly but Alice sensed that he wasn't about to let it go. There was a familiar searching look in his eyes as he flicked his fringe from his forehead.

Christ, how could I have forgotten to put a bloody polo neck on?

Alice knew that explaining the red marks as well as divulging where she'd been on Saturday would be hard going, so she decided to try to dismiss them both as casually as possible. "Just a touch of eczema. It breaks out when I'm stressed or run-down." A flush of guilt teased the surface of her skin as her eyes wandered to the take-away queue by the restaurant entrance.

"So, where were you again on Saturday? Pretty sure you told me at the press conference—" Although the words tripped off his tongue with innocent nonchalance, Alice knew he was desperate to know.

Her heart sank as she realised she'd have to churn out another little white lie.

"Just a little get-together with some girls from the office." Sensing that he was eager for more information, she continued, "A pre-hen shindig. You know, finalising the finer details over some – okay – over a *ludicrous* amount of alcohol."

There was a trace of doubt in his quiet half-laugh as he picked up the laminated menu that was slotted in between the salt and pepper pots. "Fancy something sweet for afters?"

Alice felt a flutter of relief that he'd moved the conversation on. "Nah, I'm stuffed now."

He raised his eyebrows. "Seriously? I think we both know you'll only end up eating half of mine anyway."

"That's true," she replied matter-of-factly before breaking into a wry grin. "You'd better ask for two spoons then."

Whether it was because they'd seen less of each other recently, Alice couldn't be sure. But, as she sat across the table from Pete amidst the aromas and bustle of the crowded restaurant, she suddenly saw him through objective eyes. Pete: undoubtedly attractive, funny, trustworthy Pete. A true friend – and probably always would be.

Yet now, it was as if Alice had somehow stepped back from all the memories and nostalgia and was, for the first time, appreciating him in a purely platonic way. Despite their undeniable bond, Alice understood that this was how it was meant to be between them now; their relationship had nowhere else to go.

Then, like an epiphany coursing through her; a transcendental force awakening her senses, she suddenly realised why her feelings for Pete had come so clearly and precisely into focus.

There was one abiding, inescapable truth that Alice could no longer deny; a fact she'd been reluctant to admit to herself until this very moment – he wasn't Victor.

CHAPTER FIFTEEN

"Shit." Alice scrunched the piece of paper up into a ball and lobbed it over her computer towards the wastepaper bin. This one – her fourth – ricocheted off the metal edge with a dull ping then half-rolled, half-bounced to disappear underneath the filing cabinet in the corner.

She shoved her fingers through her loose curls and pledged that this would be her last attempt of the day to draft her resignation letter. First things first, she still had a couple of features to fine-tune before her copy deadline and, no matter how pissed she might be at Alan, she was conscientious enough to still take pride in her work.

Case in point, her fracking story was proof that a little bit of extra homework and investigation can pay dividends – she knew that would undoubtedly be a highlight on her CV. And in no small part to Betty Jackson, the mysterious old woman she'd interviewed on the windswept moor, who just happened to be in the supermarket queue next to her the other day. It was such an odd reaction for her heartbeat to gallop during the banal activity of loading shopping onto a conveyor belt yet, as she mindlessly placed a packet of pasta behind the obligatory bottle of Pinot, the hairs on her arms suddenly stood on end. It was all she could do to stop her gaze from being dragged to the neighbouring check-out; that feeling of being either too scared or too embarrassed to confront the eyes you know are upon you. Regardless, this time the intensity had vanished from the old woman's eyes – replaced with an unlikely warmth and softness thanks to her gentle, unassuming smile. Betty nodded and Alice returned the gesture – knowing full well that she was acknowledging the recent rejection of the fracking proposal. And, so, their silent but meaningful connection was left at that.

Yet, Alice couldn't shake the feeling that it wasn't just circumstance or plain luck that their paths had crossed again; or that it hadn't been simply another everyday story for her to cover in the first place – but that she and Betty were *meant* to meet one another.

She shook her head and tucked the loose tail of her shirt into her trousers with worrying ease. She'd always accepted her tendency to eat less in times of stress but she had to concede that, on this occasion, the weight loss had been stealthily swift. She winced at the thought of the lecture her mum would undoubtedly give her when she next saw her.

It had just gone ten in the morning and already dense, slate-grey clouds had merged seamlessly above the city skyline to create an endless and oppressive bleak canvas. Lost in a hopeless mess of emotions, Alice gazed out of the window, beyond her ghostly, semi-transparent reflection; silently imploring the heavens for some – any – celestial benevolence.

She swivelled in her chair, past the screenful of unanswered emails, to snatch the ringing phone.

"Alice Webster speaking."

"Good morning, Alice." Just three little words but they set her pulse racing.

116

In the ensuing seconds of strained silence, the sound of the blood rushing in her head was all-consuming. Aware that she'd been holding her breath for a while, she let out a lungful of air all at once.

"Morning, Victor." The words came out like a whisper on a breeze.

"I hope I'm not interrupting anything… just wanted to check you were alright." There was a subdued tone to his voice that Alice hadn't heard before.

She wound the twisted phone cord around her fingers, barely noticing that the black, unforgiving rubber was slowly cutting off her circulation.

Victor took a deep breath. "You seemed a bit preoccupied when you left on Saturday night."

"I—" Alice placed a soothing palm onto her collarbone as an intense heat began to build beneath the surface of her skin; she looked down to see the scratch marks below her neck were as inflamed and fiery red as they'd been after she'd woken from her nightmare. "I'm sorry, Victor."

"Please, don't apologise, Alice. I was—"

Although, deep down, she was relieved that he'd called, Alice couldn't suppress her doubts and confusion any longer.

"No, Victor – you don't understand. Look, I can't speak about this right now."

"What's wrong, Alice? Have I done something to upset you?"

"That's just it, Victor. I don't know if you have…" She caught her breath. "God, look I'm just really confused at the moment."

"I need to see you."

She threw her head back onto her chair, instantly flinching at the glare from the fluorescent tube directly above her desk.

"Alice... please."

Her stomach churned at the desperation in his voice; the self-assured, dominant businessman had vanished.

"There's so much I need to know – to ask you, Victor."

He sighed. "You're right – we need to talk. There are things I have to... to explain to you."

She sat bolt upright in her chair, struggling to comprehend what he'd just said.

"Maybe we can meet tomorrow night?" His tone was hopeful.

"All right. Look, I have to go now—"

"I'll pick you up at eight."

Alice put the phone down as gently as she could, just as Alan appeared by her side.

* * *

Her skin still dewy from the shower, Alice peered through the gap in the curtains to see who'd just rung the doorbell. In the gloom of the front doorstep, she could make out two familiar shadowy figures standing side by side.

Shivering, she tossed her towel onto the bed, pulled on her clothes at breakneck speed and hurried down the stairs. She yanked the front door open, not wholly surprised to find her mum and Gordon wrapped up in their winter woollies, huddled together in the freezing night air.

"Hello, sweetheart. Just passing on our way to the cinema, don't panic." Alice's mum kissed her on the cheek before sneaking into the hallway. She stopped at the mirror to remove her hat.

"Everything okay with you then? Haven't seen you for a

while—" she said, patting down a few flyaway strands of hair.

Gordon and Alice smiled knowingly at one other as she placed her leather gloves neatly beside the telephone. Although it was rare for her mum to drop by unannounced, Alice was surprised that the impromptu visit hadn't fazed her at all. In fact, it felt quite nice, almost refreshingly normal; considering how strained and dysfunctional their relationship had been in the past.

"I'm fine, Mum. Just the usual nonsense." She nudged Gordon with her elbow. "Hey, great news about your daughter. When you seeing her?"

"Next weekend, actually. Yeah, can't tell you how happy I am about it." His beaming smile lit up his healthier, fuller face. For the first time in months, Alice felt her spirits lift as she stood beside her mum, watching her carefree interaction with Gordon. It warmed her heart to see the two of them looking so natural together; openly enjoying each other's company.

"I'll put the kettle on, shall I?"

As the three of them sat around the kitchen table, chatting over their steaming mugs, the conversation turned towards the newspaper.

"... so, after more or less promising me the features' ed job, it bloody well went to some sycophantic upstart that Mr Chalmers obviously knew *and* wanted."

Gordon huffed; his contempt of Alan clearly not diminished through time.

"Hey, you've got plenty more years in you yet, kiddo." He took a huge gulp of coffee. "But, you're right. He should never have implied that the job was yours – especially if he didn't have the final say. Pretty unprofessional."

"Spineless bastard pretty much sums it up."

119

"Alice!" Her mum spluttered on a mouthful of milky tea.

"Well it's the truth, Mum. He knew that I was more than ready to take on the job – just kowtows to everything Mr Chalmers says. No courage whatsobloodyever – it's pathetic."

"Wouldn't have happened on my watch, I can tell you," Gordon winked at her as he stood to rinse his empty mug under the tap.

"Yeah, I said you'd love it when I told you—"

"You what?" The mug slipped out of his hands and clattered into the sink. "So, he knows we're in touch?" He turned his head, his eyes straining against hers.

"Well… yeah. No big deal, though," she uttered as casually as she could.

Her mum caught the change in atmosphere. "What's going—"

"Nothing, it's all cool." Alice checked her watch. "Look, I've got to get to work soon."

"We'll have to head now anyway – don't want to miss the start of the film do we?" her mum said, eyeing Gordon curiously as she raised herself tentatively off the chair.

Seconds later, Alice noticed that the discerning gaze had switched to her waist and hips. She couldn't believe it when no comment flew her way regarding her figure. Instinctively, her hand wandered up to check the collar of her high-neck jumper.

Gordon snuck up behind her as her mum checked herself in the mirror. "Sorry, it's just the mention of his name puts me on edge—"

"Hey, I know. Sorry for bringing it up," Alice whispered, patting his arm.

A twinkle returned to his eyes. "You just hang in there,

kiddo and you'll be Editor-in-Chief in no time."

Her mum opened the front door then leaned in to give Alice a tighter-than-normal hug.

"Not planning on being there much longer anyway." As the words left her lips, Alice felt a weight lifting off her, as though vocalising her intentions had somehow been cathartic.

"Really? Well, don't be too hasty. Especially if you've nothing else lined up."

"We'll see." She shrugged as Victor's job offer prised itself from her subconscious to imbed itself in the front of her mind. A rush of guilt mixed with a growing excitement swelled inside her.

"Come on, Gordon." Her mum's high-pitched holler echoed from the gate opening out onto the frosty pavement.

"Hey, looks like you've got a parcel," he said, groaning as he reached down beside the plant pot on the doorstep. Seconds later, he placed a shoe-box-sized parcel wrapped in brown paper into her waiting hands.

Alice stood shivering in the doorway as she watched them disappear around the corner and out of sight. She gave the feather-light box a gentle, inquisitive shake by her ear before untying the black ribbon that had been secured into a perfect bow on top. There was no writing to be seen on the outside.

It's been hand-delivered.

Her eyes scoured the sudden threatening darkness. With adrenalin pumping through her, she edged backwards into the comforting warmth of the house, and closed the door.

Her shallow breathing was all-consuming in the eerily silent hallway. She dropped the hand that was pressed hard against the door and let it hover over the package for a few seconds.

Willing herself to remove the wrapping and look inside,

she prised the lid open and felt something soft to the touch; wrapped in tissue-paper and sealed with a small round label. Holding her breath, she unpicked the sticky label then carefully unfolded the rustling paper.

What the hell...?

At first glance, she thought it was a dark net underskirt but, as she lifted it out of the box, she realised it resembled a long, black wedding veil. She held it out in front of her, allowing the semi-opaque mesh to drape to its full length, barely brushing the floor.

Alice turned to look at herself in the mirror with a sudden overwhelming desire to try it on. She had ten minutes to spare before heading to the restaurant; enough time to satisfy her irrational urge. With one hand, she gathered as many curls in the nape of her neck as she could, then carefully slotted the tapered fingers of the attached comb into the hair on her crown with the other. The long, flowing train of the veil cascaded like a waterfall down her back – but it didn't look right; something was missing. She quickly unravelled the shorter section that had bunched up on top of her head. As she smoothed it out, appraising the texture with her fingertips as she went, the shorter section fell elegantly forwards to perfectly cover her face – as though it had been made just for her.

She stared through the black mesh in morbid fascination at the dark, distorted image in the mirror. A warm tear trickled down her face as a low, mournful sob escaped from her lips. Something insidious was seeping into her soul that neither her mind nor her body could deny; a hidden entity that would no sooner let her escape than it would engulf her in her own wretched, sorrowful grief.

The box tumbled off the telephone table as she stumbled forwards; her eyes drowning in tears as a small piece of paper floated down in front of her.

In frustration, she whipped the veil from her head and bent down to snatch the blank card from the floor. She turned it over, unable to tear her eyes away from the words scrawled in black ink on the back.

With compliments, Alice
One **B**lack **V**eil

CHAPTER SIXTEEN

The car purred into life with a low, inconspicuous hum; an infinitesimal vibration through the soles of her new shoes the only hint that the engine was running. She stared beyond the windscreen as Victor pulled out into the intermittent, late-evening traffic.

"Is everything all right, Alice?" He turned his head slightly but his eyes were fixed on the road ahead.

With her handbag stacked on her lap, she scanned the stylish interior and took a deep breath; the new-car scent combined with the subtle spice of Victor's aftershave was a deliciously intoxicating mix.

"I'm fine." Even to herself, it sounded unconvincing.

In the reflective green glow of the dashboard lights, she could just about make out the badge in the middle of the steering wheel; she didn't recognise the logo. All that had registered as she'd walked around the car was the pale, pearlescent exterior. It occurred to her that it was probably such an exclusive make that anyone earning less than seven figures would never have heard of it – let alone seen or sat inside one.

She shifted in the heated leather seat to sneak a look at Victor as he drew the car up to a junction; his long, perfectly straight nose and distinctive square jaw took on a haunting appearance in the harsh neon glare. His cheekbone seemed more pronounced, razor-sharp even, as it swept upwards in a perfect contour towards his temple; next to the cavernous socket that shrouded his eye in the darkest of shadows.

Her pulse was hot and tremulous in her ears as the image of herself in the black veil shot into her brain. A fleeting dizziness dulled her senses; for a few seconds it was like she was outside her own body looking back at a distorted version of herself through the fine black mesh – but it didn't feel like her, rather some doppelganger imposter who'd somehow crept inside her skin.

Then just like that, she was back; peering at the oncoming traffic as the glare from the headlights overwhelmed her eyes. She took a deep breath to steady her nerves. Victor's aftershave caught in the back of her throat, as though it had just been sprayed right under her nose.

"I'm sorry, I should've mentioned I'd be picking you up myself—"

She flinched as his voice reverberated in her ears. Was she imagining that everything seemed magnified – more intensified? Either that or she was officially losing her mind.

"I hope you haven't eaten?"

Alice stiffened as he took a sharp left turn in the direction of the quay then accelerated past his office.

"Nearly there, don't worry." His deep, velvety voice was compelling in the near-darkness of the car.

In that second, her disorientation vanished as the car weaved seamlessly around a tight bend and the quayside appeared in the distance, shrouded in a veil of thin, wisping mist.

Almost instinctively, Victor pre-empted her curiosity. "I thought you might like to see her—" He paused.

"I'm sorry, what... *who* are you talking—?" Her voice faltered as the car trundled to a halt on the cobblestones, alongside a sleek white boat.

"This is Isobel," he said proudly.

"Okaaay..." She swivelled to face him full on. "So you weren't talking about a person, then?"

"My mother's name," he offered wistfully.

Alice nodded, unable to conjure an appropriate reply. As her gaze returned to the stunning vessel in front of her, she noticed there were lights on in several different areas, both above and below deck; as though it were inhabited.

Victor unclicked his seat belt and grabbed the door handle. "Shall we?"

Hampered by her tight skirt, Alice hoisted herself awkwardly out of the low-slung car seat and closed the door behind her. It resonated with a hefty clunk along the bleak, deserted quayside. She pulled her coat tighter as they stood shoulder to shoulder on the wet cobbles in the bitingly cold mist. The low, echoing hum of the distant city was only noticeable in between the rhythmic lapping of gentle waves against the hull of the boat.

With a sweeping hand, he gestured her towards the gangplank.

Alice's breathing was visible in the icy clouds that led her, precariously in her kitten heels, up the wooden walkway. As she neared the top, she was surprised to see a tall figure dressed in full chef's ensemble, waiting to greet her on the deck.

"*Bonne nuit.* Welcome aboard, Miss Webster." The middle-aged man stepped forward to offer his hand. "My name is Leon. I look forward to serving you and Mr Davies tonight. A glass of champagne to begin, perhaps?" His soft Gallic accent had a wonderful soothing lilt to it. Alice warmed to him instantly.

"Lovely, thank you."

He presented a full flute of fizzing bubbles before leading her through a sliding glass door into a plush, cosy dining area. In the far corner was a large square table, lavishly set with an elaborate four-tiered candelabra and silver ice bucket to the side. The elegant, minimalist décor was reminiscent of an exclusive Michelin-starred bistro. It was intimate – *too* intimate.

Victor helped Alice off with her coat then pulled out a chair for her as Leon lit the tapered ivory candles, one by one. She studied Victor's clothes as he slipped out of his leather jacket and passed both coats to Leon at the side. He looked much younger in his pale blue, cashmere jumper and dark, loose-fitting jeans. She'd never seen him in anything other than a pristine suit before – the contrasting image caught her off-guard. As she took her seat, she quietly admired his casual attire; it flattered him – he seemed less intimidating.

The intricate strains of Vivaldi's 'Four Seasons' echoed delicately in the background.

"I've taken the liberty of asking Leon to prepare a few different dishes tonight. Thought it best to cover all dietary bases." His tone was almost business-like as he flashed her an awkward smile.

As they sat across from one another in the dimly-lit quiet of the room, Alice didn't know where to look. She shifted in her seat as the contrived intimacy of the situation suddenly overwhelmed her. Nerves and agitation jangling inside her, the timing had never been better to offload all the pent-up doubts and suspicions that had been plaguing her. She took a deep breath as she stared at the reflection of the moon gently rippling on the endless murky sea.

"I met Eva a few weeks ago, Victor." It was out before she could stop it.

In the short but tortuous silence that followed, she felt like her lungs might burst. She stared straight ahead, focusing on a tiny red light flashing painfully slowly on the horizon. It wasn't until the fourth flash that Victor spoke.

"Look at me, Alice." The calmness in his command was unnerving. With every ounce of courage she could summon, she turned to meet his intense stare.

Her heart lurched in her chest but she knew that if she didn't keep going now, she never would. "She told me about your secret group and that you... you... abuse her." She hung her head as the gravity of the accusation hit her with a force she hadn't expected. The soothing strains of the background music contrasted agonisingly with the tension hurtling between them.

Alice thought she saw the colour drain slightly from his face. As he exhaled slowly and deeply, the candle flames wavered unsteadily; precariously close to being extinguished before reigniting, seconds later, into full luminosity.

His grimace vanished as Leon appeared, as if from nowhere, with four steaming platters on a large silver tray. He described in mouth-watering detail what each beautifully-presented dish contained as he laid them down onto the warming plates, neatly encircling the candelabra. The glorious fusion of the freshly-cooked aromas was a welcome assault on her senses.

Victor smiled politely at Leon as he popped the cork on a bottle of champagne but it didn't mask his anxiety. He methodically readjusted his cutlery a few times so that everything was in perfect alignment, then signalled to Leon that he'd dish up the food himself.

As the Frenchman turned on his heel, the tension shot back into the room. Alice shifted in her seat, then made the mistake of meeting Victor's expectant gaze. She swallowed hard as he looked at her with the same controlled expression.

"Jesus, Victor, I don't know a damn thing about the *real* you – in fact, I should probably be running a million miles in the opposite direction right now. But I'm not... and that worries me even more. I've no idea why I'm here with you. I can't begin to explain it—" She shook her head in an attempt to rid her mind of the confusion that was flooding in.

Without saying a word, he calmly offered her a portion of veal followed by a generous serving of creamy Dauphinoise potatoes and steamed asparagus. She nodded reluctantly as he held each spoonful up in front of her. He gestured with his cutlery for her to tuck in to the food that looked so appealing, it would have deserved top billing on any a la carte menu.

Still, the doubts and confusion needled away at her brain. As if to further cleanse her soul, she recalled in breathless detail everything that Eva had divulged at their meeting that night. Victor reclined into the back of his chair with his champagne, disturbingly unconcerned.

Alice thought she caught a flicker of intolerance as he lifted the flute to his face to scrutinize the clarity of the glass; mindlessly twirling the stem between his thumb and forefinger.

As the background music reached a rousing crescendo, he

turned his head slowly and leaned in towards her – his eyes darker than ever.

"Alice, do you believe in karma?"

His apropos-of-nothing question threw her, prompting her to swallow a mouthful of the most succulent meat she'd ever tasted.

"If you're talking about your sins returning to haunt you in the next life then, yeah, seems pretty fair to me. You've been a bad person, then I think you deserve it to come back and take a chunk out of your ass."

He grinned at her passionate analogy.

"But I don't really believe in all that reincarnation crap, though. Surely we all just concentrate on making the most of the lives we're living now?"

He raised an eyebrow as he carved a slice of veal with effort-less precision. "Wise words from one so young. Interesting, though, that you wouldn't want a second bite of the cherry – so to speak." His voice was distant and mechanical as though he was lost in thought. A slow, controlled inhalation regained his perfect composure.

"Alice, I think you deserve to know that there was more to my childhood than has ever been documented. You know that I was orphaned at six and raised by my uncle – my mother's brother – for many years. That much is widely known and regarded as gospel. However—" he paused, raking his fingers through his thick hair, "there's not a single person alive who knows what *really* happened under my uncle's roof; the despicable, awful truth—" He snarled the words through tense, unforgiving lips; a tone of sheer hatred darkening his voice. "When your parents are killed and the person trusted to look after you lets you down – invades your innocence in the worst way you can possibly imagine – it isn't a natural proclivity to worship God as your one true saviour…"

Alice swallowed hard. "Victor – I… I'm sorry, I had no—"

He waved her words away. "My parents were the most devout couple you could ever meet. My father was a much-loved, respected parish priest and my mother was the doting and supportive clergyman's wife, assisting the church in any way that she could – often above and beyond the call of duty. Aside from family, the church was their life – and mine – for the few years that I can remember…" His lips hinted at a nostalgic smile. "What I'm trying to say, is that my uncle was never punished for what he did to me. The sanctimonious bastard went to his grave having carried on with his life as normal; no remorse, no guilt – only relief that his dirty secret had never been exposed. My parents' killer was never caught, either." His mouth twisted in disgust. "My father was sure somebody had broken into the house that night. He made the mistake of confronting the burglar on the dark staircase, unaware he had a shotgun, and my mother was standing right behind him. After the shots, I hid under the bed for hours, too scared to come out in case the man with the gun was still there. In truth, I just couldn't bear the thought of seeing what I knew had happened to my parents." His voice cracked. "They never got *their* retribution. The only way I can deal with the hellish injustice of it all is to presume they'll get what they deserve in the next life…"

Alice fought the urge to reach out and touch him. "There wasn't anybody you could tell? About the abuse, I mean?"

He huffed dismissively. "By the time the agonising shame had subsided enough for me to talk about it, my uncle was dead. Besides," he continued, topping up her flute with fresh champagne, "there's probably a hell of a lot of abuse goes unreported, don't you think?"

Their eyes met as he lowered the empty bottle into the ice bucket with a loud crunch. Those few seconds felt like an eternity.

He knows about my dad?

"Anyway, I'm not looking for sympathy. Far from it—" His tone turned brusque and impatient, as though he was keen to draw a line under his confession. Alice sensed that displays of emotion didn't come naturally to him; made him feel exposed and vulnerable, and, more importantly, not in control.

She was strangely relieved when Leon reappeared through the sliding door.

"I trust everything is to your liking tonight?" he asked, hands clasped tightly.

"Leon, you've excelled yourself – the food is superb, as is the champagne." Victor gestured with a smile towards the ice bucket.

"Another is on its way." The Frenchman nodded then duly whisked the empty bottle from the bucket.

With Leon out of earshot, Victor continued. "Now do you understand why I could never, *ever* – inflict abuse of any kind, on anyone?" His voice was low and indignant. A droplet of sweat glinted in the deep cleft above his top lip. "As for the secret group, which I'm assuming you've already investigated – I'd be disappointed if you hadn't – it's purely a spiritual cult. No sacrificing, no horned headdresses, nothing untoward. Just a group of like-minded guys with similar beliefs. Surely you can understand why I would turn my back on God after what happened to me, Alice? Where was *He* when my parents, who couldn't have worshipped him more, were being brutally

132

murdered?" His grief and bitterness was painfully raw despite the passage of time.

He exhaled with a solitary deep breath. "If you like, I'd be happy to tell you more about the Order – show you some literature? It really is an empowering, fulfilling mindset, Alice."

With her appetite sated, she sat her knife and fork next to one another on the plate then scrunched her napkin into a heap on top of the linen tablecloth. She watched Victor lift the last perfectly-cut, precisely-arranged forkful to his lips; transfixed by the gentle rhythmic movement of his jaw as he slowly and delicately chewed the delectable mouthful.

Alan's involvement with Kelly and the cult continued to niggle her; like an unassuaged itch teasing her skin, but she would pursue that enigma later – she had to keep the momentum going with Eva for now. She twirled a strand of hair that had fallen loose from her clip. "That's fine, Victor – whatever floats your boat, but that's not my problem with all of this. What I *really* don't get is why on earth Eva would lie about the abuse, the hotel job, in fact everything…"

He formed an open steeple with his fingertips and raised it to his mouth, as though in prayer. She sat in frustration, watching a fresh cloak of mist tumble in on the breeze.

"Coffee in the lounge?" He didn't wait for a reply as he nodded to Leon who duly opened an oak-panelled door leading below deck.

Alice let her hand glide along the cool wrought-iron handrail as she followed him down a narrow spiral staircase into a lounge area that wouldn't have looked out of place in a plush West End apartment. An oval glass table and plush, sprawling cream rug took centre stage in the middle of the room. A vintage-style silver coffee pot gleamed in the reflective light from the crystal pendant light dangling above, while a plate of colourful, artisan petit fours sat temptingly to the side.

Victor gestured for her to sit on the chocolate-brown settee directly below a tall, gaudy abstract painting. Alice guessed it was a Picasso – probably an original one at that. As her body moulded itself gradually into the warm, forgiving leather, he took a seat directly opposite her and nodded towards the canvas above her head.

"It's a Kandinsky. Wonderful, isn't it? The way the colours and shapes blend so beautifully but remain so strong and pure in themselves—"

Alice shook her head in bemusement. Craning her neck to look at it again, she saw something she could easily have painted in nursery class. "So, you're into art then?"

"Actually, I've always fancied myself as a budding van Gogh." His face broke into an indulgent grin. "I painted some landscapes a few years ago and I've done the odd portrait. Nothing special by any means but it's a passion, and I enjoy it. Just can't seem to find the time these days."

Alice's heart skipped a beat as the painting of the woman in the corridor pulsated in her mind's eye; every minute detail crystal clear as though the image had been imprinted in her consciousness.

He poured some coffee into a cup and pushed it towards her. "Black, no sugar, I seem to recall?"

"Thanks," she muttered. "But you've still not answered my question about Eva, Victor." Alice felt the blood surging through her veins as she put him firmly on the spot. He was going to answer her now – whether he liked it or not.

134

He shrugged his broad shoulders and took a quick sip of the steaming espresso.

"What I'm about to tell you, Alice, is very private. Suffice it to say, your discretion is of the utmost importance."

She nodded, shuffling herself towards the edge of the couch.

"So, Eva and I aren't a couple."

For a second, Alice thought she'd misheard him; the shocking revelation was so quietly understated, so matter-of-fact.

"She's actually Charles' granddaughter." The words hung in the air between them as his wary eyes scanned her face.

She gave his statement a few seconds to impact on her brain; she certainly hadn't seen *that* coming. Then, a niggling doubt drifted instinctively to the front of her mind. "But she lives with you?"

As soon as the question was out, Alice felt the knot in her stomach tightening. Victor sighed and tilted his head back to look up at the ceiling, as though relinquishing control to the heavens.

She held her breath as she waited for his response.

"Well, the tenacious reporter never clocks out, does she?" His caustic tone was no match for the defeat echoing in his voice. His face turned solemn as he looked at her again.

"I know how it must look, Alice – it's just a bit, well... complicated at the moment." His voice tailed off as he clocked the suspicion in her eyes. "Look, a couple of years ago Charles asked me for a favour. Would I take his granddaughter under my wing for a short while in Davies' Enterprises? She fancied a year out before starting university and he thought it'd do her good to get some work experience out in the field, so to speak." His face fell into a frown. "That *short while*, however, has been somewhat extended for—" he looked down, playing

135

with his ear lobe as he paused, "—for personal reasons."

Alice sighed at the wearisome ambiguity of his explanation; her intolerance didn't go unnoticed.

"Look, what I'm about to tell you stays within these walls – *period*." His eyes were wide and sincere.

"Eva has, for want of a better word – *issues*." He leaned in. "Has done for quite a while now. She'll often have episodes where she retreats into herself, locks herself away. Take the night of the ball, for example – she was all dressed up, mask in hand, ready to go but, at the last minute, she just couldn't face it."

Alice lowered her gaze, suddenly feeling awkward about following Eva through the house that night. In hindsight, it was blatantly obvious what she'd been doing and she was more than a little surprised that he hadn't acknowledged it.

"More worryingly, though, she's now started to *see* things, even say things that are completely out of character. I noticed she was always worse after we'd been to the restaurant. She'd barely open her mouth the whole time. She just wasn't connecting with me; it was like she *wasn't there*."

His eyes darted towards the window as the reverberating hum of a passing boat startled him. He slugged a mouthful of cooled espresso before pouring Alice a fresh cup from the silver pot.

"It all started after her mum died in a car accident. She'll have these phases where she'll essentially *become* someone else – adopt another persona – to remove herself from the trauma; protecting herself, I suppose, from the reality she can't bear to face. The medics call it Dissociative Identity Disorder: a defence mechanism that's particularly prevalent in victims of trauma."

His eyes softened as he held Alice's gaze.

"I know it might sound like a convenient excuse, that I'm making up her condition for my own ends, but it's the only explanation, Alice. I've honestly no idea why she'd even want to meet you, let alone lie to you about me."

He mindlessly inched his hand across the table towards hers, then snatched it back a few seconds later.

"Before you ask, she's only staying at my estate as a favour to Charles. He's been away on business a lot since Eva's mum died. Her dad's lived abroad for years now – got a job on the Continent soon after they divorced – so Charles has played a big part in her life for a long time now. He knows he can trust me one hundred percent to make sure she's looked after when he's not around. The girl's got real problems just now, Alice. In all good conscience, I couldn't turn a blind eye – and Charles has always been there for me. It's only right that I return the favour. Besides, she desperately needs someone she can trust – her dad's cheating really affected her. You can appreciate she doesn't exactly have a lot of confidence in men."

Alice nodded solemnly. "Sure, of course. And it's all very admirable and everything but the dinner dates every Friday? Doesn't exactly scream purely platonic to me…"

Victor half-laughed; flashing an uneasy smile. "I know how it must look, Alice – but, believe me, there's nothing in it. For years, Charles took Eva and her mum to Amo Mangiare every week – a little family tradition. It kind of fell to me, by default, to keep it going." He shifted awkwardly on the leather couch.

"Maybe she was hoping it might lead to more?" Alice said.

Victor's jaw tightened; he glanced up at the painting behind her with narrow eyes.

"Good God, no. No, I'm sure that's not the case." Although his voice was calm and controlled, there was more than enough hesitation to suggest he had his doubts. Alice was taken aback by the fluster he seemed desperate to conceal as he shook his head.

"So, how come she knows about the *obv* then?"

"I can only assume she's been sneaking around my office when I've been out. I never went out of my way to hide my meetings with the other members. She's bound to have seen them coming and going every so often – put two and two together."

"So it must have been *her* that sent me the veil then?" she said under her breath.

"The what?"

"Last night, there was a hand-delivered parcel on my doorstep. Inside was a black veil wrapped in black tissue paper with a hand-written note. There was no name—"

Victor's brows snapped together.

"There is no black veil, Alice." The disbelief in his voice made her skin prickle.

She flinched as she recalled her gut-wrenching reflection in the mirror the night before.

"It doesn't exist. At least I don't think it does any…" He shrugged as his voice tailed off. Alice couldn't articulate anything for a few seconds as she struggled with the barrage of revelations.

Victor swivelled to rearrange the row of faux fur cushions behind his back; straightening each one several times until they were all perfectly uniform and identical in height.

"I suppose her condition – or however you want to put it – would explain the lies?" she offered tentatively. "But wait—"

A light flicked on in her brain. "It wasn't all lies, though. She wasn't lying about the cult and she *did* have the pendant. I know *that* exists – I even touched it."

He spun round to face her with irises so dark they looked like infinite holes bored into the whites of his eyes. "Jesus, what was she thinking—"

His voice was so deep it reverberated through every nerve in her body. He seemed riled; lost in some kind of internal struggle as he shunted the blue sleeves of his jumper up past his elbows.

Despite the humidity in the room, Alice felt the hairs on her arms prickle beneath her chiffon blouse.

"So what's the pendant for, then? What does it symbolise?"

"It's an ancient relic from when the cult was founded. Charles introduced me to the Order five years ago and entrusted me to look after it for him. We perform all our incantations and power meditations around it. To say it's priceless is an understatement, particularly to Charles – his ancestors founded the cult centuries ago."

"Why would he give it to *you*, then?" Her challenge was loaded with scepticism.

"I suppose you could say that Charles has been like a mentor and surrogate father to me over the years. He understands my *ways* – all my foibles; my strengths and weaknesses."

His affectionate respect for the old man was evident in the warmth of his voice. "I actually felt great pride and honour that he'd handed the responsibility over to me."

As Alice recalled her brief encounter with Charles at the ball, she recognised that the admiration between the two men was entirely mutual. His comment about Victor's complexity and trust issues had been particularly enlightening; he'd obviously known him on a deeply personal, as well as professional, level for many years.

Alice was about to probe Victor further about his relationship with Charles when his mobile phone startled them both. Unsurprisingly, the ring tone was a soundbite of rousing opera. He glanced at the caller display. "Sorry, have to take this." His expression hardened as he concentrated on the words on the end of the line. "No, let's leave that for now. Too much going on with the Hoffman account just now." He turned his back for privacy, keeping his voice low.

As she checked the clock on the wall, it suddenly struck Alice how much champagne Victor had consumed – there was no way he'd be able to drive her back home. As though reading her mind, he turned to face her again after placing the phone carefully on the glass table.

"Alice, I've asked Edward to drive you home later. I hope that's all right? Obviously, I'm over the limit, but I have to deal with something urgent now so I'll be staying here to work in my floating control centre." He grinned at his overtly pretentious statement.

Alice didn't know why she was remotely surprised that a multi-millionaire would afford himself the luxury of a floating office.

"You never know when something's going to crop up—"

There was a mutual understanding that their conversation had come to a halt for now. Her head was throbbing after the maelstrom of emotionally draining confessions; it had been a tumultuous few hours and it would no doubt take at least that time again for her to even begin to process it all. Yet, at the same time, Alice felt like she'd experienced something miraculous that evening – something she was privileged to have witnessed: an insight into the fiercely-protected recesses of Victor's mind; an enlightening glimpse into the darkened complexities of his soul.

"Well, I don't want to outstay my welcome—"

He let out the breathy half-laugh that was now so familiar to her. "Oh, I don't think you could ever do that, Alice."

Fear flashed across Victor's face in the second or two before their eyes locked into one another's. Alice was sure she caught a faint blush spreading slowly across his cheeks. She lowered her head; momentarily fraught with nerves before looking back up at him from beneath the protective canopy of her lashes. Her throat begged her to swallow as his piercing gaze remained fixed upon her face.

"I'll get your coat," he said, his composure forced and reluctant. Alice let out a lungful of air as he breezed past her; his spicy aftershave evoked a familiar feeling as it lingered tantalisingly under her nose.

He was already wearing his jacket when he returned less than a minute later holding hers out. She stiffened as he sidled up behind her to guide each sleeve up and over the delicate chiffon covering her arms. His warm breath tingled the nape of her neck as his fingers brushed the tendrils that had fallen loose from her clip to dangle carelessly over the top of her collar. She'd never been this close to him before and not seen his face. Her heart was racing. She felt vulnerable and exposed – yet strangely excited.

She followed him up the stairs and past Leon who was busy clearing their table. He turned to bid them goodnight, cradling an array of plates and cutlery in the crook of his arm. Alice was in awe that his chef's outfit looked as pristine as when he'd welcomed them aboard a few hours earlier. The candles still flickered behind him; albeit less proudly and vividly than before.

She shivered as they left the warmth of the boat behind and strolled out onto the deck, into the perfectly still, bitingly cold night air.

Victor took the lead as they made their way in silence down the gangplank. A hatless Edward was blowing into his cupped hands as he waited by the passenger door of the limo. His less formal attire suggested he hadn't expected the last-minute driving call from Victor. Still, he greeted her with the same endearing chivalry as before; opening the car door for her with a warm, genuine smile. Alice lowered herself onto the firm, ribbed leather of the back seat, enjoying the glorious warmth that now enveloped her.

Victor bid her goodnight then hesitated before reaching for the handle; he looked like he wanted to say something. At the last second, she thrust her hand onto the door to stop him from closing it.

"By the way, I was wondering if the job offer was still open?" She couldn't contain her urgency.

He leaned expectantly into the half-open window; his left hand dangling casually over the top to reveal the familiar platinum Rolex. "May I ask what's prompted the change of heart?" His lips hinted at a smile.

"If you must know, I lost out on the Features' Ed job." She paused for a moment to control the pent-up frustration that was threatening to erupt again. "It's time to move on now."

He didn't react. No sympathetic expression or words of commiseration; almost as if he'd been expecting it. "Looks like we'll be arranging another meeting soon then?" Victor's presumptuous statement hung in the air, encased in an icy cloud of breath.

Her finger was already hovering over the window button when he leaned in again to rest his hand on top.

"A lot's been said tonight, Alice." His eyes flitted towards the partition behind Edward's head, checking it was fully raised. "I'm sure I can count on your discretion?"

Despite the questioning cadence in his voice, Alice understood it was more than just a polite request. He studied her with a cool, assessing gaze – for a brief moment, the authoritative, intimidating businessman had returned.

"Of course."

He nodded. "There's still plenty more we need to discuss. However, if you're sure it's—"

She cut in. "I'm handing in my notice tomorrow, Victor. I'd say that's sure enough, wouldn't you?"

"Undoubtedly." His voice was so low Alice wasn't sure if he meant for her to hear.

"But there's one thing I need to know – *now*." She played nervously with the metal buckle on her clutch bag.

"Oh?" He was looking right at her again; a smile pulling at the corner of his mouth. Victor wasn't used to being beholden to anybody else – the irony clearly wasn't lost on him.

"It's been bugging me for ages so I'm just going to come right out with it. Do you know anything about the girl that went missing a couple of years ago?"

His smile vanished, replaced by a curious almost disappointed frown.

"Why would you suppose I know anything about that?" He narrowed his eyes.

"I have evidence that she was linked with Alan. I know he's in your *group* as well, Victor."

143

Fire smouldered in her belly as she seized control of the conversation. She had the upper hand now and she wasn't afraid to exploit it.

"I don't deny it at all." His tone was indignant. "What I *will* deny, though, is any knowledge of what happened to that girl."

She scanned his face for clues, any nervous mannerisms that might unwittingly expose a lack of innocence. His effortless deadpan expression was exasperating to say the least – no incongruous twitching or mistimed blinking; nothing visible that could, in any way, be misconstrued as concealing a lie.

She bit her lip. Was she so desperate to believe him that she was willing to smother any lingering doubts? Yet, was this a man who would cover for someone else solely out of loyalty; withhold information of such importance for fear of the repercussions to another? Say what you liked about Victor but the man had morals and an unwavering sense of duty and virtue.

An unbearable tiredness washed over Alice.

"I'm sensing this is a topic I'll need to address sooner rather than later to put your inquisitive mind at ease?"

She shot him a look that promised she wasn't going to let it lie. "You bet. But I'm too knackered to think anymore so you've got a stay of execution – for now."

He smiled. "I'm very much looking forward to you joining the firm, Alice."

A flicker of uncertainty forced its way into her mind. "Although, I'm still not entirely sure why you'd want me. I mean, it's not like you know my work particularly well – or me, for that matter—"

"Look, I'm more than willing to give it a go – I think deep down you are, too." His voice was reassuringly calm; almost hypnotic. "Aren't we all searching for people whose demons play well with ours; whose beliefs mirror our own – who *get us?*"

Her heart raced as his dark eyes stared straight into hers.

"We probably know one another better than you think, Alice. I'll be in touch." He reached in to clasp his hand on top of hers before turning away to stroll into the mist. She watched as his hazy silhouette appeared to glide up the gangplank towards the deck then disappear from view.

She rummaged in her bag for her crystal as the limo trundled slowly over the cobbles away from the water's edge. Just then, a new text message flashed up on her mobile – she pulled it out to swipe the screen.

Her pulse quickened as she read it, then re-read it with a smile.

I'm sure our demons will play perfectly well together. V

CHAPTER SEVENTEEN

Alan peered over his half-moon specs at Alice; every furrow on his clammy forehead stacked into a deep, harsh crevice. He folded the letter he'd been clutching in his chubby, nail-bitten fingers and slotted it back inside the envelope – all the while looking straight at her.

He reclined slowly, almost nonchalantly into the springy back of his chair – a gesture Alice found way more unnerving than his searching, judgemental eyes.

Unable to suffer it any longer, she begrudgingly broke the silence.

"Of course, I'll honour the full four-weeks' notice…"

Alan didn't respond. Instead he grabbed his computer mouse and proceeded to shunt and click it feverishly, tutting under his breath at some annoyance on the screen. "Right, so that takes us up to the middle of next month," he mumbled to himself, as though Alice wasn't sitting right in front of him. She squeezed the arm of the chair as her breathing quickened.

He snatched his glasses from his nose and leaned forwards, hands clasped in front of him.

Alice bolted herself upright, allowing their eyes to meet at the exact same level across the desk. "Well, you can't say you didn't see it coming, Alan." It was out before she knew it; and she was well aware that the words could be the catalyst for a torrent of vitriol she might soon regret. She bit her lip, both in anticipation and dread that his reply might just tip her over the edge.

"True, Alice... true." He grinned smugly, stroking his wiry beard. "So much so, in fact, that I've been priming someone else to fill your shoes. Lynn, to be precise."

She tried to ignore his wide, goading eyes. "That's life, though, I guess. Everybody moves on eventually."

*Yeah, but some people are **forced** to move on.*

Her deep-seated bitterness about Gordon's dismissal threatened to erupt as she stared nostalgically at the chair he once sat in; now occupied by a man she'd come to despise.

"I take it you've another job lined up?" Alan's tone was too casual, too laidback for it *not* to be feigned.

"Actually, I'm going to work for Victor." She surprised herself at how routinely and confidently the words she'd never uttered before, had tripped off her tongue. She hoped that keeping her answer short and sweet would leave him craving more.

Alan sighed, lifting his eyes. "Always knew he wanted to poach you."

His matter-of-factness threw her off-kilter; she hadn't anticipated the accepting, almost gracious response. "Suppose it's a no-brainer, really. After all, a man like Victor's always going to get what he wants – isn't he?"

Alice huffed as he raised an eyebrow at her.

"If you must know, I took a while to mull it over. It's only recently – in light of *certain events*, shall we say – that I made my decision." She fiddled with her earring, eyeballing him with an intensity that was straining her tired, dry eyes. "To be honest, I wasn't sure how you'd take it – what with you two being friends and knowing each other… *socially.*" Her slow emphasis of the last word made him budge awkwardly in his seat.

"All's fair, I suppose." Wary curiosity flashed across his face and Alice delighted as his arrogant nonchalance dissolved before her eyes. Suspicion was etched all over his face. It was obviously killing him to find out what she was implying; exactly what she knew – and how much. He swallowed hard, loosening the knot of his garish tie.

"So, it's off to Davies' Enterprises then? Well, good for you." His eyes flitted towards a random press release on his desk. "Of course, I don't see as much of Victor as I used to. More of a business relationship nowadays—" He mindlessly shuffled some paperwork in front of him – anything to avoid eye contact.

With the upper hand firmly in her grasp, Alice knew there would never be a better moment to pitch her proposal: the unashamedly wicked, self-indulgent idea that had come to her as she'd removed her make-up the night before.

"You know, I was thinking, in light of the boyband statement at the press conference – which, by the way, went viral in minutes because of their ridiculously huge following – that we should run a fresh piece on the girl that went missing a couple of years ago." She held her breath, quietly studying him. "Quite appropriate, don't you think – considering it was my first-ever story for the paper. Almost like my job's gone full circle—"

Alan tutted as his eyes darted to the computer screen. "Not really news, though, is it? There's a backlog of other features to be concentrating on just now, anyway," he said crisply.

His constant averted gaze only compounded the bit between her teeth. "Yeah, but there's nothing like a fresh, emotive appeal to really resonate with the readers. I know you don't have kids yourself but just imagine if it were your daughter – the awful, heartbreaking agony of not knowing what happened to her, where the hell she is, if she's still alive? It's the 'not knowing' that would kill me…"

He coughed. "People go missing all the time, Alice. It's hardly an exclusive now, is it? Life goes on."

Alice felt her stomach shift. "Suppose we'll just have to hope the new Chief of Police doesn't see it that way when he takes the reins soon." She stared at him; waiting on the reaction she knew was coming. "Yeah, wasn't sure if you'd forgotten about that press release we got a month or so ago? A newcomer from a division up north, apparently. Good to inject some fresh blood, though, eh? I remember his statement on cracking down on corruption within the force…"

In the very instant that her words appeared to penetrate Alan's brain, the phone on his desk rang. He snatched it straight away.

"Jesus… all right, I'll be down in a minute." He slammed it down less like an irritated boss, more like it was a convenient outlet for pent-up frustration. "Sorry, have to cut this short – something urgent in the press room."

Great bloody timing…

He sprang from his seat and snatched his glasses from the top of a pile of strewn, unopened mail. It was clearly time for her to leave his office.

"Oh, say hi to Gordon for me, will you?" He glanced up at her as though it had been an afterthought; his curt tone and cold, menacing eyes betraying the convivial sentiment. She hovered in the doorway as a chill slithered through her bones. "Mind you, if the old bugger's still flitting about, more than likely I'll bump into him soon enough, eh?"

Alice's heart skipped a beat as he trudged past her, leaving an odious waft of stale sweat lingering under her nose.

With the adrenalin surging through her, she headed for the lift, strolling mindlessly through the chaotic bustle of harassed, third-floor journos.

After pressing the call button, she heard urgent footsteps behind her. Pete was hurrying towards her; his infectious lopsided grin instantly calming her nerves.

"Hey, glad I caught you." His cheeks were rosy above a navy gilet that was zipped up to the hilt. He rested his crammed satchel on the ground between his grubby Doc Martens.

"Jesus, think somebody needs a hot shower—"

"No time to chat. Look, you gonna make it for my farewell drink at the usual in—" he flicked his wrist to check his watch, "—say about an hour?"

Alice rolled her eyes. "As if I'd bloody well get out of it…"

"Great. See you then." He flashed the familiar, cheeky smile that she was already missing, then disappeared through the door leading to the stairs.

Alice held the lift door to look around her for a moment – at the office that had been such a huge part of her life; her growth, both emotionally and professionally, for the last couple of years.

But a change was coming. She could feel it in the air around her and deep within her soul – an all-consuming metamorphosis that would irrevocably transform everything she knew and everything she was.

It was undeniable closure; the end of an era juxtaposing a

new beginning – mysterious yet exciting. And she was ready for it – *more* than ready for it.

Yes, there was no doubt that this was the dawn of a completely new Alice.

CHAPTER EIGHTEEN

Emotions swelled inside Alice as she nudged the swinging door open with her shoulder for the last time.

Memories of waitressing at Amo Mangiare rolled like a slideshow through her mind as her black pumps squeaked across the polished floor. The order of steaming mains, balanced just-so in the crook of her arm, were met with gasps of delight as she lowered each one with exaggerated flair in front of the expectant female diners; a well-lubricated trio who, for the last two hours, had commandeered the sought-after circular table that took pride of place in the grand bay window. A table that was unofficially one of the establishment's best – but couldn't actually lay claim to being *the* best.

Scurrying back to the kitchen for her next service, Alice's eyes were instinctively drawn to the exclusive seats that rightfully deserved that prestigious accolade; the impressive quartet of Art Deco high-back chairs strategically positioned on the elevated stage for optimum impact yet discreet enough for sufficient privacy in the candle-lit alcove by the grand piano.

In the few weeks since Victor's last reservation, the familiar table had taken on a completely different atmosphere – it just didn't look or feel the same anymore. Alice's mind drifted to the resignation letter tucked safely inside her coat pocket in the cloakroom. Handing over the last one to Alan had been easy – a relief, in fact. But her strong attachment to the restaurant meant handing in *this* letter was a far more harrowing prospect altogether.

She couldn't put her finger on it but everything seemed more intense during her shift that night. The blast of humidity that always met her as she hurried into the kitchen was more brutal than ever. She could feel the sweat covering her face like a glistening veil; the tiniest amount pooling in the cleft above her top lip.

It was the usual eclectic mix of diners for a Friday night. The chic, perfectly-coiffured twenty-something singles, out to impress with their eye on the prize of the inevitable nightcap. The unpredictable last-minute groups of couples out on the town; all more than likely married and sufficiently merry upon arrival, bringing with them an infectious camaraderie along with the usual late-night, alcohol-induced banter. And you could literally set your watch by the familiar once-a-week regulars; the sticklers for routine: the pensioner demographic – so intrinsically content and satisfied, they could never contemplate ordering something from a different section of the menu, let alone live so dangerously as to order an alternative dessert or, God forbid, a cheeky liqueur coffee.

She paused for a moment, taking in the ambient noise and bustle of the other waiting staff, as they scurried along their way, amidst the mixed aromas of food, fine wine and perfume – all fused with that sense of collective self-indulgence and relaxation that was almost a scent in itself.

Perhaps it had been the unexpected text from Victor that

morning requesting another meeting that had filled her with a close to intolerable fluster?

Regardless, it was undeniable that she was anticipating seeing him in a few days' time with an exhilaration she was struggling to comprehend.

With her mind still reeling from the prospect of their encounter, Alice bumped into Kate by the cash desk. The sullen waitress sighed, crossed her arms then stepped back.

"Overheard you talking to Ben earlier—" She glared at Alice, her face stiff with disdain.

"And?" Alice snapped, silently berating herself for allowing Kate the smug pleasure of eavesdropping on her conversation.

"Such a shame we won't see each other again—" she whimpered sarcastically.

"Actually, it's *more* of a shame you didn't make it to Pete's leaving do the other night. It must've been so nice for him having all his close friends and colleagues there – you know, the people who *really* mean a lot to him…" Alice smirked as it became painfully obvious that Kate hadn't been invited. "Oh… so you didn't know about it, then?"

She tilted her head.

Kate's face fell.

"Yeah, just couldn't make it, that's all," she mumbled into the order pad that had been plucked urgently from her apron pocket for no apparent reason. She took a deep breath then glared past Alice towards the back of the restaurant.

"Anyway, it pains me to say but there's some old, beardy guy over there who'd prefer *you* to serve him instead of me. God knows why…"

Alice craned her neck in the direction of Kate's sneering. In the millisecond it took her to register Charles' presence, a confusing mixture of surprise and unease jangled her nerves. He was deep in conversation with his dining companion as she made her way up the steps towards the table tucked away in the farthest nook of the diner. Charles didn't look up until she was standing directly beside the blond gentleman's shoulder.

His face instantly broke into a warm, genuine smile.

"Alice, *so* lovely to see you again." He promptly leaned over the table, grabbing her hands to clasp them gently between his. "Mark, this is Alice, a friend of Victor's – at least for the time being—" He chuckled to himself as he gestured to the man sitting across from him.

His guest flashed a cursory smile before looking down at his menu. The fleeting glimpse of his face stirred a vague recognition as Charles lowered himself back into his seat with a satisfied sigh. "You know, it's a while since I've been in here," he continued, gazing admiringly around him. "I suppose it must have been before you started – forgotten how lovely it was. Anyway…" His finger hovered over the appetiser section of the menu. "I think we're ready to order now."

Alice took her chance to study Mark's profile as he reeled off his starter and main choices, all the while his nose stuck firmly in the menu.

Charles' eyes twinkled as he made his choice then handed both leather-bound menus back to her.

"Be good to give up the waitressing, though, I'd imagine?"

Victor's told him already?

"Actually, I really enjoy working here." She wanted to play her cards close to her chest.

"Come now, Alice," he chided, "you don't belong in a job like

155

this – pandering to the needs of others. You deserve better than this… subservience. It should be *you* enjoying the haute cuisine and fine wines every night."

In spite of his playful chuckle, Alice caught something in his eyes. An unnerving intensity burned behind the twinkling grey; like he had some sort of deep-seated, vested interest in her which he wanted – *needed* – her to understand.

Charles tensed as his companion stood to excuse himself.

Conscious that her orders would be piling up, Alice swivelled to check if her manager was keeping tabs on her. "Sorry, have to get back to the kitchen now—" She smiled politely as she topped up his water; the odd lemon slice and ice cube escaping to plop noisily inside the glass.

Charles slowly adjusted his bow tie.

"You know, some people find their true destiny in life sooner than others, Alice."

She looked down at the wrinkled, veiny hand, flecked with age spots, that had suddenly clutched her right forearm; gently restraining but unyielding nonetheless. A chunky cygnet ring with an illegible engraving dazzled as it caught the light on his pinky finger.

"Maybe your time is now? I only want what's best for you, you know." He let go with a perfunctory but polite smile as Mark returned to his seat.

She smiled nervously at his intimation that Victor's job was some kind of predestined higher calling for her; some sort of exalted echelon. As implausible as his notion was, her skin still tingled at the thought and she could feel the familiar heat teasing her neckline once again. She instinctively placed her palm on top of her blouse. Aware of Charles' searching eyes, she turned and hurried back towards the kitchen, breezing past Kate and Ben as they stood chatting by the swinging doors.

The next two hours ticked by in a chaotic haze of non-stop orders, the odd complaint and copious refills of alcohol. Alice did her best to avoid any unnecessary eye contact or conversation with Charles as she brought and cleared away each of their courses. It was, however, unavoidable when they stood side by side as he settled the bill at the end of the night.

"Until next time, Alice." His parting shot, as he doffed his trilby, was presumptuously matter-of-fact; as though he knew it wouldn't be long before they met again.

As the clock struck eleven, she bid the last group of customers good night and flipped the sign on the door to 'closed'. Handing her letter to her boss passed without any awkwardness or bad feeling. On the contrary, his gracious acceptance and heartfelt wishes for the future couldn't have been more contrasting to her experience with Alan. The lump in her throat remained stubbornly lodged, even after she'd changed into her boots and pulled on her coat before clocking out.

It was only as the restaurant door clicked shut behind her and the cold air hit her, that her mind began to clear and the evening's adrenalin surge slowed to a trickle in her veins. That's when her subconscious allowed other thoughts to filter in and the niggle that had been smouldering away in the back of her mind burst into a flame of realisation – that was the moment it occurred to Alice why Charles' companion seemed so familiar.

Admittedly, she'd only seen him once before so it wasn't beyond all reasonable doubt that it *was* him; what's more, his demeanour past and present couldn't have been more at odds.

But as she'd let everything marinate slowly during the bitterly cold walk home, all the loose, hazy strands had spontaneously fused together to make it all so glaringly obvious.

At first, she'd thought he was just being standoffish, rude even, yet the more she replayed his behaviour in her head, the more it appeared that he was deliberately avoiding her gaze.

What Alice *couldn't* make sense of, though – what she was really struggling to grasp – was the connection between the two men in the first place.

What on earth was Charles doing having dinner with the drunk from Bar Rio?

CHAPTER NINETEEN

She peels a stubborn lock of hair from her glistening cheek as subtly as she can.

The brutal heat of the mid-summer sun hangs heavy in the sultry air; tenacious in its oppressive, hidden density. Her chest glistens above the embroidered, rib-crushing corset he demanded she wear to sit for the portrait; the one he's commissioned the artist-in-residence to paint. To commemorate her 25th birthday.

He casts a cursory glance at her from across the room – blatantly apathetic to the weak, shallow breathing that's slowly stifling her blood flow; weakening her pulse by the second. Yet, he is far from apathetic when it comes to his own selfish, primal wants; his sickeningly debauched needs in the suffocating privacy of their boudoir. She takes small comfort from the fact that his proclivity is such that her back is always turned for the fleeting duration of the abhorrent deed.

Her heart sinks. How can so much have changed since they exchanged their vows only a year ago? As she'd gazed up at him before the altar – so full of hope and naïve expectation – her heart and soul had been laid bare. She'd believed every word of the sacred verse before silently praying to the heavens above for him to love her; cherish her as much as she'd always dreamed her husband would.

As he'd turned reluctantly towards her to mutter his vows, she'd searched his glazed green eyes for a flicker of emotion; a twinkle of excitement or anticipation. Nothing. Dead.

There and then, she knew her love would never be reciprocated.

She glances down at the feather-tipped fan dangling in a bejewelled hand by her stiff, brocade dress. With a deft flick of the wrist, she spreads it open by her side then raises it to waft delicate streams of gloriously cool air across her face.

*Then **he** walks into the room. She prays that the burgeoning heat smouldering deep inside her and creeping up slowly through her body, will stop before reaching her already flushed face.*

She moves the fan closer so that with each waft, the downy feathers delicately brush the tops of her cheekbones. Her eyes peer cautiously over the feather tips as she tries desperately to conceal her fluster, as well as the rash that sweeps mercilessly across her décolletage, as though to callously highlight her anxiety.

She cannot deny the guilty pleasure in their stolen glances; the intimacy known only to them – the unadulterated thrill of their secret connection. She is drawn to him on such an improbably deep, elemental level that it defies all reason; she can't describe it simply because she cannot understand it.

But a secret it must remain. At least, until she can somehow free herself from his despicable, ruthless clutches. As much as she knows that she was chosen purely as a vessel to carry the Comte's future heir, she struggles to accept the harsh reality that once she has fulfilled her maternal duty and their child is born, they will never be a proper family.

The haunting image, as she'd stumbled unnoticed upon his intimacy with the stable-boy in the orchard, only compounded her hopelessness; the pathetic futility of the façade that was their arranged marriage.

160

He *often joked about his 'plan' for the Comte in the lighter moments they'd shared as he tutored her in her water-colour painting and charcoal sketching. What had once begun as a routine but enjoyable distraction to while away an afternoon after a morning's needlepoint in the garden, had soon blossomed into a hotly-anticipated, deliciously-forbidden encounter in the privacy of her drawing room. Yet, it was only their lips and hands that had brushed and caressed one other until now; in those stolen moments of quiet devotion when his eyes would feed upon her; savouring every detail of her face; drinking her in as though his sight had just been restored that very second.*

In the beginning, she was burdened with guilt; tormenting herself more with each illicit episode – but, like her love for her husband, that remorse had swiftly faded.

She reflected again upon his seemingly innocent witticisms about 'doing away' with the Comte. Many a true word uttered in jest? No, surely he couldn't be serious; wouldn't begin to contemplate ever actually going through with it? Yet, there was a part of her, locked away somewhere deep inside that was already bracing itself for the regret; the bitter disappointment, if he didn't eventually act upon those words. And she couldn't deny her own musings, either; the increasingly bad thoughts that gnawed away at her conscience more and more with every passing hour...

He took his place in front of her; easel and palette at the ready – primed for the portrait he'd been commissioned to paint.

At first, the broad, uninhibited smile lit up her face as she sat, perfectly composed, on the cushioned chair by the ceiling-high window, surrounded by a sea of towering, flickering scarlet candles. But as she foresaw the miserable, loveless future that lay ahead of her, her gently-curled lips collapsed into a hopeless melancholy and the sparkle faded from her warm, brown eyes.

Yet, he continued to paint, mesmerised by the beguiling sorrow on her beautiful face; desperate to capture it in all its mournful, haunting glory.

As he dabbed and swirled his brush with wild abandon in the blend of colours on the palette, she glanced down at the pendant embedded in her sweltering cleavage; the glistening symbolic charm that had been passed down to her from his mother - the charm he had kissed countless times as it lay across her chest.

As the sun set slowly through the tall window behind her, all twenty-five candles surrounding her appeared to burn more fervently; as though compensating for the diminishing daylight with their passionate radiance.

It was only then that she vowed, no matter what, she would keep it close to her heart.

Forever...

* * *

Alice woke with a start; clutching the warm, plump pillow to her chest and letting her tired, heavy eyes adjust to the crisp, early-morning light streaming in through the small chink in the curtains.

She gazed blearily at the meandering cracks on the ceiling above her bed, letting the surreal vividness of the dream flood over her once again. Nothing was clear at first – not even the faces, but as the thoughts tumbled through her mind, making and breaking alliances as they went, it slowly began to piece itself back together again.

As she rubbed her eyes back into focus and pushed herself upright on the bed, everything suddenly made perfect sense.

All that she'd been feeling, thinking, dreaming about – all

hinged on one undeniable, inescapable truth.

She was the girl in the portrait.

CHAPTER TWENTY

Alice could feel Gordon's steely eyes boring into her as the full force of her job announcement impacted like a bullet in his brain.

His shoulders and arms were rigid with tension, as though she'd pressed pause in their tense exchange – but it didn't last long. She wasn't sure why his hand began to tremble as it tentatively carried the spoonful of chicken broth to his mouth. Was it his condition or the fact that he was so utterly consumed with rage?

It was the conversation she'd been dreading from the moment she'd handed in her notice; the prospect of having to justify her decision to her ex-boss when she couldn't even justify it to herself.

"That sounds exciting, sweetheart." Her mum's naïve enthusiasm only compounded the awkwardness in the snug dining room.

Alice smiled at her for longer than was necessary before snatching the last slice of buttered baguette from the china side-plate. Gordon's stare was unrelenting in the corner of her eye as she ripped the warm bread in half then rammed it into her mouth – allowing herself a stay of execution from further discussion for the next thirty seconds or so.

"Anyway, this meal's not supposed to be about me—" She raised a congratulatory half glass of wine in front of her. "Happy birthday, Gordon. And here's to a fresh start with your daughter." She turned to look him in the eye with all the self-assurance she could summon; praying that her emotive words might go some way to soothing his raw indignation.

She was counting on the fact that her mum wouldn't pose any awkward or probing questions; sufficiently satisfied in the knowledge that her daughter was happy and content with her decision. Still, Gordon's disapproval remained carved into an expression of such determined belligerence, all she could do was endure the agonising wait before his inevitable questioning.

"You know he's also offering a great private healthcare package that extends to relatives—" Alice took a hearty gulp of the crisp, chilled wine and placed the near-empty glass back down beside her soup plate. She sighed as the refreshing buzz of the alcohol surged through her. "No more costly physio sounds like a pretty good perk to me." She smiled at her mum. "Fingers crossed, we might even get your operation fast-tracked."

Her mum ran a preening hand over her hair and turned towards Gordon with the wide-eyed excitement of a child. "So, what exactly does this Vincent man do? He must be awfully important – and rich." She winked at Gordon as he tore a chunk of bread and rammed it into his mouth. Alice watched as he ground it manically with his teeth, as though taking his frustration out on the soft, warm dough.

She took a deep breath. "His name's Victor Davies and he's a—"

Gordon cut in. "He's a megalomaniac businessman with a

lot of power and a *lot* of influence, June."

He turned towards her mum with a sardonic smile that said far more than his imperious statement ever could.

Alice watched her mum's naïve enthusiasm dissolve before her eyes; shifting into an uneasy confusion. Her wary eyes searched his face, as though she'd just witnessed a new side to his personality; a side that surprised her but unnerved her even more. In the ensuing few seconds of silence, she mindlessly brushed some scattered crumbs off the tablecloth into the palm of her hand.

"I'm guessing you don't have much time for Mr Davies, then?"

Gordon shifted in his seat, clearly regretting the words that may just have opened up a can of very awkward worms. He said nothing as he clenched his hands together in front of him on the table. Alice guessed he was doing this to stop them from shaking.

"You just hear things about people sometimes, that's all—" Alice sensed his sudden casual indifference was an attempt to placate her. He caught her eye as he stretched over for her soup plate. "Anyway," he continued, hesitantly, "I'm sure Alice will be more than a match for the multi-millionaire."

Her mum sighed as she relaxed into the back of her chair. "I've no doubt Alice will succeed whatever she does. Pretty determined, this one."

"Yeah, tell me about it – I had to work with her, remember?" He raised an eyebrow before gesturing her into the kitchen. "Roast beef, coming up."

Alice followed him through the archway and made for the sink that was close to overflowing with fresh, soapy bubbles. As she slid their empty plates carefully into the hot water, she let her eyes wander over the feminine-inspired surroundings: floral, tie-back curtains framing the window that overlooked the slightly unkempt back garden, a small cracked-glass vase crammed with artificial flowers on the white window ledge, a couple of hanging wooden plaques with scripted heartfelt quotes and witticisms about love and family. Alice was shocked by the wave of emotion that swelled inside her as she stood for a second or two, gazing at every inch of the room that appeared to be a shrine to his late wife. In spite of the mouth-watering aroma of cooked beef saturating the air, she could almost smell the delicate, lavender perfume from the trio of unlit lilac candles that decorated the otherwise bare kitchen table.

"What the hell are you playing at, Alice?" Gordon's seething sliced into her daydreaming.

Before she'd taken another breath, he was standing right in front of her; eyes blazing, as he yanked open the top button of his checked shirt.

Alice fixed her gaze firmly on the wooden mug tree sitting forlornly in the far corner of the work surface, sparsely adorned with its top two branches displaying matching his 'n' hers ceramic cups. Her heartbeat already galloping, she turned to meet his wide-eyed stare.

"I've been nothing but helpful and supportive in all the years I've known you but this… this is too much, Alice."

"Look, I know what you must be thinking—" Her dry throat barely croaked the words out.

"No, Alice, you can't begin to imagine what's going through my mind just now—" he whispered, sneaking a look behind him towards the dining room.

"You know, the only reason I haven't said anything about

any of this to your mum is because I know it would worry her sick."

She stiffened at the emotional blackmail. "Jesus, Gordon – do you honestly think I'd take a job from somebody I didn't trust or was afraid of? You know, if anything it's Alan we should be worried about. The man's a sleazy, malicious creep."

Considering his current temperament, Alice knew she had to strike the perfect balance in relaying the facts about her meetings with Victor.

"Please, Gordon, just take my word for it that Victor's not the man you and I both thought he was. There's more to him than meets the eye – a lot more – and it isn't bad, you've got to trust me on this." Alice struggled for breath as she gave her all with every heartfelt word.

An uneasy silence fell on the kitchen as Gordon carved the beef as precisely as his trembling hands would allow. Alice figured this was as close to tacit acceptance as she was likely to get.

"You two needing a hand through there?" Her mum's high-pitched trill echoed in the fragrant steam of the kitchen.

"Everything's under control, Mum," Alice hollered through to the dining room. She blew a curl off her face and caught a look from Gordon. His lips hinted at a smile as he flung a set of tartan oven gloves at her before thrusting a casserole dish crammed with roast potatoes under her nose.

There was a definite warmth in his otherwise weary eyes and Alice let out a relieved sigh, sensing that they would now sit down around the table to eat, drink and just enjoy each other's company.

By the time they'd devoured her mum's home-made lemon meringue pie, the conversation was flowing freely and the earlier tension had faded. But only until Gordon seized a second chance as they stood by the boiling kettle in the kitchen.

"I'm not going to let this lie, Alice. You know that, don't you?" he said, flipping open a stainless-steel canister filled with coffee granules.

Alice rolled her sleeves up and shot Gordon a wry grin. As she grabbed a teaspoon from the cutlery drawer, she pondered that perhaps the timing was right to announce her plan concerning Alan and the missing girl.

"Anyway, I wasn't sure if you knew we'll soon be getting a new Chief of Police—" Gordon shrugged as he turned his attention to the remaining dishes in the sink. Alice quietly studied his profile, her heart sinking a little as her eyes caught his gnarled fingers as they struggled to pick up the last few dirty plates from the work surface. She flinched as he dropped them into the bubbly water with uncharacteristic impatience.

She took a slow, deep breath.

"So, I was thinking—"

"Why do I get the feeling I'm not going to like this?" Gordon sighed, his arms suddenly motionless in the bubbly water. He turned towards her as her mum moved about in the dining room.

Alice tutted under her breath, frustrated that she may have missed her chance to talk freely.

"Just nipping out to the car to get my bag." Her mum poked her head through the archway. "Just realised I haven't had my second lot of pills today." Her voice faded away as she disappeared into the hallway.

Alice leaned in. "Look. Cut a long story short, I want to put my last couple of weeks at the paper to the best possible use.

169

And run a fresh piece on Kelly." The last sentence tumbled urgently from her mouth. The kettle gave a timely click.

"Oh, Alice. Kiddo…" Gordon raised a wet hand to his forehead; his affectionate nickname for her instantly taking on a patronising tone as he closed his eyes and soapy water trickled down onto his wrist.

She glared beyond her blurred reflection in the window out towards the slatted wooden shed at the edge of the garden; the early evening dusk was descending as rapidly as her mood. The sliver of hope she'd been harbouring that Gordon might just support her idea, had plummeted like a leaden weight of despair.

"For God's sake, can't you just leave this alone. Why are you so hellbent on pursuing things that no good can possibly come of?"

Alice chewed her lip, desperate to quell the frustration that was burning inside her.

"I just think that if I can at least get the new police chief on my side, it'll only be a matter of time before Alan gets what he deserves. Surely after he sees the photograph of him and Kelly together the night she went missing, it'll be plain sailing. You know, after I read the guy's statement on stamping out corruption, it really got my hopes up. We can't let it lie anymore."

Gordon choked back the dregs from the whisky tumbler by the sink. "You know, I bumped into Kelly's parents again the other day. Hadn't seen them in a long time—"

His eyes were intense as he turned towards her.

"They're slowly coming to terms with the fact they'll probably never see her again – let alone find out whatever the hell happened to her." He rested a hand on her stiff shoulder.

"This gets dredged up again and nothing comes of it – *again*, I just think it would kill them all over again, Alice. Sometimes, you just have to let things go..."

Alice stomped over to the table and bumped herself down onto a cushioned chair.

"You know, I never had you down as a defeatist."

He dragged the chair out next to her and sat down.

"Listen, I care about you very much, Alice – but, please, enough's enough—"

She huffed. "Don't you get it? This guy's fresh blood, with no connection to the cult, nothing to hide. He can't possibly dismiss your photo this time around."

"My photo?" He fell back in his chair. "What photo?"

For a second, Alice didn't appreciate the joke but as a look of genuine confusion contorted Gordon's face, deepening every wrinkle, line and furrow, she suddenly felt sick to her stomach. "You know, the photo of Alan and Kelly...?"

She studied him for a moment or two, quietly but desperately searching for even the slightest trace of recognition – but the agonising bewilderment remained etched on his face.

"So, I took it, did I? When was that then?" Gordon looked at her to prompt his memory. "What is it, Alice? What's wrong?"

My God, he really doesn't remember.

A shudder of dread pulsed through her as they stared at one another. Alice was itching to say something – *anything* – that might make the awful reality of the situation magically better, but it was as if the shock had somehow blocked her brain from making any connection to her mouth.

Alice jerked herself off the seat as she heard her mum walking towards the kitchen. This time, she was secretly thankful for the interruption.

Despite trawling through hours of often traumatic Parkinson's research to prepare them for the inevitable decline in his symptoms, Alice was still shocked by the brutal swiftness of his memory loss.

How long would it be before he started forgetting everyday things: what he'd eaten for breakfast, what he'd gone to the shops for, where he was meant to be, people's names? Then, God forbid, the people themselves?

Alice forced a smile at her mum, trying desperately to erase the heartbreaking images that were bombarding her mind.

Then a sickening and unimaginable dread surged through her – if they didn't find that photo; the one and only shred of damning evidence connecting him to the missing girl, Alan was off the hook forever.

* * *

With a throbbing head and waves of nausea ebbing and flowing in her belly, Alice kicked off her slippers and fell back onto her soft, puffy duvet. The fraught emotion of the evening swirled dizzily in her head as the heat oozed out from underneath her back, slowly seeping its way across the bedspread to envelop her in a glorious, soporific warmth.

And so it returned – the familiar craving pricking her conscience; seeping into her soul and infusing her senses; a need so strong and pure yet fraught with a pain that was mercilessly but unmistakably sweet. Alice closed her eyes to stop herself from once again succumbing to her new addiction but, as with every other night, the yearning was so powerful that it shamelessly prised them open, dragging her helpless gaze up and behind her. It only took a second for her twitching hand to surrender and reach for the bedpost – towards *it*.

It was only then that she realised she hadn't reached for her beloved crystal in weeks. That need had long been usurped by the lure of the fine black mesh.

With her eyes half-closed in anticipation, she lifted the veil from the bedpost and delicately caressed it between her thumb and fingertips. Alice could feel the skin on her neck getting hot and agitated – but she was too absorbed in the near-spiritual gratification to care. Like a junkie after a fix, an all-consuming torrent of relief flooded her body; sating her like the most intoxicating drug; quenching her mind and soul with a euphoria like no other.

As she lay on the bed with the veil softly kissing her face, Alice willed herself to drift off to sleep. Although she couldn't understand why she felt – no, why she *knew* – she belonged there, her desperation was undeniable. She *must* succumb to her need; her innate desire to return to the sacred place she visited every night – her adored sanctum, her own private utopia – locked away in the mists of time…

CHAPTER TWENTY-ONE

Victor passed the crisp sheet of headed paper to Alice then eased himself back into his chair. He mindlessly adjusted a cufflink before straightening some folders on the desk in front of him.

He seemed preoccupied – nervous, even.

As they sat across from one another with the late morning sun pitching long rectangles of golden light onto the plush, cream carpet and oak furniture, he finally looked up. Alice reached for the cup of espresso he'd just poured, watching as the tiny foam bubbles of the crema layer slowly drifted and separated to form an irregular but unmistakable dark brown heart at the centre.

She looked down at the sheet of A4 in her hands; unable to stop the warm flush sweeping across her face as he stared at her.

"I trust the terms are acceptable?"

Alice scanned the bold print on the contract and looked back up at him. She knew that her expression laid bare her shock at what was being offered to her, yet she was powerless to hide it.

A double-knock on the office door startled her. She fixed her gaze out of the window at the sun-tipped skyscrapers a few blocks in the distance and tried to settle her nerves. Victor bristled as the door whooshed open. Her eyes darted back towards him.

"Yes, Amanda?" he snapped, eyeballing the female Alice pictured cowering in the doorway.

"Sorry, Mr Davies." The girly apology was saccharine sweet. Alice could feel the woman's eyes boring into her from behind. "I *did* try to call you from reception a few times but it kept going straight to voicemail—"

Silence. Victor's frown deepened.

"My phone has been on silent... as it will continue to be for the duration of this meeting."

"It's just your 11 o'clock is waiting in the foyer. Mr Banks arrived early on the off-chance that—"

Any sympathy Alice had for the female vanished as it dawned on her that the disingenuous, high-pitched voice belonged to the obnoxious, Bambi-lashed receptionist she'd encountered on her first visit to Davies' House. As she recalled the brunette's unashamed ignorance that day, she allowed herself a smug, inward smile.

Victor's gaze slid from the doorway, his eyes instantly warming as he looked at Alice.

"No off-chances today, I'm afraid." His face softened as they made contact for a second or two. Then he shot another steely look back towards the door. "Show Mr Banks to Eric's office for now. I'll meet them both in the conference room when I'm finished here." His tone immediately closed the subject.

"Of course, Mr Davies." The door closed with the softest of clicks.

"Honestly, you can't get the staff these days," Victor huffed under his breath, the corners of his mouth hinting at a smile which didn't quite transpire.

"Remind me never to get on the wrong side of you, then," Alice said, nodding towards the door.

Sensing a deeper undertone to her banter, Victor rested tightly-clasped hands on the polished desk in front of him. Alice crossed her legs and tucked a loose curl behind her ear as a sudden restlessness washed over her. As he sat facing her, his charcoal gaze focused firmly on her face, she turned to look as nonchalantly as she could towards the coat stand in the far corner – afraid that if she so much as caught his stare, her blush would give her away. An unsettling mixture of awe, respect and infatuation engulfed her; an attraction and magnetism so intensely raw, so deeply-rooted within her, she almost feared it – yet nowhere near as much as she feared not ever feeling that way again.

She purposefully laid the contract down on the desk in front of her. It made a high-pitched whoosh as she slid it back towards him across the smooth walnut of the desk.

"What is this, Victor? I mean, this is a lot of money – way, *way* more than I was ever expecting." She put a hand to her mouth, shocked by the amount of sweat that had pooled above her top lip. "It just seems a bit over the top. I mean, there's no way you could ever justify that amount on me—"

Victor pushed himself off his chair, shoving his hands into the pockets of his perfectly-pressed, grey trousers. He stood with his back to her, looking out of the window – his shoulders slowly rising and falling in his white shirt as his breathing became deep and full. He shifted his head slightly, allowing her a glimpse of the profile she'd come to know so well.

"Am I to assume you're having second thoughts?" Although

his back was turned, his defensiveness cut through the air. Alice slowly raised herself off the soft, warm leather chair and joined him by the ceiling-to-floor window. As they stood side by side, soaking up the sprawling view before them, he raked a hand through his hair – allowing a subtle waft of musk to breeze past her.

"I have to be honest with you, Victor, I'm finding the whole salary issue a bit—"

He tutted. "Look, that's a technicality for now." He tilted his head towards the ceiling. "If it's too much for you, I'll happily reduce it – but I believe you'll be worth every penny of it, Alice." His tone was unashamedly curt, as though her worth was such a crystal-clear, foregone conclusion, it was tedious for him to defend it.

But it was his implication that he *knew* she would be of great value to him that Alice found the most intriguing. The more she thought about the almost prophetic statement, the more ominous it seemed to become. She had no problem with any of the duties detailed in the job description – on the contrary, she was more than proficient with press releases, copywriting, liaising with the press – after all, these were talents she'd honed over the years at the *Gazette*.

No, it was the fact that Victor was putting so much un-founded faith, such unconditional trust in her, that unnerved her. She'd rather *prove* her worth first before accepting anywhere near the six-figure pay packet.

"No, I'd be happier with a probation period first," she said politely but firmly.

He nodded in acceptance, yanking loose the knot on his lavender tie. "As you wish. Actually, there's one other thing we have to discuss before you leave."

His voice softened as he stared straight ahead. "Charles and I are attending an important conference this weekend. It's always very productive – usually reaping big benefits for some of my companies."

He turned towards her. "We'd very much like you to join us. I appreciate it's over the weekend but it's a great way to get to know some of the big-shots in the business – get an insight into exactly what Davies' Enterprises is all about."

Suspecting that his request was merely a formality, she bowed her head, suddenly overwhelmed by the magnitude of what she was getting herself into. Then, like a light-switch had suddenly flicked on in her brain, a bolt of adrenalin surged through her veins, instantly sweeping away any lingering doubts or insecurities.

"I finish at the *Gazette* on Friday, so the timing's good."

Victor flashed his first relaxed grin of the morning. "So your diary's free all weekend?"

Alice huffed. "No hot dates or wedding invites to cancel, that's for sure."

Victor half-laughed then dropped his gaze as she caught his eye. He stepped back to open the top drawer of his desk. "Oh, by the way, is your passport up to date?" he asked, noisily rummaging around for something.

She hadn't considered the possibility that they might be travelling overseas.

He nudged the drawer with his knee; it glided effortlessly shut by itself. "Sorry, forgot to mention the conference is in the South of France. Quite near the Pyrenees, actually – convenient for staying at Charles' cousin's chateau—"

Alice was only thankful she didn't have a mouthful of coffee at that moment, as she'd undoubtedly have spluttered it out in shock.

"Look, Alice," Victor lowered his voice as he beckoned her to join him on the chaise longue. "I know I haven't properly addressed the—" he paused, "the – *misgivings* – you shared with me that night on the boat."

She shot him a look as she lowered herself onto the soft, cream leather.

"You beat me to it. You were just about to get the Spanish Inquisition any second—"

Despite her determined talk, all her previous, pent-up desperation for any explanations vanished for the moment; replaced by a firm, inexplicable belief that Victor would stay true to his word and lay her doubts to rest in the fullness of time.

She glanced up to sneak a look at him; hoping to catch some sort of spontaneous, instinctive reaction – but he was already looking at her. For what seemed like forever, she sat helpless to move as his dark eyes slowly traced every detail of her face; caressing each feature in turn; engulfing her in a relentless swell of longing.

A sudden soundbite of opera shattered the silence – and the moment. Victor growled under his breath but his face relaxed when he looked at the caller display on his phone. He indicated one minute with his finger.

"Charles, great to hear from you." He paced the floor by the window, chatting animatedly for a minute or two before half-turning towards her. The second she leaned forwards into her bag for her phone, his eyes swooped upon her.

"I'm pleased to say she's with me now actually – we've just been discussing the France trip. Yes, it looks like it's all finally falling into place, Monsieur Laconte…" He single-handedly loosened his tie and let out a sigh that Alice could only describe as the perfect agreement between relief and satisfaction.

Victor's whimsical emphasis of the French moniker instantly roused her attention. For some reason, discovering that Charles had a foreign surname threw her – although, admittedly, it wasn't beyond all deduction considering that his cousin lived in that part of the world. Yet, somehow, she didn't equate the distinguished Etonian professor image with a French ancestry.

The one thing she *did* accept, though, was how cathartic and therapeutic the imminent trip would undoubtedly be for her. On her less than generous journo salary, Alice couldn't remember the last time she'd had a weekend away, let alone left the country, so there was no doubt that Victor's invite would be the perfect excuse to recharge her batteries – work-related or otherwise.

It would also force her to put some distance between herself and a certain possession that was now controlling her every night; dominating her conscience, invading every fibre of her being as darkness fell at the end of every day. How was it possible, in such a short space of time for her to become so utterly dependent? Yet, as much as this addiction, this nightly necessity confused her, she had never once failed to succumb to its glorious and passionate powers of persuasion. The pull was too overwhelming as it sucked her like a vortex into her *other* existence; the place where she felt – *she believed* – she truly belonged.

"Great, let's talk tomorrow." Victor's voice jolted her back into the moment as he made his way towards her from across the room. "I'll have the jet ready for Friday evening, then.

CHAPTER TWENTY-ONE

Speak to you soon, Charles."

Just as Alice was beginning to wonder if she'd misheard him, he uttered a phrase she never dreamed she'd ever hear.

"How does it suit you to fly out Friday evening? My pilot's looking at just after eight for a take-off slot..."

The shock that she'd just been invited to fly on a private jet, coupled with the ease with which the words had tripped off his tongue, completely halted any interaction between Alice's brain and her mouth. After a few seconds, she let out an involuntary laugh.

Victor eyed her with a mixture of caution and mild amusement.

"Is this all okay, Alice?" He narrowed his eyes. "I understand if it's a bit much to—"

She sprung to her feet; a sudden nervous energy overcoming her. "Look, Victor, it all sounds fine – really it does. You just have to accept how utterly bizarre this all is for me right now..."

She shook her head as the surreal reality imbedded itself in her conscience, then slung her bag onto her shoulder. "Anyway, I'd suggest you get your ass down to that conference room pronto – Mr Banks is probably losing his rag by now."

She smirked at the genuine shock on his face as she reminded him of his delayed appointment. True to form, Victor's composure returned following a long, perfectly-controlled sigh.

"You do know it's true what they say about the wicked, Alice? There's no rest for us..."

The subtle look he shot her as he pressed the lift button set her pulse racing. Even after he'd stepped into the air-conditioned glass cube beside her and they began their slow, seamless descent, the rush of blood continued to thrum in her ears.

Seconds later, the doors slid quietly apart, connecting them once again to the rest of the world in the bustling hum of the lobby.

As Victor reached forwards to clasp her hands, Alice caught the curious looks from a trio of suits passing the lift, along with the lingering gaze of a woman seated across the foyer.

"I'll email you the full itinerary tomorrow. I promise you it'll be an experience to remember—"

Alice once again felt the steely gaze from the reception desk.

Victor's hand cupped the small of her back as he escorted her across the pale, gleaming marble of the foyer.

As she admired the revolving doors' sparkling panes of glass, each adorned with *D.E.* in the centre, he leaned in. His breath was surprisingly warm against her cheek as he uttered the words that would jar every nerve inside her.

"Oh, think I forgot to mention that Eva will be joining us on the trip. Hope that's alright?"

Alice stiffened then turned to face him. But he was already making for an open door behind the reception desk; towards a tall slim blonde in a razor-sharp black trouser suit.

The second Victor disappeared through the doorway, the young woman's eyes focused on Alice, standing motionless in the revolving doors. For a beat or two, they stared at one other through the perfectly-polished, engraved glass. Then Eva's lips curled into a subtle, controlled smile.

But, unlike her smile as she'd left the restaurant all those weeks ago, this time Alice *could* put her finger on it.

It wasn't a smile that comes from the eyes or a grin that lights up the face – this was a cold, hard look of unashamed conceit – the epitome of self-satisfaction.

In that instant, it hit Alice exactly what that smile signified.

Eva had finally got what she wanted.

CHAPTER TWENTY TWO

Alice typed her last ever byline for the *Gazette* with mixed emotions.

Her finger hovered over the *save* button as she looked around the dingy, minimalist office she'd soon be leaving behind. Then, a brief pang of nostalgia; a momentary wistfulness as she gazed at the seat in the far corner – the one below the dodgy fluorescent tube that flickered often enough for it to irritate Pete whenever he'd pop by for one of his impromptu chats. Alice still couldn't believe he wasn't here anymore, let alone get her head around the fact that this would be the last day she'd sit in this chair or force herself to smile politely at Lynn and all the other journos she'd never really got to know that well – admittedly, through choice more than circumstance. Aside from a select few who shared her off-kilter sense of humour – the head typist and a couple of layout artists – Alice certainly wouldn't be upset to bid farewell to her work colleagues.

And then, of course, there was Alan. Yes, Gordon's successor was arguably the primary reason for her departure, rife with a behaviour and attitude that had ultimately been impossible for her to endure. Yet, despite all her deep-seated loathing and contempt of the man, she wasn't finished with him yet – not by a long shot.

If only she could get her hands on Gordon's photo and show it to the new police chief, she knew that it would finish his career, or worse. Withholding the truth about his connection to a missing girl would undoubtedly be his undoing – she could feel it in her bones. But her pursuit of retribution would have to wait until Gordon and her mum returned from his daughter's wedding.

She flinched as Alan's office door shut with a slam; her hackles rising as clumping, heavy footsteps grew louder. She didn't brace herself in time for his shiny, flushed face to appear from behind the partition.

"Got a minute, Alice?" He avoided eye contact as he bumped himself down onto the edge of her desk, forcing it to shudder and tilt under his bulk.

"Not going anywhere yet, Alan." She eyed him with polite disinterest and, she hoped, a touch of disdain. She'd always known he'd wait until the last gasp to say his goodbyes, wish her well, tell her to keep in touch – all the painfully perfunctory, wholly impersonal clichés that his arrogance and lack of empathy deemed acceptable.

"You know, I really did see you climbing the ladder here someday soon." His voice took on an unsettling genuine tone as he fidgeted with the grubby cuffs of his shirt.

Alice bristled. "A bit late for that now, don't you think?" She slid Victor's itinerary to the side, away from his prying eyes. A frisson of excitement pulsed through her as she remembered exactly where she'd be and what she'd be walking across the tarmac towards in a few hours' time.

"Look, Alice. Just know that I wish you well in your new job with the megabucks businessman." He let out a long, stale sigh. "He's lucky to have you – I mean that."

She instinctively recoiled as he leaned in towards her; her body stiffening as he maintained his overly-familiar hug just a little too long. Just as she was about to wriggle free from his sweaty hold, he dropped his grip, but remained close enough to invade her space. She let out a lungful of air when he finally turned to leave before swivelling on his heel at the last second.

"Oh, say hi to Gordon again for me, will you?" His disingenuous pleasantry followed by a long, drawn-out pause, made her skin prickle. "Top bloke. Such a tragedy getting Parkinson's just after you've retired – and living on his own as well. Can't be easy…"

"Who told you about that?" Any attempt to conceal her shock was futile.

"Why, the man himself, of course. Bumped into him a short while ago," he said half-grinning, as though he'd somehow seized the upper hand. "Yeah, we had quite the chat – about a few things actually. Have to say, though, I think his mind might be going a bit." His last words hung in the air as he stroked his goatee but Alice was too on edge for it to irritate her this time. Instead, she couldn't take her eyes off the sweat beading above his brow.

"Such a shame. But you do have to wonder if you can actually believe – *or trust* – anything he says anymore." His hard stare went right through her.

"What do you think, Alice? I mean, you must speak to him a fair bit these days, what with him and your mum's cosy little friendship." He ran his fingers across his forehead, soaking up some perspiration as he went. "Has he said, oh, I don't know, *anything*, that might make you doubt his mind at all…?"

She could barely shake her head as confusion and the

sudden injustice of it all overcame her.

"Just be very careful what and *who* you choose to believe, Alice. Sometimes trouble can be closer to home than you think—"

And with that, Alan walked out of her office for the very last time.

* * *

A good half hour after his parting shot, Alan's words continued to gnaw away at Alice's conscience.

Even the frequent distraction of third-floor colleagues popping in to say goodbye and wish her well couldn't lessen their impact or diminish their potency. Neither did the mindless clearing of cluttered desk drawers or the packing away of random photos and miscellaneous personal belongings make any headway in allaying her doubts. Yes, there was no denying that Alan's mind games, whether intentional or not, had left Alice with a close to intolerable sense of foreboding. It was as though he was deliberately holding something back from her; a revelation perhaps, of such magnitude, such personal importance that he simply *had* to wait until the timing was right to deliver the earth-shattering blow.

It was only when she glanced out of the window to catch a solitary ray of sunshine splitting the dense, slate sky, that Alice's mind relaxed and allowed itself, and her gaze, to drift out into the distance. Instinctively, her eyes settled on one building – one building alone. The rest of the geometric urban skyline as good as gone; unregistered, insignificant in the daunting presence of Davies' Enterprises. It was only as she took one last look around the office that Alice allowed herself a reluctant smile.

With thoughts of her French weekend buzzing in her head, she wheeled the cracked leather chair back under the desk, grabbed her box of belongings and hoisted her bag onto her shoulder.

Time to move on.

CHAPTER TWENTY-THREE

"You're on your way *where*, sweetheart?" Her mum's voice grated with a tinny echo against the low hum of the engine.

Alice tutted, flipping her head to shove the mobile between her ear and shoulder.

She'd need both hands to clean the stain she'd just noticed on her new shift dress; the unlikely designer purchase she'd justified to herself as a reward for bagging her new job – and, of course, the small matter of looking like she belonged on a private jet was a slight contributory factor.

"The south of France, Mum. Thought I told you before you left?" A few manic scrubs later with a barely-damp wet wipe she'd plucked from the murky depths of her handbag, and the unidentified stain was fading. The complete opposite to the nerves and excitement that were building at an alarming rate in her empty stomach.

"Yes, yes, I think you – sorry… just a minute—" Her mum's fading voice was drowned out by muffled cheering and a burst of rousing music. The wedding reception was clearly in full swing.

Alice craned her neck to watch the streetlights shrinking into the distance in the rear window, just as the limo accelerated into the oncoming darkness. She knew it wouldn't take long to reach the airport on the outskirts of the city; not even ten minutes until Victor was scheduled to greet her at the car and escort her across the tarmac. Yet, despite playing the scene out countless times in her head, she just couldn't get to grips with the idea of being ushered onto a private jet by a multi-millionaire.

Just then, the driver's blacked-out partition slowly lowered.

"Only a few minutes now, Miss Webster." As she sat admiring Edward's wonderfully soft, reassuring tone, her mum's voice cut through the air like a shockwave.

"Sorry about that, sweetheart… should have phoned you from outside. They're just away to have their first dance, so better go. Gordon and Sally seem to be getting on great. Think they've finally put it all behind them." She laughed. "So happy for him."

Alice smiled, said her goodbyes then took a last generous swig of champagne from the flute on the ledge. Up ahead, she could see the myriad of twinkling, coloured lights heralding the entrance to the airport terminal. She snatched her compact from her bag to give her appearance a quick once-over.

As she smoothed her hair in the smeared mirror, the reflection caught a glimpse of the skin below her neck – the strangely-familiar, red rash had flared up yet again. It felt like no time had passed at all when the limo drew to a halt beside a long line of towering floodlights. Alice quickly buttoned her boucle coat and swung her pink cashmere scarf across her shoulders – praying that a blast of cold night air would calm the rash before they boarded the plane.

Seconds later, the passenger door opened and Victor ducked his head to lean inside. As he held his hand out towards her, a gust of wind whipped his dark coat up behind him.

"Glad to see you're suitably wrapped up." Despite flashing her a dazzling smile, Alice couldn't take her eyes off his unkempt, wind-swept hair. In the oddest of moments, she reckoned that it suited him far better than his usual neater style.

"Well… shall we?"

Alice shuffled herself along the leather seat to grab his outstretched hand. In the bitter night air, it was surprisingly warm to the touch. An icy squall blasted her face as Victor helped her out of the limo. Grimacing, she dropped her head and scrunched her scarf tightly around her collar. It wasn't long before dense droplets of rain were buffeting about in the strengthening wind – yet Edward still stood to attention by the bonnet and doffed his cap as they hurried across the tarmac.

"I hope you're okay with a bit of a breeze—" Victor leaned in to make himself heard over the storm, his warm breath like a naked flame against her cold cheek.

"Nothing I can't handle, I'm sure," she replied, trying desperately to conceal the fear she'd harboured for way too long. But despite her best efforts, her legs trembled more the further she climbed up the metal walkway. As she took her last step, a vision from her dream the night before flashed into her mind. She lost her balance and stumbled into the entrance as it all came rushing back.

The flickering shapes and images were hypnotic in their intensity; penetrating her brain as though she could feel them in the deepest recesses of her soul. Most were ephemeral and blurred, yet one remained constant and most vivid of them all.

She'd had the same vision over and over towards the end: a never-ending tortuous loop of raging fire and twisting flames, so uncannily real she could hear the hissing and crackling as the veil melted then disintegrated in gut-wrenching slow-motion before her eyes. Then came the heat. The god-awful, agonising heat…

With the vision still burning in her mind's eye, she brushed Victor's hand from her arm. Staring down the length of the plane, she shoved her bag back onto her shoulder; her agitation rising as the familiar cloak of claustrophobia insidiously smothered her senses. Recalling the advice to look at a single point in the distance, she focused on Victor's logo; the metre-high, initialled grey emblem dominating the rear wall.

"Alice?" Her mind still hazy, she couldn't decide if the urgent whisper was a gesture of concern or Victor merely ushering her forwards into the cabin. Either way, it startled her back into the moment and she was suddenly aware of a smartly-dressed, smiling brunette sashaying towards her.

"Good evening, Miss Webster," she trilled in the unfeasibly upbeat tone that only members of cabin crew can get away with.

"Please." She gestured with a tanned, slender hand towards four enormous gold silk brocade seats: two sets facing each other, separated by a glossy walnut table that Alice figured could easily accommodate eight diners, with elbow room to spare.

"Marie, lovely to see you again." Victor leaned in to plant a single kiss on both her cheeks. Alice had to concede that she looked every inch the glamorous femme fatale, with her perfectly shiny bun, sleek red pencil skirt and bosom-hugging blouse.

"A pleasure as always, Mr Davies." Alice was sure the dulcet voice had risen at least an octave or two, post-kiss. But it was only when she half-laughed to reveal a smear of scarlet lipstick on her otherwise immaculate, gleaming teeth, that Alice permitted herself a wry smile.

"I'll be back with the menus in a minute." As Marie slinked her way towards the front of the plane, Alice gave her own dress a quick once-over – thankfully, the stain was all but gone. Victor settled himself into the oversized seat across from her and let out a contented sigh.

"Straight here from the office – I'm famished." He whipped off his tie and yanked open the top button of his white shirt, instantly transforming from the distinguished business mogul. "A bite or two to eat, once we're airborne?"

"Sounds good." Alice bit her lip, suddenly aware that it was just the two of them on the plane. "So, I thought you said Charles and Eva were joining us?"

"Oh, they're already here," he replied nonchalantly, unzipping the small black case beside him and pulling out the thinnest laptop she'd ever seen. "In fact," he said, twisting round to look behind him, "I'm pretty sure they're on the other side of that door right now."

He swivelled back towards her, his expression turning serious as he rested his elbows on the table. "It's usually better for Eva to be first on the plane. No distractions or anything that might... *unsettle* her."

Alice nodded, understanding the delicacy of the situation.

"I'll give Charles a bit longer. Make sure she's properly settled." Victor's voice oozed genuine warmth and softness; his tact and patience concerning Eva were clearly well-practised.

Marie shimmied her way back down the aisle with their menus; her fulsome, sickly perfume wafting under Alice's nose as she sidled up to them.

Just then, the cabin lights dimmed and the plane moved gently forwards.

"If you could both fasten your seat belts now, please." She rested a hand on top of Victor's seat and leaned in towards him; exaggerated smile and all. Alice glanced at the other beautifully-manicured hand resting on her thigh and huffed knowingly. Of course, not an engagement or wedding ring in sight.

"A glass of your usual Chilean red coming up, Mr Davies." She turned towards Alice, instantly straightening; the softness in her face all but gone. "Some champagne after take-off, Miss Webster?"

"That would be lovely." Alice couldn't bring herself to say thank you.

Marie shot her a curt, perfunctory smile before turning around to sway her voluptuous hips back up the aisle.

Alice stiffened as a mighty gust of wind battered the fuselage.

"You know, you probably won't feel a thing anyway – she's pretty robust, this one."

Alice couldn't help but relax a little at Victor's affectionate description of his jet.

"Sorry – just one quick email to send then it's switched off. I promise."

Alice continued to watch him as he typed, scanned the words, then typed some more. She was mesmerised by his face as he concentrated, not because she hadn't seen him looking so intense or focused before, but because the reflective glare of the screen made his glowing skin look so wonderfully translucent; almost other-worldly. He tutted then punched some words impatiently on the keyboard. Alice dragged her gaze away and looked outside. Beyond the rivulets of rain meandering aimlessly on the oval window pane, she could see that they were already taxiing parallel to the lights of the runway. As the plane veered slowly to the left, a fork of lightning split the distant night sky. Feeling the panic rise, she leaned over and tugged the window blind down beside her. Without saying a word, Victor stretched out to shut all the ones within his reach.

"There," he whispered, with a reassuring smile.

Within seconds, the noise from the engines rose to a vibrating, roaring crescendo and Alice was forced into the back of her seat. She focused on the portrait in the far right-hand corner as the plane finally thrust itself off the ground. She half-closed her eyes, waiting for the inevitable dizzying, disorienting sensation that always washed over her seconds after take-off. But, nothing.

A few minutes into the air, she gradually loosened her grip on the fabric of the seat. No hint of turbulence; not a single disconcerting shake or shudder – only the smoothest, most relaxing take-off she'd ever experienced. There was a small ping above their heads.

"You can unbuckle now. Told you it'd be plain sailing, didn't I?"

Despite concentrating on the picture from the second they'd left the tarmac, Alice sensed that Victor hadn't taken his eyes off her the whole time. She could feel the familiar heat prickling her skin once again. His narrow eyes followed her palm as she raised it tentatively to her collarbone.

"Nervous rash?" he asked quietly.

"Probably. Never been the best of flyers."

Marie appeared, as if from nowhere, to place their drinks on the coasters in front of them.

The silence was excruciating as Victor rolled up the sleeves of his crisp, white shirt – his dark eyes fixed firmly on her rash. She budged awkwardly in her seat.

"So, shouldn't we be going over the itinerary for the conference—" She dragged the glass of champagne towards her and took a hearty gulp. The sensation of the chilled bubbles fizzing on her tongue and sliding down her parched throat instantly relaxed her.

"How about we leave that until the morning – good night's sleep, fresh heads and all that?" He pressed one last button on the laptop, closed the lid and slid it to the side under the window. "I've looked forward to this all day." He raised his drink in front of him, gently cupping it where the stem met the bulbous glass. Alice watched as he swirled the opaque burgundy liquid around and around, making it undulate with a rhythmic precision that was almost hypnotic.

"Look, Victor, there's something I'm not exactly sure how—" Alice looked down at the plush grey carpet, feeling her throat tighten. "Well, it's just that Eva and I... I mean we've not spoken since that night in the pub and I don't really know how to behave towards..."

Victor took a generous swig of wine and grinned, as though he'd been anticipating her concern.

"I mean, obviously now I know she has *issues* but—" She groaned inwardly at her woeful choice of words. "Jesus, what she said about you, though, Victor—"

She looked him dead in the eye, imploring him to respond;

to throw her something – or maybe just to hear him denounce Eva's awful allegations one more time.

"I think it's best if we leave that alone for now." He turned away to look out the window. A few seconds later, he looked back at her. "She's been back staying with Charles again for a bit recently. From what I've seen of her at Davies' House, she seems more – dare I say – *balanced* these days. Charles thinks they've finally got her on the right meds now. Been a bit trial and error, by all accounts…"

He blew out a lungful of air, instantly closing the subject. "Anyway—" He picked up the menus they'd forgotten to look at and passed one to Alice. "If everything looks fine to you, I'll chivvy the food along."

Still dwelling on her imminent encounter with Eva, she gave the menu a cursory glance. The bruschetta, mushroom risotto and dark chocolate mousse were already whetting her appetite.

Victor stood up and strode down the aisle towards the cockpit, disappearing through a tall door at the far end of the cabin.

As she took a first proper look around her, soaking in the luxurious walnut and gold-trimmed interior and admiring the lavish silk brocade furnishings, Alice felt a momentary shudder under her feet. Not a tremor to set the pulse racing, by any means, but the panic began to swell regardless.

Realising the windows on the opposite side still had their blinds up, she launched herself across the aisle. As she raised her arm to yank the first one down, a blinding flash of lightning zapped the wing of the plane. She stumbled backwards, tears welling in her eyes. Through the blur, she could see the lights flickering on and off – then on… off…

on… off – finally, on again. Panicking, she reached across the aisle for the edge of the table just as a figure hurried towards her out of the corner of her eye. She bumped down into her seat, rummaged for both ends of her belt and clicked them together as quickly as she could.

A few deep breaths to slow her heart, she squeezed her eyes shut and rubbed them back into focus with her knuckles.

"Are you alright, Alice?"

She gasped and lowered her hands.

"Charles?"

"Just wanted to check you were okay after the… incident."

"Yeah – think so," she said, shaking her head.

"Oh, Victor's with Eva just now, by the way. He came to see us just as the lights went off and, well, she asked him to sit with her for a bit. I suspect he shouldn't be too long." He lowered his half-moon specs, peering over them to look at her. "He's always been *so* good with her…"

She nodded tentatively, unease creeping through her as she realised this was the perfect opportunity to bring up Eva's lies and slanderous allegations. Christ, maybe even the veil on the doorstep, if she was brave enough. She bit her lip, trying to suppress the confusion and unanswered questions that were desperate to escape.

Whether it was the effects of the alcohol or simply a surge of post-lightning adrenalin coursing through her, Alice couldn't contain it any longer.

"You know, Victor wanted me to leave this but I'm going to say it anyway." She took a deep breath. "Did you know I spoke to Eva a few months ago?"

The old man reclined in his seat, tilting his head as he watched her. His grey eyes were wide and intense, as though he was studying a piece of art for the first time.

"Okay—" The inflection in his voice made it more questioning than confirmation. He cleared his throat. "Not exactly out of the ordinary, though."

"We met in Bar Rio. She told me Victor was abusing her then showed me a silver pendant with the letters *obv* on it." Alice couldn't read anything from his deadpan expression. "I know all about the cult, Charles – Victor *enlightened* me, shall we say?"

The plane banked slowly to the left as Victor walked back down the aisle towards her. As soon as he heard the approaching footsteps, Charles' solemn expression vanished and the avuncular old gent reappeared.

"You know, I'm so glad you decided to join us on the trip, Alice," he said; his usual perky, affable manner oddly exaggerated as Victor planted himself on the seat across from them. But the sudden change in his demeanour couldn't disguise the fact that she'd obviously hit a nerve with Charles – a very raw one at that. She watched him spinning his cygnet ring around his pinky finger like it was some sort of compulsive, meditative ritual; all the while looking at nothing but the air in front of him.

"All good with Eva now, Charles – she's just fallen asleep," Victor said with more than a hint of relief.

"Great news." The old man leapt to his feet and patted Victor on the shoulder. "Anyway, I'll leave you to it. See you both after we land, then."

He nodded politely then flashed Alice a cool, cursory smile.

"Should only be another hour or so now. Just enough time for us to finally get some food." Victor winked at her, missing the look on Charles' face as he turned to walk back up the aisle towards his granddaughter.

But Alice didn't miss it; the fleeting, agitated scowl on his creased brow that would ordinarily go unnoticed yet for some reason played out in slow motion before her.

CHAPTER TWENTY-FOUR

Two dull, booming clock chimes jerked Alice awake.

Hazy and disoriented, she forced open her heavy, bleary eyes. In the shadowy darkness, she struggled to make out anything in front of her; in the gloomy vastness she could *feel* surrounding her body.

She blinked her eyes back into focus and looked up at what seemed like an endless vaulted ceiling above her. Her short, sharp breaths echoed in her ears, as she subconsciously pieced together where she was.

Bedroom... castle... must be two in the morning?

The back of her body and legs were gloriously warm, as she lay half-sunken into the soft, silky plumpness underneath. The heady scent of rich, dark wood and aged leather was all-consuming in the cool air, but there was another scent fading in and out; something evocative, intoxicatingly sweet – and instinctively recognisable.

A chill began to creep across her bare arms and neck, and she realised she was lying fully clothed in her shift dress and tights on top of the bed. She'd obviously had more to drink on the plane than she'd thought as it suddenly occurred to her that she couldn't remember anything about the journey from the airport.

As she propped herself up onto both elbows and peered into the darkness, her fingers brushed something small and hard beside her. Thankful that she'd found her mobile, she snatched it from the silky bedspread and swiped her index finger across the screen. A message flashed up.

Hey you! Just checking in on my favourite lady. All good here with the new job, so far – more money and less work. Result! Hope you're staying out of trouble? Maybe we can meet up when I'm back in town next month? P x

The familiar, warm fuzziness bubbled up inside her as she read the text Pete had sent her yesterday. Although her feelings for him seemed a world away now, she knew there would always be a part of her that regretted not trusting him more; a pang of guilt that, at the very least, she could have given it a go with him. But in her heart, she knew she was only fooling herself. Deep down, she knew the *real* reason and had done for some time – probably longer than she cared to admit.

Relieved that it was all working out well for him, she glanced at the battery level and realised she wasn't getting a signal. Her reply would have to wait until later.

Desperate for decent light, she pushed herself towards the edge of the bed and held her phone out in front of her, sweeping the luminous glow from the screen in a controlled arc around the room. The ghostly yellowish cast danced along an enormous marble mantelpiece flanked by two ornate chairs before sweeping across a writing bureau, a glass-topped wooden table then a tall chest of drawers adorned with curved metal handles. She rested the glow over a ceiling-high wardrobe before easing it up and down the intricate carvings on the huge panelled doors. A set of red velvet drapes hung next to the wardrobe, as tall as they were wide; like the oversized curtains on a West End stage.

With her right arm straining, she swapped the phone to her other hand where the glow settled on a large lamp on the bedside table; to the right a huge door lurked in the shadows.

A quick flick of the phone to locate the light-switch, Alice leapt to her feet, index finger poised. When the first click produced no light, she tried again – this time pressing slower and harder. Flustered, she flicked it on and off; faster and faster, eventually giving in and thumping it with a frustrated fist. In the cold stillness, she felt a growing vibration beneath her stockinged feet. She pressed her ear to the door and held her breath as she realised it was footsteps approaching her room.

She dropped her hand and fumbled for the door handle. The cold, smooth knob wouldn't budge so she threw her phone onto the bed, thrust her other hand on top and squeezed it as tightly as she could. After turning it so vigorously that both hands were stinging, the handle gave an abrupt loosening turn, finally relenting with a low, satisfying click. A couple of hefty yanks later and the door creaked slowly open towards her.

Peering out into the dim, cavernous hallway, she caught a dark figure disappearing around a tight bend at the top. She crept out of the bedroom, her throat tightening as she was confronted by a sea of candelabras adorning the various ledges and alcoves along the walls.

"Power cut…" she whispered, watching the gentle, wavering reflection of the candles against the dark red walls.

Her eyes were drawn upwards to the enormous portraits tilting slightly forwards off the wall, looming down on her;

forceful and intimidating. There was a striking similarity between all of them: each subject's head tilted to the same side, at the same half-profile angle; each solemn, aristocratic face etched with the same superior intolerance, screaming from the same taut, unforgiving lips. Whoever had been commissioned to paint the small but impressive gallery had obviously been kept busy over the years.

Alice crept across the hall to look at the signature on the portrait of the elderly gent staring down at her – the prolonged creak of the dark wooden plank beneath her foot was amplified ten-fold in the cool stillness. She leaned in to peer at the initials scrawled in the bottom left-hand corner when a voice startled her. All the snatching glance had registered was what looked like a beautifully-scripted *H*.

"Ah, Alice – you're awake." As if from nowhere, Charles stood beside her. Dressed in a long, green velvet smoking jacket, he was dangling what looked like a golden orb on a thin chain in front of him.

"Yeah… a bit confused, though—" She shook her head, distracted as he rhythmically swung the metal ball to and fro; the shiny surface glinting in the candlelight on each downward swing, like a giant shimmering pendulum. A few seconds later, an intoxicating sweetness redolent of burning lavender and cinnamon, seeped out of the small, patterned holes to drift underneath her nose. Alice thought she recognised it.

"Just a touch of incense. Helps an old insomniac get some decent shut-eye. A necessary evil, I'm afraid—" He spoke earnestly, not quite making eye contact.

"So, I'm assuming this isn't mood lighting?" She nodded towards the candelabras.

"Would you believe a freak blizzard's cut the power? Came from out of nowhere apparently."

Alice's skin prickled as she studied his nonchalant, almost carefree, expression.

Charles sighed and turned his head to look down the long corridor she couldn't quite see the end of.

"So, it would seem that we're not going to make the conference this weekend – at least not today, anyway."

Alice narrowed her eyes.

"All roads to and from the chateau are snowbound – pretty much impassable, I'm afraid."

At that moment, an arid dryness choked the back of her throat before creeping up into her mouth. The incense was now eye-wateringly potent; almost embedding itself in the lining of her nose.

"A stroke of luck we got here when we did last night." Charles' half-laugh seemed almost inappropriate in the circumstances. "Oh, before I forget, I must apologise for not bringing your bag up earlier."

Alice couldn't believe she hadn't looked for it as soon as she'd woken – considering the precious black item she'd decided she couldn't leave behind; lovingly wrapped and carefully secreted in the middle pocket.

"I didn't even notice. Don't even remember getting here from the airport—" Her pulse quickened as she realised how utterly bewildered she was.

"Why, I think you're definitely needing more sleep, my dear. You did seem very tired when you got off the plane. Perhaps with all the exhaustion, you've lost an hour or two along the way?"

Alice shrugged. "And Victor? Where's he?"

Charles peered over his glasses, a twinkle in his grey eyes. "Well, why don't we go and see?"

They took a sharp turn into a narrow vaulted corridor; barely visible in the fading glow of the distant hallway candles. Alice's heart was beating in time with the rhythmic whoosh of Charles' slippers as he shuffled across the wooden floor towards a door at the bottom.

As they passed an arch-shaped window on the left, she was strangely relieved to look out onto a wintry landscape bathed in the light of the most glorious full moon she'd ever seen. Scores of trees sparkled from root to tip, their densely-covered branches wilting under the twinkling white mass. Behind them endless mountains rose sharply and majestically up to the midnight blue sky. It was a scene of such awe-inspiring, natural beauty, she couldn't help but stand and stare.

Charles was already waiting at the door, looking back at her. "Didn't believe me, did you?"

Alice forced a smile, embarrassed that her scepticism hadn't gone unnoticed. She took one last look at the stunning view before walking towards him. As if on cue, he gave the door a gentle nudge then beckoned her to enter. She left the narrow corridor behind and wandered into a breathtakingly enormous room. The feeling that she'd been instantly shrunk was overwhelming.

Gazing up at the dome-shaped, patterned ceiling and the surrounding bookshelves that were so tall they almost kissed the soaring cornices, she knew exactly how her namesake in Wonderland must have felt. But something was unsettling her even more; something visceral pinging her brain, somewhere just below the level of consciousness.

She stared into the roaring flames of the huge open fire, trying to rein in her growing angst. All the while, she could feel Charles watching her intently. "You'll find any book on any subject in here, you know," he boasted, unashamedly.

She turned to face him, the vivid imagery of the orange flames still wavering in front of her eyes.

"More than a few on cults, I'd imagine?" The words were out before she knew it.

Charles took a deep breath, ripe to reply when his eyes darted behind her. A short sharp click followed by distant footsteps made her turn around.

Victor was standing on a raised platform by a small staircase at the back of the room; a half-empty glass of amber liquid clutched in one hand, the other resting casually on the handrail beside him. He was still in his white shirt and suit trousers, looking as fresh and charismatic as ever. Alice stiffened as he made his way slowly down the few steps to the main floor of the library. It was the same relentless churning of awe and admiration deep inside her but this time it was more intense – *too* intense.

She teased a stray curl around her finger as she glanced down at the toes peeking through the thin, sheer denier of her tights. When she looked up, Victor was standing right in front of her.

Without saying a word, he raised his glass and downed the contents in one swift gulp. He let out a curt, gratified sigh and shot her a look that she couldn't quite read.

"Will you join us in a nightcap, Alice?" Charles poured himself a whisky by the mantelpiece then collapsed into a huge leather chair by the fire. "I hope you didn't mind me putting you to bed earlier but you really were out for the count when we arrived—"

Victor gestured for her to take a seat next to the old man. His calm smile made her hackles rise. That was when the surreal reality of the situation struck her full force.

"You see, that's what's bothering me about all this." She hung her head; painfully aware that she was about to unleash a torrent of pent-up emotion.

"No, actually, it's not just *bothering* me – it's confusing me – *really* confusing me and, quite honestly, it's scaring the crap out of me."

Her face felt like it was on fire and she knew she was about to lose any remaining self-control she had left – but there was no going back now.

"I chose to come on this trip with you, Victor – this *supposed* business conference that I'm now starting to realise was just a figment of your imagination. I'm here of my own volition, I accept that—" Her train of thought vanished as she watched him meticulously roll back one cuff, then the other, exposing first the dark hair on his wrists then up towards the thicker hair on his broad forearms.

She shook her head to force herself back on track but the momentum was gone. In desperation, she changed tack.

"And where the hell's Eva, anyway? That girl's about as real as a bloody urban myth. You know, I'm beginning to wonder if she even got on the plane..."

"Hmmm—" Victor tilted his head as he stared at her. "I think you need a drink, Alice," he said calmly.

"Christ, stop offering me drinks, will you? I don't bloody want one, I just want answers – and I want them now." She yanked open the hair clip that was hanging loose at the nape of her neck.

"How about we start with the girl who went missing, Victor?" She meant business now – she had the bit between her teeth and she was damned if she was going to let it go.

Charles got to his feet, facing the fire.

"I'm wondering if you really know what happened between her and Alan that night? You know, the night she vanished into thin air after one of your *meetings*…"

Victor strode towards the bookshelf next to the fireplace, stopping before a section crammed with foot-high, leather-bound volumes. He ran the tip of his finger over a few before prising a thick burgundy tome from the shelf running level with his waist.

Alice swallowed hard, about to demand a reply when he strode back towards her with the hefty book gripped between his hands. He stopped in front of her, ceremoniously holding it out, like a prized possession.

"This will tell you everything you need to know about the Order, Alice."

"Jesus, you're really not getting it, are you?" She marched towards the bookshelf.

"I couldn't give a damn about your cult, Victor; what it stands for or whatever the hell it is you all *do*—" Despite her indignation, she couldn't tear her gaze away from the books in front of her eyes; she felt utterly compelled to stare at them.

In the mingling of light and gloom, she could just make out the title running up one of the thick, embossed spines: *The Order of the Black Veil – A Complete History.*

Before she knew it, she was cradling the book in the palm of her hands and instinctively lifting the cover to her nose. Within seconds, saliva began to seep into the sides of her mouth, quickly pooling over her teeth and tongue as she inhaled the glorious, distinctive fustiness of the old leather.

"First edition – good choice." Victor's voice dragged her back into the moment.

She bristled, annoyed that she'd allowed herself to get distracted from her questioning. "Maybe read it later," she huffed, tossing it onto the plump seat of the armchair beside her. She looked across at Charles who was still standing with his back to them, shoulders hunched and unnervingly quiet.

Her eyes flitted back towards Victor, hoping for some – *any* – reassurance about the old man's strange behaviour when, finally, he spoke.

"For your information, Alice, Eva is fast asleep in bed." His tone was deeply disapproving. He turned slowly to face her; his chin tilted downwards, almost to his collarbone. She could barely see his eyes in the dark shadows slicing across his face, from forehead to mouth.

"I wasn't saying—"

"You know," Charles cut in, "I'm sensing a distinct lack of patience, perhaps even a lack of compassion, when it comes to my granddaughter?"

She could feel her previous bravado draining away; slipping downwards and out through the soles of her cold feet.

He hoisted his chin abruptly, his eyes glaring past her. In that instant, she sensed Victor walking up behind her. Seconds later, he appeared out of the corner of her eye to take his place in the armchair by the fire. Alice watched the two men throw each other a look; a fleeting, blink-and-you'd-miss-it look yet so unequivocally surreptitious, so knowing, she couldn't shake the feeling that she wasn't meant see it.

"Please, Alice, take a seat while I *enlighten* you—"

She was too on edge to refuse the old man as he poured

a small whisky and held it out towards her. She pushed the book to the side and lowered herself gently into the armchair; the merciless heat from the roaring flames instantly blasting her face. She turned towards Victor in the chair next to her. He was sitting motionless, staring into the wild, crackling flames; eyes wide and unblinking, like he was steeling himself for what was to come.

It had never occurred to her before but suddenly it was glaringly obvious to Alice who the dominant, controlling force in their relationship was. She flinched as Charles placed a gentle hand on her shoulder.

"I know you have questions and doubts, Alice, but you really mustn't worry, you know. This is exactly how it should be."

Her disbelief escaped as a sharp, high-pitched huff. Charles continued unfazed, lost in his passionate discourse. "Relax, put your trust in fate and the fact that everything happens for a reason. There are no accidents or coincidences, my dear – it's all predestined. Fate's design is infallible." He let out a long, wearisome sigh. "And, I'm afraid, the sooner you accept that, the better."

"So what about Kelly? She was *meant* to go missing, then? Is that what you're saying?"

Victor shifted uncomfortably as Charles ran the silk belt of his jacket through his gnarled fingers.

"And now we get to the good part…"

Every nerve in her body grated as she listened to him dismissing the girl's disappearance as though it were an unfortunate incident.

"Jesus, cut to the bloody chase. Surely you must know what happened between Kelly and Alan that night…" Her heart felt like it would burst through her chest. "… I mean, you were all

211

there, right?"

She yanked her shoulder from his hand, unable to bear his touch any longer.

"And why do you assume Alan had anything to do with it?" He shot a look over her head. Nausea stirred in her gut. She turned behind her towards Victor – he was already looking at her.

"Well… I've seen a photo of them together. Taken the night she went missing—" Realising she was still talking at Victor, she spun round towards Charles, who was pacing the floor with both hands behind his back, following the same invisible line up and down the marble. His eyes were fixed firmly on the ground in front of him, like a lawyer parading the courtroom before a jury.

"My old boss, Gordon, took it… the photo, I mean. When he showed it to Alan, he was fuming. The guy apparently looked as guilty as hell. Not long after, Gordon gets shafted at work, is forced to leave his job, his house gets ransacked for the photo…"

The hellish series of events replayed so frantically in her brain that her mouth could barely keep up. Without thinking, she knocked back a mouthful of whisky, probably to steady her nerves or bolster her courage – maybe both. But she wasn't prepared for the burning as it slid like a trail of molten lava down her gullet. Her eyes brimmed with tears as the alcohol kicked in, along with a distinct edge that wasn't there before.

"Are you telling me that sounds like someone who's innocent?" she snapped.

Charles stopped in his tracks then lifted his head.

"Alice, my dear…" He made his way across the marble

towards her. "I was never sure how this was all going to come out, if I'm honest—"

A sudden dread jolted through her.

"It seems you were so intent on blaming one person that you were blind to the possibility of… well, other options—" He raised a silver eyebrow. "Oh, come on… the day Kelly went missing must surely have stuck in your mind for another reason." He leaned over her shoulder, his mouth brushing her ear. "A tragedy closer to home, perhaps—" His whisper was warm and soft yet it shot a chill right through her. For a second, Alice's mind went into shutdown – no thoughts flowed, no connections made – nothing; like her brain had flicked to self-preservation mode.

But she knew she couldn't suppress it for long. At first, her conscious mind staggered feebly back into the moment but as soon as it gained momentum, there was no stopping the race towards clarity; towards finally unlocking the truth. The truth that she'd chosen to dismiss and bury deep in her subconscious – too afraid to ever confront it.

"The truth is, Alan wasn't involved with Kelly. He was just the go-between – the delivery guy, really. You see, Alice, her boyfriend had *way* too much at stake to get caught – a wife, a daughter, top job in the police…" His voice tailed off as Victor walked to the back of the room.

Then he turned, his judgemental eyes swooping upon her. All she could do was stare at him as the lump in her throat swelled with such ferocity she didn't think she could breathe, let alone speak. She squeezed her eyes shut with a sudden urge to just run – somewhere, anywhere – but as fast as she could and as far away as possible from the nightmare she was drowning in. When she opened them, Victor was walking back towards her – each stride shorter and less purposeful than before. She couldn't stop her head from shaking as the reality embedded itself in her brain. "Christ, we didn't even know dad was in the cult, but an affair as well…?"

"It would seem he had rather a lot to answer for." Charles sighed through the steeple of his fingertips; his cygnet ring glinting like a tiny beacon in the candlelight. "Perhaps her threat that she might be pregnant tipped him over the edge…?"

Alice's head fell into her hands. She felt like breaking down; releasing all the hellish, pent-up emotion but she was too numb to do to anything.

"He left a suicide note. He was sorry for what he'd done and he couldn't live with himself anymore—" She was muttering to herself, frantically trying to make sense of the barrage of revelations. "I figured it was all about the way he'd treated me and mum but now… well, maybe that's not all he was apologising for?"

She looked back up at Charles – a hot tear spilled down her cheek. "What did he do to her?"

"That is something nobody knows, Alice. There isn't even any proof that he actually did anything at all. All I know is that they were arguing before they got in his car to leave that night. It's all circumstantial—"

A light flicked on in Alice's brain. "And, of course, Alan wouldn't want to be seen in a photograph with a missing girl…"

"It would seem that your father may have taken this to his grave, Alice."

Another thought crashed into her brain.

Jesus, mum…

As though reading her mind, Charles turned towards her as

he poured himself another large whisky. "Are you *sure* your mother didn't know what he was doing, Alice? There must have been a lot of unexplained trips out of the house—" He threw back his drink and smacked his lips together. "And she did strike me as quite the doting wife—"

For a split second, the thought that her mum might actually have known all along was frighteningly plausible. No matter how many times she tried to dismiss it, the idea seemed to make more sense by the second. She rubbed her forehead as she watched Victor leaning casually against the bookcase by the fire. "You know what, I can't deal with this right now."

She pushed herself out of the chair to make for the door, but her legs were like leaden weights and she stumbled, falling back onto the curved edge of the velvet seat.

"Alice—" Victor rushed forwards as she grabbed the arm of the chair. She shoved his hand away, glaring at him.

"Oh, don't worry about me – too much shock, I guess. You know, a heads-up about my dad wouldn't have gone amiss." She marched towards the door, grabbed the handle – then stopped. "So, it's all true then, is it?" She stared at the dark wood in front of her; bile rising in the back of her throat as her heart pounded against her ribs. The ensuing few seconds of silence was all the confirmation she needed.

"Alice, I—" Victor called after her as she yanked the door open and rushed out into the corridor. A welcome blast of cool air hit her face as she picked up the pace across the creaking floorboards. Each breath was coming sharp and fast as she fought to quell the tears stinging her eyes. As soon as she heard Victor's footsteps echoing close behind, she hurried past her bedroom towards a giant set of double doors at the end of the hall.

As she stood in front of the grand mahogany entrance, hand poised to grab the wrought-iron handle, she turned to look behind her – just as Victor appeared around the corner. They stood in silence for a beat or two, staring at each other in the distance. He rested his hands on his hips, as she slowly pressed the stiff handle down behind her.

"Please, Victor – just go away. I want to be on my own..." Her hand trembled as she pushed it down as far as it would go. She flinched as the grandfather clock beside her let out a shrill piercing chime. Victor strolled towards her as the fourth and last chime faded away. "Why are you going into that room, Alice? Do you even know what's in there?"

She was damned if she was going to admit her irrepressible urge to enter a random room in a castle she'd never set foot in before. Then, just as she took a breath to reply, the snib clicked sharply and, without any persuasion, the door creaked open.

Victor held her gaze; his chest rising and falling heavily beneath his unusually crumpled shirt.

"I'll say it again, Victor – *leave me alone*." But deep down, she knew she didn't mean it.

And with that, Alice took a deep breath and stepped into the room she knew was waiting just for her...

CHAPTER TWENTY-FIVE

Alice stood transfixed beyond the open door. Warm, un-expected tears spilled over, pooling onto her top lip before slowly trickling into her mouth.

As her bleary eyes drank in the surreal, overwhelming beauty in front of her, a recognition began to stir; raw and intense, resonating in the depths of her soul as though something had just been reawakened. Row upon row of towering red candles bordered the room; the casting glow of their hypnotic dancing light making each wall almost come alive. Sensing Victor was right behind her, Alice turned to face him.

"Why didn't you tell me about my dad?" she whispered. "Jesus, why would you keep that from me?" Out of nowhere, a gut-wrenching sob escaped from deep inside her.

Victor grabbed her shoulders – she flinched but couldn't bring herself to move away. He gave them a firm, comforting rub. "I had no knowledge of your father and the girl – you have to believe that. It was only Charles who knew about the affair before she went—" He paused.

Alice huffed, wiping away the wetness on her cheeks. "—missing? It's okay, you can say it." She glanced at the row of candles to her right and instinctively began counting them, before adding the ones behind her then those along the last wall.

"Oh my god… twenty-five." She let out a disbelieving sigh as her eyes came to rest on the last candle.

Victor slowly guided her face back towards his.

"So, you remember the birthday card, then?" His expectant eyes stared into hers.

"It wasn't just the card I remember them from, though…" She glanced at the oversized bed only a few feet from them; a surge of heat flushing her cheeks as she recalled the most vivid and erotic dream she'd ever experienced. She closed her eyes as his finger brushed a stray curl from her forehead.

"Why am I here, Victor? Why do I feel like I've been here before?"

Without taking his eyes off her face, he laid a cool, flat palm against her collarbone. "I think that might be flaring up again—"

But she was barely aware of the smouldering heat sweeping across her chest. "Please, Victor, I need to know why I'm here. Why I have these dreams, these feelings that I can't explain—" She stiffened as he cupped her face with firm, reassuring hands. Her heart was racing; it felt like electricity was firing through every nerve in her body.

His grasp unrelenting, she slowly relaxed into his hold. He slowly loosened his grip and trailed delicate fingertips down her cheeks.

"I think the real question is, do you *want* to be here?" His voice was soft and low as he leaned in towards her, pressing his chest against hers.

"I don't think I want to be anywhere else…" The words spilled out without a moment's thought.

"That's all I needed to know," he whispered, edging closer; his mouth barely brushing hers. She pushed herself up onto shaking tiptoes to finally meet his lips. And then they kissed, gently and barely moving to begin with; simply relishing the first exquisitely soft, sensual touch. After a few seconds, the urge to explore was too much and Victor clasped her face and pushed his mouth hard onto hers; their lips urgently but seamlessly merging into one. Alice grabbed the back of his head, shoving her fingers through his thick, dark hair. Victor's breathing was hard and fast as he scooped her up into his arms and laid her down on top of the red silky bedcover.

His eyes were hungry and intense as he kneeled at her side, impatiently yanking at the buttons of his crisp, white shirt. She gasped as he straddled her hips then lowered himself forwards to place a hand either side of her head. She drank in his taut, naked torso as it escaped through the unbuttoned white cotton.

A sudden panic and vulnerability washed over her as she lay there on her back; pinned to the bed by a distinguished, wealthy businessman – then he leaned in to kiss her again and all her insecurities vanished. His mouth was hard and desperate as he forced her lips apart with his tongue. Urgent passion swelled inside her as she felt his fingers on the zip of her dress then listened to its teasingly slow, stuttering release. She arched her back as his fingers followed the zipper all the way to the base of her spine. All she could do was take shallow sips of air, full of expectation, as he slowly pulled the sleeves off her shoulders and slid them down each arm, trailing soft, featherlight kisses along her skin as he went. She instinctively raised her hips to let him pull the dress – and her tights – down over her thighs, before giving one final tug and tossing the fabric on the floor behind him. She could feel his hardness pressing against the delicate lace of her pants and, before she knew it, her fingers had released the catch on his waistband and she was slowly unzipping his trousers.

He stared down at her, his mouth parted and wanton, his dark, lustful eyes penetrating hers with such intensity she could feel the blood rushing to every inch of her body. She knew right there and then, that she'd never wanted anyone more.

"I've waited so long for this," Victor moaned as he eased himself slowly inside her.

Suddenly, Alice couldn't breathe – the exquisite pain as he pushed deeper into her, filling her completely as his mouth licked and kissed its way across her breasts sent all her senses into shock. Just when she thought she couldn't take any more, he raised her up towards him, his hands frantically grabbing and squeezing her buttocks, supporting them as he thrust himself harder and faster inside her.

Everything felt so natural, so right – each writhing twist, every entwining movement of their glistening limbs completely synchronised, in perfect unison. Almost as if their bodies had been made for each other – had *always* known each other.

Alice was helpless as the furious momentum of their grinding hips forced out gasps of endless, breathless pleasure. Then, as though sensing she'd reached the point of no return, Victor grabbed the back of her hair, forcing her to look him straight in the eye. Although hers were half-closed, the sheer intensity of his stare tipped her over the edge and she dug her nails into his back as her body stiffened then convulsed in wave after wave of ecstasy. Just as her trembling body was starting to recover, Victor suddenly tensed all over and seconds later thrust into her so much harder and faster than before. Alice didn't think she could take any more of the relentless but glorious pain when Victor collapsed on top of her, his rapid heartbeat thudding against hers in perfect unison.

Just as the full weight of his languid body was starting to crush her, he rolled over onto the satin bedsheet beside her and slid his arm under her neck.

Their breathing began to slow as she lay with her head resting gently on his chest. Although she was desperate to break the candlelit silence, she knew there was nothing either of them could say – no words that could possibly do justice to what they'd just experienced.

But there was something she had to know, *had* to ask him before she lost her nerve and he fell asleep and the moment had passed. As his breathing became heavier and slower, she knew it was now or never.

"Victor, what did you mean when you said you'd waited so long for this?" She held her breath as she stared at the gently flickering shadows on the ceiling above them.

He turned his head slowly towards her, his eyes lightly closed as he rested his chin on her forehead.

"I had to wait all that time... Charles said... it had to be this way—" She could tell by the slur creeping in that she was going to lose him any moment – she had to keep going.

"But it's only a few months since we met. You make it sound like you've been waiting for years."

The next few seconds of silence felt like an eternity.

"I have been waiting for years..." His voice faded to a husky whisper. "... hundreds of them."

CHAPTER TWENTY-SIX

Alice opened her eyes and reached across to the other side of the bed.

For a second, she'd no idea why she'd done it. Then, the memories hazily dredged themselves up as she pulled her knees to her chest in the fading candlelight – each emotionally intense scene from the night before, slowly sparking and fusing together; making her stomach knot with both pleasure and pain.

But was it all just another dream?

As she stroked the cool, crumpled sheet with her fingers, she lifted her head and saw that the red satin bedspread had been smoothed down and folded back neatly on the other side. The pillow was plumped up and set perfectly and precisely against the headboard. She allowed herself an indulgent grin as she realised that she was completely naked under the covers.

Definitely not a dream, then.

Panic rose in her belly as she watched the last remaining candle give a hesitant flicker, before fading to nothing but a single, slow-motion wisp of smoke. She stretched her arms and legs out beneath the endless satin, letting the delicate material caress every inch of her. As each rapturous memory came flooding back, consuming her all over again, something pinged into her subconscious. Yet bizarrely, without giving it another thought, she dismissed their lack of protection completely out of hand.

She raised herself up onto her elbows and caught a shard of daylight slicing the wooden floor beside her. Desperate to get out of the room and find Victor, she crawled to the end of the bed and reached out to grab the edge of one of the tall, velvet curtains. She tugged it open, unable to contain her excitement at what might lie behind it – and she wasn't disappointed. She held her breath as her eyes drank in the beautiful, sprawling landscape surrounding the castle. The snow had stopped, melting in places as flashes of green and brown poked through the sparkling white expanse.

She hurriedly threw on the clothes that were strewn in a heap on the floor then opened the glass doors leading out onto the balcony.

The air was bitter but perfectly still as she rested her hands on the frosty metal rail and gazed out across the sweeping, multi-layered gardens below. Alice wasn't sure if it was her body acclimatising to the cold or the breathtaking scenery bathed in the crisp, clear daylight that was covering her skin with goosebumps. Either way, she could have stood there staring forever.

A deer, quickly followed by another, darted over a small fence and disappeared into the distance at the bottom of the meandering driveway. As the graceful animals fled the scene and not a single form of life remained, it occurred to Alice that she should be feeling isolated and vulnerable – stranded as she was, deep in a desolate, mountainous valley in a foreign country. Yet, curiously, she felt nothing of the sort.

Instead, the warmest familiarity flooded her senses; a

natural awareness and understanding encompassed her – almost as though she'd looked out onto the stunning vista before. In that instant, she felt like she'd been brought here for a reason; some sort of higher purpose.

But what?

As the clock in the hallway echoed its ninth and final chime, a dull ache began to spread below her belly button. She massaged it for a few seconds, passing it off as hunger pains and strolled back into the room. Standing alone in the silence, she decided it was time to get out and explore the castle – and maybe seek out some much-needed breakfast.

Before pulling the door shut behind her, she gave the light-switch an opportunistic flick – but the fact that there was still no power was irrelevant as she tripped and stumbled over something at knee-height behind her. After a quick scan of the hallway to check if anyone had seen her, she picked herself up then bent down to grab the familiar worn leather handles of her favourite travel bag.

Desperate to freshen up and run a comb through her hair, Alice quickly unzipped it and rummaged inside for her toiletries case. But just by touch alone, she could tell something was different; that the contents had been displaced and jostled around. Panicking, she began tossing and flinging everything to the side; eventually pulling out every item it could be hiding under. She held her breath as she stared down into the empty bag.

He's taken the veil...

Frustration boiled inside her as she shoved everything except the toiletries case and a pair of pumps back inside the bag and tossed it through the doorway onto the floor. She pulled on the shoes and marched towards the bathroom in the far corner – all the while playing out in her head how best to confront Charles about the veil.

Then, it struck her that, if Charles *had* left the bag outside the door, he must have known she'd stayed the night in that very room. Alice shuddered as she wondered exactly how much he knew…

She stood in front of the mirror and yanked the hairbrush through her flattened waves, barely flinching as the bristles caught and tugged tangle after stubborn tangle. But it was only minutes later, when the mouthful of toothpaste she spat into the bowl was riddled with blood, that Alice realised her frustration was getting out of control. In that instant, she realised just how important the veil was to her.

Refreshed and with a renewed conviction, she stepped out into the dim hallway – her long, purposeful strides guiding her in the opposite direction from the night before. Instinctively, she turned and walked down a short, wide corridor with ceiling-high scarlet walls, stopping in front of a spiral staircase surrounded by huge sash windows. She craned her neck to look up at the towering, whorling coil above her – the vertigo building as her eyes followed it until it disappeared like a never-ending, hypnotic corkscrew of muted blues and greys. Just then, the faint smell of toast wafted under her nose. She closed her eyes and dropped her dizzy head, suddenly aware of muffled voices and the faint clinking of cutlery on china in the distance. Her eyes were drawn to the only door on the right-hand wall; closed over but not tightly shut. As she inched forwards, the voices became clear and more recognisable. She took a deep breath and pushed the door open just as a high-pitched voice surprised her. Before she knew it, she was standing awkwardly in the doorway – staring at Eva.

Three pairs of eyes swooped upon her. In that instant, it was as if every noise had been dulled and she was drowning in a scene of suspended animation. She shuffled, eyes low, towards the dining table – too edgy and unprepared to deal with any judgemental looks just yet. She focused on the generous spread of cooked food, toast and silver jugs covering the oval table.

Victor made a low, garbled noise through a half-chewed mouthful as he stretched over to pull out the spare chair beside him. She turned as far towards him as her nerves would allow – her polite smile finishing somewhere between his breakfast plate and the v-neck of his blue sweater.

Still, everyone's gaze persisted; intense and searching – none more so than Eva's. But it was only when she reached across to offer Alice some toast from a half-empty silver rack, that their eyes finally met. There was an unsettling sweetness in her instant smile; the abrupt, harsh curl that settled on her naturally plump, crimson lips.

"Thank you," Alice croaked, desperate to clear her throat.

"Think somebody could do with a nice, hot cuppa, mmm?" Charles half chuckled as he poured the steaming, dark brown liquid to the brim of her cup.

"Lovely, yes—" The glorious aroma of the rich roast lingered under her nose as she mindlessly scraped a curl of slowly-melting butter this way and that across the crisp golden triangle. Out of the corner of her eye, she saw Victor pick up a small dish of jam then reach towards her. It was now utterly impossible not to look at him.

She nervously rammed the corner of toast into her mouth and turned to him with a nod. At least, that's what she thought would happen until she caught the subtle smile on his lips as he watched her. She stopped mid-chew to take in the flecks of stubble peppering his usually smooth, flawless skin. Instinctively, her eyes followed the coarse, dark path as it spread upwards from his mouth and jawline to merge with the short, tapered hair by his ears. She forced herself to keep chewing as she recalled just how good that roughness had felt against her skin only hours before. She cringed as a warm flush swept slowly but surely across her cheeks.

"I trust you had a good night's sleep, Alice?" Charles' tone was light and nonchalant – *too* nonchalant for someone who either knew or seriously suspected that something intimate hadn't long occurred between them.

Then something made her look up at Eva. The young woman instantly shifted her gaze from Victor to her. No words were needed as she caught the fleeting look of suspicion that flashed across her face. Eva glanced back at Victor as he looked down at his plate, concentrating on arranging another generous forkful of sausage and egg. The young woman stared into space for a few seconds before her eyes flitted back to meet hers. For some reason, she looked older than Alice remembered. The azure eyes were still child-like and undeniably mesmerising but there was a distinct maturity; a discernment behind them that she hadn't noticed before.

And then, just like that, Eva spoke. "Victor, remember you promised me that walk through the woods today?" Behind the light-hearted tone and sweet, hopeful smile, there was an urgency in her voice.

Victor grinned as he swallowed his last mouthful. "Of course. How could I possibly forget?"

Eva's shoulders instantly dropped and a beaming smile lit

up her face.

"But we'll have to limit the walk to the stream today," he craned his neck to look out the arched window behind him, "still lots of fresh snow underfoot." He dabbed his mouth with a napkin and patted it into a scrunched heap on the table beside him. "Actually, I was wondering if Alice might like to join us."

The chair leg screeched against the wooden floor as Eva budged in her seat; her stare fixed firmly on Alice.

"Seeing as we won't be making it to the conference now…" Victor pierced a couple of sausages with a fork and, without asking, slid them off with a knife onto Alice's plate. She shook her head as he made to do the same with a small pile of leftover bacon from the same dish. She looked down at the paltry arrangement on her plate. Even the slim pickings of a half-eaten slice of toast and two small Bratwurst seemed insurmountable to her vanishing appetite. Was nobody else aware of the glaring looks being shot at her from the other side of the table? Or were they simply ignoring the resentment that was so intense she could have reached out and grabbed it?

"So, the conference is dead in the water then?"

She knew Victor was watching her as she hacked her way through the soft, meaty filling.

"Afraid so. Hopefully, tomorrow afternoon we'll be able to make tracks and I can at least keep some of my Monday appointments." He paused, quietly studying her as she lifted the fork to her mouth. "I'm assuming you'd be happy to stay here a bit longer?"

She shrugged, savouring the juicy tenderness that had suddenly rejuvenated her appetite. Then, she made the mistake of glancing across the table again. Eva's glare, although surreptitious, was unrelenting from beneath her lashes.

"Victor, with all due respect, I may have to sabotage your plan." Charles smiled as he leaned over to cup Alice's hand. "I'd like to borrow this young lady myself for a bit, if that's alright—"

She flinched as the old man gave her hand a quick, tight squeeze. Then he leaned in closer. "Thought you might like a private tour of the chateau and grounds from a wise and learned guide?"

She couldn't ignore the intensity in his pale grey eyes. "Great, yes." Despite her unease, the agreement tumbled readily from her mouth. She could almost hear the sigh of relief from the other side of the table. "But maybe a shower first? Oh, and I'd really like to call my mum but I don't seem to be getting a signal on my mobile—"

Charles tutted and shook his head. "You young people, always got to be in touch." He rolled his eyes. "That's why I love this place – it's my sanctuary from everyday interruptions; a haven from all the stress and chaos of the outside world. Just relax and enjoy the peace and quiet for a change, my dear. It's good for the soul…"

Alice was ready to protest when Victor caught her eye and cut in. "Look, if you're still keen to phone home tomorrow, you can borrow mine. My network's usually pretty good here." He nodded, suggesting that the subject was now closed.

"So we're agreed, then?" Charles shunted his chair back from the table and stood up. "Don't rush, Alice. How about we meet at the front entrance, say," he glanced at his watch, "eleven o' clock?"

"Fine, yeah." She stuffed the last forkful into her mouth before placing the cutlery together on the side of her plate.

"Okay then, Miss," Victor said, turning towards Eva, "shall we say the same time for us, as well?"

Eva nodded and grinned at him with the unashamed excitement of a young child. But Alice couldn't place the look in her eyes as she gazed up at him. Whatever it was, there was no denying her behaviour was a far cry from her tense, nervous disposition in the restaurant all those months ago. She watched Eva's blonde ponytail swish out of view into the corridor and made to follow when a tug on her wrist pulled her back. The grasp was unyielding as she spun around to meet Victor's dark, searching eyes. The desperate, stinging hold faded into nothingness as she found herself unable to look away.

"I have to see you again tonight—" he whispered; each short, sharp breath in perfect unison with hers. "Please…"

She glanced behind her to see Eva leaning against the spiral staircase. Aware that their secret discussion would only add fuel to the young woman's fire, Alice nodded as she slipped behind the door to kiss her fingertip before pressing it gently onto his lips. Without saying a word, he released his grip on her wrist and slowly trailed his fingertips up the inside of her arm, only stopping when he reached the sensitive crease of her elbow. Alice forced herself to turn her back on him and stride out into the corridor. She smiled politely at Eva who flashed her a cold grin in return. As she made her way back to the bedroom, her heart was pounding in her chest at the thought of spending another night with Victor. But at what cost? And was she mad to even consider mixing business with pleasure?

First things first, though, she had more important things to deal with in the next few hours – yes, the private tour of the chateau with Charles couldn't have come at a better time. Whether it was the clean, crisp mountain air or just the cathartic release from everyday life back home, Alice felt like she was being slowly revitalised here; as though the chateau was breathing new life back into her soul. It felt like a reawakening of her spirit; empowering her with something so deeply-rooted that it might just change her forever.

No, there wasn't a hope in hell that Charles wasn't going to tell her everything she wanted to know...

CHAPTER TWENTY-SEVEN

"Something the matter, Alice?" Charles' voice hauled her back into the moment as she watched Victor help Eva on with her coat by the front door. She studied the young woman as she hoisted a rucksack onto one shoulder and secured the strap on top of her parka. "You seem a bit distant today—"

Victor shot her a look as he buttoned his coat and ushered Eva outside. Hats and gloves were pulled on as they chatted in the hazy sunshine that streamed between the stone pillars at the entrance and on through the stained-glass windows at either side of the door. Eva quickly linked her arm through his and they disappeared from view down the frost-covered steps.

Alice turned to catch Charles watching her; the front of his body up to the top button of his tweed jacket was bathed in the luminous glow of the sun filtering through the multi-coloured glass. "Just daydreaming, that's all," she lied, her mind buzzing and tumbling with endless thoughts and scenarios – and even more unanswered questions.

He narrowed his eyes. "Nothing wrong with that," he said, gesturing for her to follow him as he walked ahead. "Thought we'd do the interior first then take a wander outside after?"

By the time Alice had nodded, he was half-way up the wide

wooden staircase that dominated the front entrance.

"1714 this place was built," he hollered over his shoulder as he planted both feet on the top step. "Francois Laconte, my extremely talented ancestor, designed it single-handedly around the end of Louis XIV's reign. He had a keen eye for Neo-classical, architectural symmetry—" He raised a hand to the ornate cornices bordering the ceiling. "Amazingly, three hundred years later, it's still in the family and *still* in near-perfect condition – give or take the odd fire and the small matter of a partial roof collapse…" He winked at her.

"So, your cousin—" Alice couldn't contain her curiosity any longer, "I take it he's not staying here just now?"

"Yves always takes a family holiday this time of year. He's more than happy to give me free rein of the place while he's away, though." Charles rubbed his hands before launching into a lengthy monologue about how challenging the construction had been on such a perilous ledge deep in the Midi-Pyrenees.

As interesting as his spiel was, Alice couldn't stop her mind from drifting to Victor and Eva. The more she thought about the young woman's erratic, obsessional behaviour, the more peculiar and unnerving it seemed. She just didn't have the first clue how to take her. Realising that the perfect moment to broach the veil wasn't likely to present itself any time soon, Alice decided to take a leap of faith. But just as she was steeling herself with a deep breath, Charles stopped in his tracks and turned to look at her.

"This, my dear, is where the tour starts to get *really* interesting—" He whipped his specs off, snapped them shut and slid them into his top pocket. "Come with me. There's something I want to show you."

She followed him along the lofty walkway overlooking the entrance below; each creak and groan of the floorboards beneath grating louder and sharper as they neared the arched double door at the end. Alice felt an instinctive comfort and reassurance in the noises that only served to highlight the age and weathered beauty of the building. Although she didn't recognise every room and not every detail was familiar to her, Alice *knew* this place. Like it was somehow a part of her – ingrained in her soul and embedded so deeply within her, she could almost feel it bubbling in her blood. A feeling of belonging washed over her as her eyes soaked in the rich colours of the lavish embossed wall coverings and thick mahogany cornices that soared up towards the impossibly high ceilings.

Truth be told, she'd felt like that from the moment she'd set foot inside the castle walls. Then, as she'd wandered the corridors, soaking up the ancient atmosphere, breathing in the history that was so rich she could almost touch it, all the vague subconscious snippets and strands slowly began to interlock and make connections; fusing and sparking into focus to finally make themselves known to her memory.

Just then, a wave of dizziness flowed over her, dulling her mind; blurring her vision. She lost her balance and stumbled into the bannister, clutching onto it to steady herself until the lightheaded feeling passed seconds later. She pretended she was admiring the view below when Charles looked back again.

"Shall we?" He was holding a door open a few yards ahead up the walkway. The knot in her stomach tightened as she slowly made her way towards him. Charles was watching her every step of the way – the unbridled anticipation on his face leaving her in no doubt that what she was about to witness was something of the utmost importance.

Her heart was pounding as she brushed past the open door and stepped into the surreal half-darkness. The perimeter of the room was cloaked in the blackest of shadows; in sharp contrast to the near blinding rays of light streaming in through the stained-glass windows. The peak of the tallest arched window soared towards a domed ceiling adorned with intricate symbols and pictures that she couldn't quite make out in the gloominess above her.

It was the colourful fusion of light from that window that shone most intensely onto a circular altar that rose up towards an enormous candle holder dangling by a thick chain from the roof.

And then she saw it.

Alice swallowed hard as slow, steady footsteps echoed closer on the marble floor behind her. There it was – the black veil draped over the edge of the altar; trailing majestically down the side to kiss the marble below. Her eyes slid to a huge pentangle inside a circle on the floor. She recognised it instantly as the symbol on the silver pendant.

Charles was standing right beside her now but she couldn't take her eyes off the veil. An awkward silence filled the room as they stood shoulder to shoulder before the altar; even the blood whooshing in her ears couldn't detract from the all-consuming stillness.

Alice jumped as Charles cleared his throat with a single, loud cough. "I must apologise, but I had to take it back for a while." He turned to face her full on. "I hope you didn't miss it too much. I know how important it is to you—" His eyes were wide and searching, boring a hole deep into her soul.

"So *you* left it on my doorstep, then?" The accusation lost none of its bite through the breathless whisper.

"Alice, Alice…" He paraded slowly in front of her – hands locked behind his back, a chilling grin fixed on his lips. "It's taken so long to get you back here, my dear. You've no idea how much planning it all took, how painfully slow it's been to reach this point—" He raised his head to the ceiling and let out a wearisome sigh. Alice flinched as he swooped in towards her ear; his shallow breath hot against her skin. "But all good things come to those who wait. Isn't that right?"

She pulled away and walked towards the altar. "It's no secret I feel like I've been here before." She turned to look at him then reached out to touch the veil. "Why me, though? What do I have to do with all of this?" She gestured around the room that was a mind-bending mix of glorious, multi-coloured light and spine-tingling, hypnotic darkness. Her breath caught in her throat as her eyes locked onto the huge painting on the wall behind the door. Even in the dim light, she recognised it straight away. Twice as large and framed with embellished bevelled gold a foot wide on each side, it was more regal and imposing than ever. It was undoubtedly one of the most impressive paintings she'd ever seen.

"Ah, yes—" Charles began, "I'm guessing you've seen this portrait before?"

She swallowed hard; grief and despair bubbling up inside her, threatening to take control once again as the familiar rush of fiery heat burned across her chest.

"I… yes, I saw it upstairs at Victor's party—"

"Of course you did, my dear, but this is the original. Victor was so obsessed with it when he last visited that I ordered a framed print for him. Rather beautiful, isn't she?"

Alice swallowed hard as she stared into the hopeless eyes of the woman who looked just like her. "Who is she?"

"Why, Alice, I think you already know the answer to that. Don't you?"

The image became blurred and distorted as hot tears pricked her eyes. She brushed away the moisture dangling from her bottom lashes and dropped her head into her hands.

"Why did you come here, Alice?" He snatched her hands away from her face and looked her dead in the eye. "I mean, *really*?"

She flinched and drew back from him. The adrenalin was surging through her. "There's no ulterior motive to me being here, if that's what you're getting at—" She took in a gulp of air. "Look, Victor's my boss now, I'm about to start a new job with him – I was hardly going to refuse his offer, was I?"

"Of course you weren't… absolutely not." He huffed as he walked towards the altar and carefully lifted the veil from the edge. He held it out in front of him, shaking it slightly as he made his way back towards her. "It's all because of this, you know—" He trailed his fingers slowly down the length of the black mesh. "Don't let this soft, delicate fabric fool you – it yields more power than you can possibly imagine right now."

Alice swallowed hard as he edged closer. It took every ounce of self-control to stop her twitching fingers from reaching out and snatching it from him. Charles' eyes swooped to her hands that were already locked in a grasp by her side; like claws frozen in time; poised and ready to pounce.

"I can't let you touch it, I'm afraid… at least, not for now. There's something I need you to do first."

Alice shook both hands back to life as the sunlight faded through the windows and darkness descended on the room.

"You see, I had to make sure it was you all along. My God, it's uncanny, isn't it?" He nodded towards the portrait on the wall behind her head. "After you touched the pendant in the bar that night I was pretty much convinced. Of course, I had to get Mark to check you were there."

"The guy in the bar…" She tried to swallow but her throat was too tight.

"But I had to be sure the book was right. The veil not only confirmed my belief, it also restored some of the power – the power that's been lying dormant in you, Alice."

"This is either seriously crazy shit, Charles, or you're playing me for a fool. What the…?"

Without looking at her, the old man grabbed her arm and dragged her to the other side of the room. Seconds later, he shoved a palm against the white wall and pushed against it to open a secret door that was concealed in the stone. At first, it was pitch-black as they walked through the narrow entrance then her eyes detected a glimmer of light at what looked like the end of a long, low tunnel. Charles' vice-like clutch on her arm was unrelenting as he dragged her through the cold, dank darkness; the uneven stone flooring beneath her soft pumps making her drop and sway uncontrollably. Angry and confused, she yanked her arm free from his grip only to lose her balance and fall shoulder-first against the damp tunnel wall.

"Jesus, calm down, will you?"

The old man said nothing as he hurried towards the growing sphere of light up ahead, his swiftness and sure-footedness belying his years and small, frail stature. Despite her protest, Alice continued to follow him; a few paces behind and slightly out of breath as nervous exhaustion drained her lungs.

"Nearly there." Charles' voice echoed with excitement in the darkness.

The blood was pumping hard and fast as she shuffled and swayed towards the end of the tunnel. A veil of clamminess covered her face as she squinted into the swelling circle of light up ahead, her eyes struggling to adjust as her weary legs carried her slowly towards the blurred silhouette at the end. Before she left the darkness behind, she paused to catch her breath – just as some birds swooped past the exit of the tunnel, close enough for their passing breeze to waft a few loose strands of hair across her cheeks.

Charles walked out first into the fading daylight; his skin looked ashen as he turned to gesture her up the short, steep hill ahead of them. The surrounding trees were draped in fresh unblemished snow, so dense that their long, spindly branches remained motionless in the cool breeze. The only sound was the gentle crunching of powdery snow underfoot.

Alice shivered as the sky grew darker with every lumbering step towards the top of the hill. "Charles, please… leave me alone. Just let me rest here in—" She stumbled and fell to her knees as she spoke. She couldn't remember thinking the words, let alone forming them and releasing them from her parched mouth.

Charles stopped, yanked up the cuff of his jacket and checked his watch. He looked back up, staring into space – at first thoughtfully, then anxiously as his eyes darted to a spot over the brow of the hill. The intensity of his stare made Alice push herself up and trudge as fast towards the summit as the slippery ground would allow. She neared the top, chest heaving, drinking in the bleak expanse of rolling hills and snow-covered trees in the fast-descending darkness; the sudden vulnerability of her situation scaring and intriguing her in equal measure.

Cursing her flimsy shoes and trying desperately not to slide back down, she planted a damp squidgy foot on the first piece of flat land at the top. A sudden gust of wind took her breath away as her eyes focused on a large rectangular fence in the distance. As she wondered what could possibly be concealed within the tall spiky railings, she suddenly realised Charles was nowhere to be seen.

A thick cloak of darkness was looming overhead, an imminent threat to the remaining shards of daylight drifting precariously in the western sky. Alice gasped as a flock of jet-black birds shot out of the dense woodland to the right. Far greater in number than before, they fluttered carelessly for a moment or two in the charcoal sky before diving down, one by one, with terrifying speed and accuracy, hurtling into the ground inside the railings.

The surrounding air was eerily still and lifeless, yet the urge to keep walking was too overpowering – she just *had* to see what lay beyond the railings.

"No, no… it can't be—"

Alice could barely hear the distressed, muffled voice but she could tell it was coming from somewhere low down. With her heart thumping against her ribs, she stopped in front of a half-open black metal gate – the only visible entrance in the perimeter of the fencing.

A few hefty shoves on the rusty metal bars and it jerked open with a high-pitched, grating squeak. She looked down to see Charles doubled over, head in hands, kneeling beside what looked like an open crypt. Creeping closer, she could see it was empty.

"Gone." His breathless voice was raw with anguish.

"What is it?" She peered down into a shallow grave recessed several feet into the ground. It was surrounded by large moss-covered stones, randomly interspersed with sprouting weeds shooting up between pockets of fresh snow.

Charles ran a careful, wrinkled hand along the seal of the black marble tomb. A discoloured white angel with clasped hands and bowed head, chipped in places, knelt in prayer at the top end. He was mindlessly caressing the black stone as he craned his neck to look up at her. "This wasn't meant to happen. No, this *can't* be happening…" he snapped, shooting her an accusatory look.

Alice shook her head.

"She's gone. Do you have any idea what that means?" Alice stepped back from the edge as he sprang to his feet.

"For God's sake. No, I don't know what that means because I don't have a fucking clue who you're talking about." Alice bristled, her heart pounding as he stared at her, his eyes almost bursting with fury.

He closed them, as though to compose himself and took a long, slow deep breath. When he opened them again, his lips curled into an unsettling grin.

"Why… she's our whole reason for coming here, my dear." His voice was lower now and controlled. Too controlled.

Alice walked to the other side to look at the unearthed headstone that lay unceremoniously on the ground. Weather-beaten and in serious disrepair, she could just about make out the last few lines of the epitaph.

… & beloved daughter of Juliette and Francois
February 20ᵗʰ 1692—June 13ᵗʰ 1717

"My birthday," she muttered under her breath. But it was only when she calculated how old the woman was when she died, that her blood ran cold.

"I'm assuming you've noticed her age, as well." His tone was smug, mocking even, as he delighted in her reaction. "Is it all falling into place now, Alice?"

She spun round to face Charles, but he was already walking towards her.

"So, where are you?" He thrust a hand out towards the empty grave. The interior was so black that it looked like a bottomless pit. "Reincarnation can be such a pain sometimes." He tutted under his breath. Alice couldn't tell if he was being serious or not.

"Me? No... no. It can't be true—" She shook her head rapidly to reinforce her defiance.

"I think you know who she is, don't you, Alice?"

"The woman in the portrait." Her voice was cracking now. Charles laughed unpleasantly, forcing a smile.

"You see, she fell in love with the artist at the Chateau – not long, in fact, after marrying my ancestor, the Comte." His tone was matter-of-fact as he continued. "Then one evening a fire blazed through his private chambers, ruthlessly incinerating every possession, every piece of artwork, every item of stunning antique furniture – and, of course, him." His voice tailed off as his eyes strained against hers. "You know, for some reason he couldn't escape – or perhaps he chose not to? Maybe he knew all along that his wife was in love with another man and the heartbreak was simply too much to bear?" He paused, his mouth twisting in disgust. "Or, as *I* believe, he was murdered in the most brutal of ways by a coward who couldn't stand the thought of spending the rest of her life with him…"

Alice couldn't tear her eyes away from the hatred on his face. The persistent churning in her gut was making her nauseous.

"Fortunately, the worst of the blaze was contained to his quarters and the rest of the chateau escaped relatively unscathed, bar the roof collapsing in the neighbouring suite."

Alice fell back against the metal railings unable to fight the realisation any longer. All the dreams, the strangely intense feelings, the fateful meetings that had combined to lead her here had been far from coincidence. But had she really been powerless to resist or could she have – *should* she have – put up more of a fight? Couldn't she have resisted the urge just that little bit more? But as soon as she accepted that the real reason – the one true reason – for her being here was Victor, she couldn't deny it any longer. There was no resisting any of it. That was the cold, hard truth and every inch of her knew it. She simply *had* to be with him.

Darkness was descending fast as another flock of birds swooped and swayed overhead before diving at breakneck speed into the dense woods up ahead of them. Just then a blood-curdling, high-pitched wail cut through the still air. They looked at one another as it echoed into the distance. Charles rushed towards the exit and flung the metal gate open with such force it slammed against the outer railings. The ground trembled beneath their feet.

Just then, a slow-moving shadow stumbled out of the trees towards them. Seconds later, a faint male voice echoed in the distance.

"Eva! Eva, please…" Victor was running down the hill towards them. He was panting as he stopped dead at the fencing, steadying himself on the railings with both hands as he took in deep gulps of air. "Eva's gone…" His hand was trembling as he rammed it through his hair.

Just a few seconds later, Charles was directly in front of him, eyeballing him like a parent chastising a disobedient child.

"How in God's name could you let this happen, Victor?" Alice figured it was the most vulnerable and anxious she'd ever seen the old man. "You know she's never been here before – she'll never find her way back to the castle in the dark. My God, was that her screaming…?"

Then, as his worry gave way to anger once more, a second piercing scream reverberated out of the woods, shattering the sky. A low rumbling quickly followed and seconds later a sliver of lightning sliced through the charcoal clouds. A single large droplet of rain sploshed onto Alice's face before rivuleting down her nose. Then another one, and another until the heavens cracked open, releasing an almighty torrent battering them from above.

Victor whipped off his jacket and wrapped it around Alice's freezing shoulders. "Quick, follow me." The sudden, almighty downpour drowned out his command as he grabbed Alice's soaking hand and pulled her up the sodden grass hill towards the densely-packed trees. They were halfway to the top, legs aching with the punishing slippery ascent, when Alice craned her neck to see Charles still standing by the railings.

Through the cold, harsh spray blasting her screwed-up eyes, she watched him turn and hurry back towards the tunnel they'd left less than an hour before.

"Why isn't he coming with us?"

"Alice, come on." Victor tugged at her wrist and yanked her forwards through the driving rain, just as a thunderous crack split the air, making her ears ring and her head throb.

A harsh gust of wind forced her hair-clip loose, whipping dense sopping curls against her cheeks. As she fought to peel them off her saturated skin, she looked up to see a bright green glow rising up from the base of the forest. The slow-moving, hypnotic rays gently illuminated the trees upwards and outwards before spreading to fan out as far as the eye could see. It couldn't have lasted more than a matter of seconds so when the mystical light suddenly vanished, Alice wondered if she'd imagined it.

"Jesus, this can't be... not now—" Victor's voice faded away to nothing as they ducked their heads and scrambled under the nearest canopy of trees. With wet hands loosely clasped, they stood shoulder to shoulder, completely sheltered yet barely inches away from the torrential downpour – as though they were standing behind a giant, gushing waterfall. Alice's freezing feet squelched inside her soaking pumps as she turned towards Victor, her fast, shallow breathing forming warm, rhythmic clouds between them.

It was a moment of such extreme intensity that Alice figured she should have been breaking down or at least collapsing into Victor's arms, weak and feeble with nothing left to give. But there was something else blowing in on the stormy air that night. Something unknown, but also something potentially empowering, potentially life-altering. In the depths of her bones, she could feel herself growing stronger and more confident. Something was shifting deep within her that she couldn't put into words but could feel with all her heart and soul.

Then, in the bitterly cold twilight, against the backdrop of the wild, unrelenting weather, Victor whispered into her ear, "There's not much time left now."

CHAPTER TWENTY-EIGHT

Alice frowned and snatched her hand from Victor's grasp. "Time left for what, Victor? Jesus, you're creeping me out…" She edged back further under the cover of the tall pine trees – dry twigs and spindly branches cracking and snapping beneath her feet. The heady scent of pine needles in the crisp, clean air was all-consuming under the low canopy of the trees.

"Alice, it's time you knew why we came here. But it wasn't meant to happen like this, you have to believe me." Victor's voice was pleading but in the fading light she couldn't tell if his face reflected the sentiment. He grabbed her hands and looked into her eyes. "The practice of love offers no haven of safety – we all risk loss, hurt and pain. But even more so, we risk being acted upon by forces beyond our control."

It was as though he was reciting some prose or text from a book.

Despite wearing cold, damp clothing for the last hour or so, Alice shivered for the first time as he slowly traced her backward footsteps into the depths of the forest. She flinched as a single bright light appeared from out of nowhere to shine a spotlight onto Victor's face. She gasped when she noticed deep scratch marks, red and raw, running diagonally down both his cheeks. One was clearly still weeping as it dripped to form a small pool of pusy blood just under his left cheekbone.

"What the…?" She couldn't get the words out as the light behind her began to shake and bounce before stabilising to become strong and focused within seconds. Alice turned to see a hazy figure clutching a torch. Both hands were outstretched, like a stalker with a gun, silently targeting their prey.

"Sorry to disappoint you, Victor…" Alice couldn't believe that the self-assured, mocking voice was Eva's. She strutted towards them with long, confident strides, clearly angling for confrontation with her petulant lips and wild, staring eyes. "Hoping you wouldn't see me again, eh?"

Alice looked to Victor for a response. But nothing.

"Look, I'm sorry if I upset you earlier, Eva, but I've tried—" His voice was cool and controlled as he edged slowly towards her. She instantly recoiled.

"Upset me? *Upset* me?" Her hands were shaking so much that her arms were struggling to control it. "No, Victor, I'm not upset…" A high-pitched shriek escaped from her taut, grimacing lips. "I'm not upset, no, no, no – I'm afraid it's *way* past that now."

The words hung in the air as she swivelled to stare at Alice.

"And then there's *you*, isn't there? There's always been *you*, hasn't there, Miss Alice." The sinister, childish way she spat her name made Alice's skin crawl.

"You ruined it for me, you know that, don't you?" Her once-youthful, innocent azure eyes burned with rage. It was obvious now to Alice how Victor had got the scratches on his face. She took a step forward to challenge Eva but Victor instantly placed a hand across her stomach.

"Leave it, Alice." His tone was non-negotiable.

"Yeah, leave it, *Alice*. Just like you should have left it a long time ago, then none of this would've happened." Eva muttered something incoherently at the ground beneath her feet. The torchlight shining up under her face cast a harsh glow, making her features appear unnaturally sharp and contorted – and her eyes look like empty black slits.

Alice shoved Victor's hand away and strode towards Eva who was standing by a large tree stump. Panic flashed on the young girl's face as she pulled her parka tightly around her collar before dropping her rucksack. She cast a lingering look at it lying carelessly on the ground. Occasional droplets of rain from the overhanging trees splashed onto the navy canvas.

"What the hell are you playing at, Eva?" Alice was standing right in front of her now, their faces inches from one other. Eva grinned wickedly as she leaned in to bump her nose onto Alice's before planting a fleeting kiss onto her taut lips. She threw her head back and laughed.

"You know, I think I probably fancy you a bit myself. Not as much as *he* does, of course. But then nobody could ever love you as much as *him*."

Alice's brows snapped together as she wiped Eva's spit from her top lip.

"What's in the rucksack, Eva?" Victor's tone was curt as he walked up beside them.

"Shouldn't you be asking what *isn't* in the rucksack any-more?" She eyed him with playful delight. The young, naïve girl had returned for a split second, revelling in her mind games. "You know, I still can't believe you didn't ask me what was in it before we left the chateau? You must really trust me, I guess." She shook her head. "Bit of a mistake, you see…"

248

"Eva, for God's sake, let it go now. I've already told you I'm sorry if you thought I led you on, but I had no idea you were—"

"No, no, please, let me finish – in love with you. Is that what you were going to say?" Eva raised a brow, her face shimmering with sweat. "How could you *not* have known, Victor? Seriously, I've been in love with you for years…"

As she uttered the words, she collapsed to the ground, falling against the tree stump then onto the rucksack. She dropped her head in her hands and began to sob – her back was heaving as she rocked back and forth on the ground as though she'd lost her mind. In the torchlight, she resembled a dying animal, slowly writhing and convulsing in pain.

"So, what was in the bag then, Eva?" Alice was shocked by Victor's cold detachment as he watched the young woman curled up, weeping in front of him. Then, she remembered the raw scratches on his face. Eva slowly lifted her head to look up at him, her wounded eyes peering through the matted blonde hair that had fallen onto her forehead.

"He didn't tell me this was going to happen. This wasn't meant to happen, it's just not fair…"

Forgetting his frustration, Victor knelt down beside her. Eva looked up at the hand held out in front of her and placed hers gently on top of it. Tears shimmered in her eyes as her lips curled into an innocent smile. She bent forwards to rest her head on Victor's coat then giggled as he soothingly stroked her hair.

It was suddenly all too clear to Alice that this troubled young woman was obsessively, even dangerously, in love with Victor. As he twisted round to look up at her, a silent but grave recognition passed between them; a sickening dread churned in her stomach as they both acknowledged the intensity of Eva's devotion.

"It was the book…" Eva's voice was weak and muffled against Victor's jumper. "I took the book from the library and—"

Victor tilted her chin to look up at him. "And what? What did you do with the book?" His voice was wavering. "Tell me now, Eva." A wave of dread washed over Alice. As blacker than black clouds growled across a churning sky, she could feel her neck and chest burning beneath her skin.

In the mystical torchlight, Eva opened her mouth to answer him but nothing came out.

"Eva, I'm not kidding now – where's the book?" Victor clenched his jaw.

"After we argued, I went to the hill, you know where the stake was all those years ago…?"

Alice reached inside her cardigan and placed a cold, soothing palm against her burning collarbone. The desire to tear at her skin was almost unbearable. The instant relief was like a long, chilled drink to a parched throat. Seconds later, though, it returned, stronger and more fiery than before. In the distance, the air grumbled, fierce and furious, like a wild beast barreling towards its prey.

Victor got to his feet and walked towards Alice. Eva's unblinking eyes followed him all the way.

"I've been reading a lot of it recently. You never knew but I read it when you and Grandad weren't around. I really liked it – it felt important and mysterious. Like something exciting that was missing from my god-awful life." She bowed her head. "All the incantations, the spells, the promises—" Her eyes pleaded her case as she raised them. "Yes, it was the promises

250

of a better, more fulfilled life, they just mesmerised me. I guess I needed something to make up for what I didn't have…" She looked wistfully at Victor as she reached inside the top of her zipped-up jacket to pull something out; something Alice instantly recognised as it twinkled in the dim glow of the torchlight.

Victor's face fell as he stared at the pendant cradled in her hands. Alice watched as a green halo of light spread from underneath it; the exact same colour as the lights they'd seen earlier in the forest.

"Why the hell have *you* got the pendant?" Alice flinched at Victor's booming voice. "Charles should never have let you take it. What in God's name was he—"

"Oh, he doesn't know I took it. Or the book for that matter." Eva laughed as a sudden gust of wind howled through the treetops above them.

"Jesus…" Victor shoved his hands through his hair and dropped his head. "You can't just do as you like with the book. It isn't a toy – some sort of casual distraction." He flicked his wrist. "Look, we have to go back now. Charles will know what to do."

"What is it? What's wrong, Victor?" Alice shook his arm.

"I'm sorry, but I didn't think reading a bit of it out loud would do anything," Eva said. "It all seemed a bit silly – something about making the body rise up…" The helpless, innocent young girl had returned.

Alice's chest tightened as the realisation hit her. "The crypt was empty." She nodded towards the grave at the bottom of the hill. "Charles was furious—"

"And he had every right to be." Victor shot his anger towards Eva. "You've no idea what you've just done." He snatched the torch and rucksack from the ground and headed for a clearing in the trees.

"Come on, we have to go." He shook the bag. "I'm assuming you were lying and the book is still in here?" Eva hung her head and nodded as he tossed the rucksack into her arms. Alice caught a fleeting look of shame on her face.

As the three of them stood by the forest's edge, he flashed the torchlight out into the sleety drizzle. The light was weak and short, casting no more than a few feet in front of them as they shuffled down the slippery hillside. With Victor a few steps ahead and Eva falling behind, Alice turned to hurry her along. The young woman yelped as she lost her footing and slipped a few metres on the heels of her boots. Alice bent down to grab her arm and haul her to her feet. As they stood side by side on the slushy grass peering through the rain at the blurred light streaming through the chateau windows, Eva pulled her hand away.

"Thanks," she mumbled, before sliding ahead to catch up with Victor. In the blink of an eye, she'd already linked her arm into his.

Alice scoured the vast surrounding countryside as she paused a short distance behind them on the hillside. Fear and adrenalin coursed through her as the thought of running away shot into her brain. Surely she should just get out of here now; take the chance to disappear into the murky distance while she still had it? After all, there would probably never be a better opportunity to do it. What the hell was she doing in a remote chateau with people she barely knew, anyway? No normal person could possibly justify staying here... could they?

Icy breaths were coming hard and fast as her head and her

heart battled it out for what felt like an eternity. But her cold, aching legs clearly had other ideas as they slowly lured her down the slope – towards the blurry silhouette of the couple linking arms in front of her.

She swallowed hard, realising that, although she didn't fully understand it, her decision had been made. Something outwith her control had made the choice for her.

Then came the lingering glance over Eva's shoulder...

CHAPTER TWENTY-NINE

Soft amber light filtered through the first-floor windows of the chateau. Alice could see they were standing just metres away from the secret tunnel they'd left no more than a couple of hours before; the entrance to it now closed off with an impenetrable black iron grate.

Eva stood, arms folded, as Victor opened a latched gate leading onto a dark pathway that meandered down the side of the building. An icy wind hit Alice's face as they turned a corner and the mountains that had long been obscured by the harsh weather suddenly came back into view – more breathtaking than ever.

The sprawling jagged prisms glinted in the flawless moonlight, like an enormous majestic barrier protecting them from the outside world. The view was so pure and clear that Alice was sure she could make out the myriad of valleys rivuleting down the sides of each craggy hill face. It was as if all her senses had suddenly become heightened and she was acutely aware of everything around her. In the damp chilly air, the faint rustling of leaves and dull shuffling of her wet shoes on the concrete path seemed to ring in her ears. Even her rapid, shallow breathing felt like it was pounding against her ribcage. Somehow, she just felt more alive…

Eva broke the silence as they stopped in front of a dark wooden door. "I'd like to go to my room now," she muttered at her feet.

She didn't look up as Victor forced the handle down and the door creaked open. Power had clearly returned to the building as the intense brightness beyond the doorway seared into Alice's eyes. She squinted in the glare as she swept away the sopping curls that had fallen onto her cheeks. Warmth enveloped her from head to toe as their footsteps echoed across the tiled floor; past deep empty sinks, large white machines, storage containers and small metal trolleys. As they left the vast utility area, Eva sneaked through a doorway on the right.

Victor called after her as he craned his neck around the slowly closing door. Alice could hear a muffled exchange of words then a door slamming in the background.

Seconds later, he reappeared, pale and subdued, with Eva's rucksack dangling from his wrist. "Come on, we should get going," he said, sounding too measured.

Alice stood rooted to the spot as he strode towards the double doors leading to the main hallway.

"No... sorry, but I'm not going anywhere until you tell me what the hell you were talking about back there." She folded her arms. "What the hell isn't there much time left for, Victor?"

He paused for a few seconds with his back to her then looked up at the chandelier above him.

"Well?"

Alice caught her breath as he turned and walked slowly back towards her; the intensity on his face was unsettling but exciting at the same time. Every nerve-ending tingled as he dropped the rucksack and stood in front of her, his jumper

255

barely brushing her body.

"Do you trust me?" He cupped her face with both hands and looked deep into her eyes.

"That's hardly the point. This is seriously crazy shit."

As she fiddled with her earring, he pulled her towards him and kissed her with such force that she was powerless to breathe.

"I can't live without you." The raw desperation in his voice made it more of a statement than a declaration of love but Alice didn't care – it was all she needed to hear.

"I trust you, Victor." As she leaned in for a second kiss, something red caught her eye. The misty glow was coming from a room upstairs – and Alice knew exactly which one. Sensing that she'd seen something, Victor looked behind him into the distant shadows of the first-floor landing.

"Charles is in that room, isn't he?" she said matter-of-factly. "The altar room, the one with the portrait of the woman who looks—"

Victor grabbed her hand, whisking her up the staircase and across the creaking floorboards of the top landing to the end of the corridor. Red mist seeped through the gap at the bottom of the door, wisping out onto their shoes as they stood just inches away. Victor's hand hovered over the handle as he placed his ear against the door. He shot Alice a look that said they were going in. She nodded and held her breath as he forced the handle down with a loud, jerking clunk. The door swung open on its own.

She turned to see Victor bathed from head to toe in a translucent blood-red glow. A familiar sweetness wafted under her nostrils as the door creaked to a halt, fully opened.

Through the wisping red mist, a figure lurked in the

shadows beneath the portrait. Alice stood transfixed – a mixture of fear and exhilaration rushing through her. She grabbed Victor's hand as they stepped into the room.

"Genevieve… such a fine woman." Alice flinched as Charles' voice echoed across the room. "Such a damn fine woman. You'd be hard-pressed to meet someone like her in this day and age, you know." She squeezed Victor's hand as the old man's slow, methodical footsteps clipped the marble underfoot. The smell of incense was pungent as he flicked his wrist from side to side, leaving transient clouds of vapour in the air in front of him. Seconds later, he stood before them; his gaze dropping to their clasped hands as he adjusted his bow tie with one hand.

"I see you finally relented, then?"

Alice bristled at his smug grin.

"Good, all good. It's just like I said, though, isn't it? You can't escape fate, my dear. Your destiny will always find you in the end. You were meant to be together, you know that now?"

"I think we have slightly more to be concerned with just now, don't you, Charles?"

Alice sneaked a glance at Victor as he challenged his friend. Something was dividing the two of them – that much was clear.

The old man humphed as he marched back towards the portrait. "Yes. Yes, we do indeed have a slight concern now, my friend." He threw a hand out towards the painting looming above him.

"Look, can you see? She's fading away. Something's happened and it isn't good, believe me. Somebody has upset the dynamic… interfered – and that is *not* good. Actually, it's

257

far from good." His narrowed eyes darted to Alice.

"So, might you know anything, my dear?"

Victor gave her hand a reassuring squeeze. A dull, throbbing ache began to spread across the side of her head as she stepped forwards to stand next to Charles beneath the portrait. Through squinted eyes, she noticed that the detail had faded slightly; almost as if the top layer of coloured oils had been wiped away.

"All I know, Charles, is that I'm standing here with both of you in this ridiculously creepy room in a ridiculously creepy castle and I must be a bloody fool for even being here in the first place. So, unless one of you—" she looked over her shoulder at Victor, "tells me right now what the hell is going on, I'm out of—" Her pulse raced as the dull ache became a sharp piercing pain before fading away. If ever she needed her crystal, it was now.

"Look, I'll explain it all soon, I promise," Victor said, nodding reassuringly before turning back to Charles.

"It was Eva. She already had the pendant and she put the book in her bag before we left for our walk this morning." He looked straight at the old man, expecting an instant reaction from him – but there was only silence.

"She read from the book. The part about raising the body up…" Alice offered, feeling brave. Only then did Charles react, squeezing his eyes shut before laughing up at the ceiling. She wasn't sure whether the sharp cry was resigned acknowledgement or blatant disgust at what he'd just heard. Either way, it didn't sound good.

And that's when she saw it: the veil dangling majestically and tantalisingly from the stone altar. The fingers on her right hand twitched as the familiar heat spread like wildfire

258

through her body. She was barely aware of Victor's voice in the background.

"Alice. Alice, are you listening to me?"

When she turned to look at him, she was already standing on the top step in front of the altar. But she couldn't even remember walking towards it. Her clammy fingers stretched and contracted of their own accord as she made to grab what was so close to her grasp.

"I… I don't—" She shook her head. "Yes. Yes, I'm listening. I think I…"

"You look pale, I think we should get you some water." He placed a gentle hand on her back as she stared down at the veil just inches away from her desperate fingers. The temptation was unbearable.

She was agonisingly close to it when a curt double knock startled her. Charles tutted as he made for the door. All the while, his eyes locked on Alice as Victor guided her down the three narrow steps onto the marble floor.

The door creaked open – just enough for them to see Eva standing in the doorway. Sneaking a backwards glance, Charles stepped out of the room and promptly closed the door. Alice held her breath on the other side.

"… so, I figured I should give you the pendant back." Eva's distressed voice filtered through the tiny gap at the bottom.

"Honestly, Eva, we talked about this, didn't we? Well, *didn't we?*"

Alice pictured her shamefully nodding her head in the ensuing silence.

"I know, Grandad. I'm so sorry, but I couldn't help myself…" Genuine or not, the desperation in the young woman's voice tugged at Alice's heart.

259

"I really thought you understood your boundaries this time, that you knew where your responsibilities ended…"

More silence. Time for a forgiving hug?

"I'm so sorry…" Her breath hitched. "Just tell me how—" Her voice tailed off, finally giving way to helpless, endless sobbing.

Victor stared at the door, shaking his head.

"I'm afraid it's too late for tears now, Eva," Charles continued. "You've really let me down – and after all I've done for you…"

Alice swallowed hard, shocked by the old man's coldness towards his own flesh and blood. The handle gave an abrupt squeak then slowly lowered.

"I'll deal with you later." His last words as he left Eva in the corridor made Alice's skin crawl. In a panic, she reached for the wrought-iron handle just as Charles pushed the door open; they stared at one another in awkward silence. Alice bit her lip, painfully aware that he knew she'd overheard him.

"Just going to fetch something," she muttered at the floor-boards. Charles' eyes followed her as she edged out into the corridor. She heard Victor mutter something under his breath as he breezed past him. Eva was nowhere to be seen as they hurried down the stairs.

"Perhaps a light refreshment in the dining room before we proceed…?" Charles hollered over the bannister as Victor snatched the rucksack off the floor.

"Up in a minute," Victor said crisply.

"So, what was all that about Eva's boundaries?" Alice was bursting with curiosity.

"I honestly have no idea," he said, grabbing her hand. "But I'm sure as hell going to find out."

CHAPTER THIRTY

Alice threw her mobile onto the crumpled red bedspread. Still no signal and probably a mountain of missed calls and messages – the majority more than likely from her mum.

She ran her fingers through her squeaky, freshly-washed curls and dabbed on some lipgloss. She cursed at the zip that was stuck on her pink linen shift dress, trying to yank it up time and again behind her back. Then cursed even louder when she realised why it wouldn't go up any further. Date-wise, the bloating made perfect sense but, considering she'd barely eaten in the last twenty-four hours, it was amazing that her stomach wasn't concave.

There was a double knock on the door. "You ready?" Victor's voice echoed from the hallway.

She opened the door a crack to speak. "Just come in. I need a hand with something." When he walked into the room, all tall, muscular frame in a crisp white shirt and dark grey trousers, it was a few seconds before she could say anything.

She turned away as she tugged at the zip. "Can't get this bloody thing up—"

"Here, let me." His warm fingers brushed her skin as he gently swept her hair to the side and grabbed the tiny metal fastening. Two firm tugs later, the zip was secure just below her shoulder blades. Before she could turn to thank him, he'd already placed a slow, gentle kiss on her bare shoulder.

They stood in silence for a second or two, admiring the full moon through a small chink in the curtains. Alice was convinced he must be able to hear the heartbeat pounding insanely in her chest. She let out a sigh when he finally ushered her towards the door.

"Come on, we'd better go. He'll be waiting on us."

As they strolled down the hallway, past the gallery of portraits staring down from the walls, she watched him from the corner of her eye.

"Amazing paintings," she offered nonchalantly.

In profile, his face hinted at nothing. But as he turned, his eyes told a different story. He pulled her to the side, beneath a portrait she hadn't noticed before. Her throat tightened as her eyes locked onto the sombre face of the male subject. Despite the fairer hair in a slighter longer, sleeker style, the dashing likeness was irrefutable. Adrenalin rushed through her as she soaked in his features; from the shimmering depths of copper in the soulful eyes, down to the perfectly distinguished nose across to the sharp cheekbones then down to the full lips.

Victor's fingers brushed her cheek as he pulled her face towards him.

"It's you…" She could barely whisper the words. Then, the warm tears that had been threatening finally spilled from her eyes – as the proof of what she'd felt deep inside for so long was finally staring her in the face.

"It's a self-portrait," he said.

But he didn't have to tell her. It was all falling into place. "So, that wasn't a dream about you painting me? It was a memory—"

He turned to her with a smile. "A very old, repressed memory locked deep in your subconscious. But yes – a memory, nevertheless."

She swallowed hard. The lightning spark of realisation that flowed between them was as true and powerful as anything Alice had ever known.

"Something wasn't finished as it should have been all those years ago." He wiped a fresh, running tear from her cheek. "That's why you're here again now."

She nodded. "I think I know that. Part of me feels like I *should* be here… like I've been here before. But what is it I have to do?"

She looked up at the painting again; her eyes soaking in each feature one by one as though she couldn't bear to tear them away. The bleakness of the background was the perfect contrast to the pale blue jacket and diffused light that kissed his perfect complexion and no more. Alice was sure the brown eyes were watching her as the most intense, powerful emotion emanated from the canvas.

With his hand resting on the small of her back, Victor guided her gently down the corridor. "It's written in the book. Look, don't worry, I'll be with you the whole time. I promise." He grabbed her hand. "It's just something that needs to be done. Sometimes you have to atone for things you've done in the past – kind of like rebalancing the universe in a small way. Some call it karma…" He swept some fallen strands of hair from his forehead as the last word hung in the air. As he looked straight ahead, Alice could see the tension in his jaw. "I always left Charles in charge when it came to the book. He knows it so much better than me – the history of every incantation, every ritual – inside out and back to front."

263

He stroked the palm of her hand. "Look, he's got your best interests at heart, don't worry."

"Jesus, Victor. What did I do?"

"You'll find out soon enough," he said, ushering her forwards.

The wall lights flickered as they walked towards a gleaming bronze bust perched proudly on a narrow marble column. Alice shivered as the beady, lifeless eyes seemed to follow them as they turned the corner.

"Anyway, I think it's time we got some food in you," he said, changing the subject. "You barely touched anything at breakfast – you must be starving."

She tensed as he playfully patted her stomach. But, oddly, she wasn't hungry in the slightest. She took a deep breath as saliva pooled inside her cheeks then covered her mouth to try and conceal the next bilious deep breath.

By the time they saw Charles up ahead hauling open two towering double doors, the feeling had passed. His narrow grey eyes watched them as they approached down the long red carpet. He smiled politely then ushered Alice into a room adorned with twinkling crystal wall lights; their shimmering radiance casting an ethereal glow upon everything it touched.

"I have to tell you, I've warned her about—" Victor began under his breath, but Charles cut him off with a wave of his hand.

"No need for that. On the contrary, I think it's better if it comes from you anyway."

Alice had a feeling she wasn't meant to overhear them but her new heightened awareness of everything made the hushed tones impossible to ignore.

Charles turned his back for a second.

"No, not yet?" Victor muttered, flashing her his best reassuring smile.

This time, Alice was convinced she wasn't meant to hear.

"Not yet *what*, exactly?" she said, crossing her arms.

The two men looked at one another.

"Well, here's what I think. Like you say, I could do with feeding up, so how about we all sit down, fill our faces then get on with whatever it is I'm bloody well here to do?" She eyeballed Charles as they stood in silence.

"Quite the feisty one today, aren't we?" he chuckled, a touch too patronisingly. "Please." He gestured to the large centrepiece table that was strewn with dome-covered silver platters. She couldn't bring herself to thank him as he pulled a chair out for her.

"You know, you could've organised this whole façade with a bit more dignity." She snatched the goblet he'd filled with red wine and took a hearty slug, forgetting that she didn't even like the stuff. She grimaced as it trickled like molten lava down her gullet.

"You see, there's been a slight change of plan, Alice," he sighed. "A rather unfortunate complication in the proceedings. Something I just didn't see coming, I'm afraid."

She grabbed a small bunch of green grapes from the nearest platter, snapped a few off and shoved them in her mouth. The sweet, juicy coolness instantly soothed the burning in her throat.

"Where's Eva? Why isn't she eating with us?" Alice was suddenly aware of her absence.

Charles topped up the wine in his goblet, almost to the rim. "In her room. She won't be joining us."

Victor caught the look on her face. "She's got food, don't

265

worry."

"Didn't want to join us or *wasn't allowed* to join us?" She tutted as she stared at the old man gleefully ripping a mouthful of chicken from a drumstick. "And where's all this food come from anyway? I haven't seen anyone else the whole time we've been here." She stabbed her knife into a large triangle of brie then slid it onto her plate.

Charles swallowed hard then dabbed his mouth with an oversized napkin.

"Questions, so many questions, Alice. Doesn't the intrepid journalist ever clock off?" His smirk set her pulse racing.

Victor reached over to place a calming hand on hers – she immediately snatched it away. "No, this isn't right." She shot a cold stare at Charles. "So, Eva did something in the woods that upset you, something that's somehow inconvenienced you? But, Jesus, the girl's got serious issues, you know that – *and* she's your own flesh and blood. Doesn't that mean anything?"

He tore a last chunk of meat from the bone, fully exposing his stained, uneven teeth. The furrows in his brow deepened with each slow, exaggerated chew – as though the grinding motion was only fuelling his anger.

"You know, Alice, everyone has to be accountable for their wrongdoings. There's no getting away from it, regardless of who you are or how old you are."

She covered her goblet as Charles reached over with a carafe of wine. He glanced at his watch, sweat beading on his brow.

"The clock's ticking now." But his words weren't directed at her.

Victor edged his chair closer to hers. "Eat." He slid a dish of chicken breasts coated in a thick creamy sauce in front of her.

She eyed him warily as he got to his feet then strolled to the back of the room. She froze mid-chew when he reappeared seconds later with the veil draped over his arm.

"I believe this belongs to you." He was standing close enough for the veil to lightly brush her shoulder. She could hear the blood whooshing in her ears as her hand edged towards it.

"Go on, Alice – it's all yours now." Charles' voice faded into the background as she focused on the black mesh now pinched between her fingers. "It's time. We need to know where the body is, otherwise all of this is for nothing. It's for the greater good, trust me."

Every ounce of logic and sanity urged her not to do it, yet Alice couldn't resist lifting it onto her head. The familiar musty smell of the delicate fabric intoxicated her as she slid it slowly, inch by careful inch, through her trembling fingers.

By the time she'd adjusted the veil to drape perfectly over her face, she was already lost in another world, another time…

CHAPTER THIRTY-ONE

Alice screwed her eyes shut as a blast of air whipped up like a whirlpool around her. With the bitter wind strengthening, the sudden sensation of floating and weightlessness was all-consuming. Surrendering to the feeling was the only option.

Gazing down upon the moonlit grass below, a sense of infallibility washed over her. Every muscle, tendon and sinew flexed in perfect harmony to propel her further into the sky, pausing just below the misty vapour of the clouds. From this high up, the panoramic view was glorious; capturing the full moon hovering above the tallest mountain peak in the distance.

Then, the breeze around her stopped dead – everything else fell still.

A surge of air blasted up from beneath her feet. Then a beat of silence. Adrenalin coursed hard and fast as her eyes swooped upon the target, lying deathly still on a small grassy mound by the edge of a stream. A flock of birds swept up into the air, wheeled in perfect synchronicity for a few seconds then disappeared into the dark, distant sky.

Then, with a single violent spasm, her body began to plummet. The harsh velocity tore at her skin as the surrounding air sucked her into a vortex of wind. Just as claustrophobia started to take hold, her body jerked to a halt. She slowly opened her eyes again.

As the soles of her feet sank into the damp grass beneath, her breath caught like glass in her throat. The face she was staring at was too dark and blurred to be normal in the flawless light of the moon. No features were recognisable as she soaked in the empty, bottomless sockets and the withered, charcoal skin.

Then it happened.

Alice felt a pain like no other coursing through her, like the sun was being ripped from her heart and her soul thrust into the most brutal, eternal darkness.

All light and conscious being was sucked away as she was catapulted into the corpse in front of her. She opened her mouth to scream…

* * *

All she could remember as she opened her eyes was Henri's hands gently cupping her face.

"How long have we been...?" She blinked hard a few times, forcing them back into focus.

He smiled, sweeping a fallen curl from her forehead. "Don't worry, I checked – all the servants are outside preparing for the party."

"You wear me out, my love," she whispered. "There's nothing else for it but sleep…"

Henri grinned and leaned over her on the sunken chaise longue when a muted cry startled them from outside. He hurried to the window and forced it open. More voices joined the frantic wailing, then one word was all-consuming.

"Fire!"

Genevieve swallowed hard as the chorus of piercing screams reverberated around the room.

Henri leaned out of the window. "Good God..."

She stood up, adjusting her underskirt and smoothing her hair with her palms as she walked towards him. "It's his room, isn't it?"

He turned to look at her. "We need to get out of here."

The smoke nipped their eyes as they opened the door and peered down the hallway at the dense black plumes slithering out from under Gabriel's bedroom door. Henri grabbed her hand and whisked her through the spreading grey haze towards the servants' staircase.

She coughed, almost choking, as the smoke caught the back of her throat. She couldn't be sure if the tears welling in her eyes were due to the toxic fumes or the shock at what was happening.

"He caught me reading the book a few times." She croaked the words out as they hurried down the spiral staircase. "He knew about us, but I was more worried he might know about my powers. He wouldn't think twice about using it against me..."

Henri paused before opening the door in front of him; his body was rigid.

"Did you hear what I said?" She was standing on the bottom stair, knuckles white as her hand gripped the edge of the wrought-iron bannister.

His broad shoulders lifted suddenly, then fell.

"What? What is it? Please, Henri – say something, anything..." She trembled as he turned towards her. She couldn't place the look on his face but she knew that it frightened her.

"Do you know what you've done, Genevieve?"

She reached out to grab his arm. "But I didn't mean it, really I didn't."

270

He slowly lifted her hand off his shirt then held it to his face. She gasped as he kissed it; the soft dark hairs of his beard gently caressing her skin. In that instant, she fell into his arms.

"It's just that I can't control it sometimes. I didn't want this to happen, you have to believe me."

*He tilted her chin to look up at him. "But you **did** think about it, didn't you? You must learn to control your thoughts – you know that."*

"Yes," she sighed, feeling for the pendant beneath her bodice. "But it's only because I'm so in love with you."

As he leaned in to kiss her, the door leading outside swung open, shoving them back against the wall. A bald, portly man rushed in; sweat glistening on his ruddy face as he struggled for breath. Genevieve recognised him as the head gardener.

"Thank God we've found you," he panted. "There's a fire upstairs – it's the Comte's quarters, up like a bonfire. I suggest you get outside now – both of you." His wide eyes flitted to Henri. "I trust you'll look after m'lady while we deal with it?"

Henri nodded as they hurried through the door and outside to a melee of noise and chaos. Men and women, servants and gentry, running and screaming in the castle grounds. As they reached the gated entrance to the garden, Genevieve stopped and looked up. She grabbed Henri's hand as she stared in horror at the scene before her. Thick black smoke billowed up into the cloudless blue sky as endless twisting, crackling flames shot upwards and outwards from the main roof. Hot tears spilled down her cheeks as a shrill voice startled her from behind.

"Genevieve, my love—" Gabriel's mother hurried towards her. "Is he in his room? How can this be happening?" The tall, willowy blonde shook her shoulders before pulling her in for a stiff hug.

"Marguerite, I—"

271

Henri shook his head as she caught his eye. "I... I don't know, I haven't seen him since breakfast."

He placed a calming hand on Marguerite's trembling arm. "I'll see what I can find out."

"Thank you." She smiled politely but it fell away as her narrowed eyes darted between them. Genevieve looked away as she recalled how her mother-in-law had caught them laughing together in a secluded corner of the garden only a few days before.

A male courtier appeared at Marguerite's side. The furrows on his brow deepened as he leaned in. "Madame, I'm so sorry... something about the key or lock being broken. By the time the servants managed to break down the door, the fire was too intense—"

Marguerite let out a blood-curdling wail then stumbled backwards. The courtier lunged to catch her as she passed out in his arms.

Unable to suffer it any longer, Genevieve fled into the orchard, her heartbeat thrashing in her ears as each panicked breath caught in the back of her throat. She hitched up her skirt then ran as fast as she could across the lush, sun-dappled grass towards the farthest apple tree. Blinded by her tears, she collapsed like a ragdoll against the narrow unforgiving trunk.

"God help me. What have I done...?"

* * *

The noose hung loosely around her collarbone, brushing the precious silver chain she'd sworn to him she would wear.

As desperation took hold, she focused on the stocky, grey-haired priest strutting arrogantly in front of her. Anything to blot out the harsh binding rope that cut deeper into her wrists and ankles with *every nervous, agitated movement.*

He paraded up and down in front of the stake, spit pooling in the corners of his mouth as he spewed his scathing monologue. She fought back the tears as she recalled the moment he and Gabriel's beloved stable boy had confronted her in the drawing room about the book – and her 'inherent hatred of God'. She'd never been able to erase the look of smug, unashamed glee on the boy's face when it was confirmed that his disclosure had surely sealed her fate.

It wasn't long before the priest had goaded the baying rabble into a frantic chorus of chanting and screaming. "Burn the witch! Burn the witch! Burn the—"

He held his hand up – the crowd fell silent.

"Genevieve, sister of the coven – you have been tried and duly convicted of witchcraft following the will of God. As a confirmed abettor of Satan, you shall burn at this very stake. Hereby repent, and God may have mercy upon your soul. Fail to do so, and you will endure a suffering like no other – just as you will suffer for all eternity in the darkest pits of Hell!"

Every pair of eyes was staring at her; she struggled to breathe.

"Well? Do you repent then, witch?" The deafening baritone echoed in her ears. Her teary eyes scanned the hushed crowd; a tall, dark-haired figure shifted at the back. In that moment, she prayed that Henri had broken his promise and secretly come to watch her; to be with her until the end. But, in her heart, she knew it wasn't him. He'd already honoured their pact by supplying the poison she held in her mouth; from the vial she'd secreted in her bodice then supped from seconds before she was dragged towards the stake.

The tears flowed as she silently thanked the apothecary friend that had slipped him the drug the day before. In a couple of moments she would be unconscious – a few minutes more and she would painlessly slip away.

273

The priest marched to the edge of the stake; only stopping when his shoes brushed the faggots that would soon be burning around her.

"So, I'm afraid your belligerent silence leaves me with no option." He nodded to the side; a cloaked figure appeared, brandishing a solitary burning torch.

"Of course, we could have made it easier for you by hanging you first..." He shook his head. "All you had to do was repent and I would happily have granted you that small mercy."

His mocking smirk was more than Genevieve could bear. She took a slow, controlled breath in through her nose then swallowed the warm, viscous poison in a single gulp. A single, harsh cough eased the burning in her throat as the toxic liquid slid further down her gullet.

She exhaled slowly, a wave of confidence washing over her; as though the very act of swallowing had stoked her defiance. In that moment, she focused on the old woman standing motionless at the front; small and rakishly thin but with intense pale eyes that seemed to stare into her soul. She nodded at her, as if making one last connection.

"Bring on the flames," she croaked.

"Aaah... the witch speaks." He turned to address the frenzied rabble before leaning in towards her. "Too late now, though, isn't it?"

He clicked his fingers; Genevieve held her breath as the cloaked figure knelt to place the blazing torch against the first faggot. It only took a second or two for the flames to spread like a burning ring up towards the soles of her bare feet. The heat on her face was suffocating as she peered out through streaming eyes at the faceless crowd in front of her; the strangers that had gathered here to watch her die.

If only she could have worn it one last time – the precious black mesh that had once draped so elegantly and carelessly behind her. Yet, she was strangely thankful she couldn't find it before being marched out in front of the crowd – in her heart she knew she could never bear the thought of it being destroyed. At least, that part of her could live on...

Her throat tightened as each tortuous, panicking breath became unbearable.

The last thing she felt before her eyes closed was an excruciating burning in her chest, as the molten heat of the pendant seared like a brand into the skin above her heart.

Then, a dream-like serenity flooded her senses – a peacefulness unlike anything she'd experienced before.

A soothing darkness cocooned her, then everything faded away.

Everything except one abiding image; the last thing she would ever remember – Henri's face.

"Until we meet again, my love."

CHAPTER THIRTY-TWO

Alice tore at her chest; her nails clawing and gouging every inch of inflamed skin. Her eyes twitched and rolled in her head as she felt herself drifting back, like she was being thrust towards the light at the end of a tunnel.

Her neck flexed as something tugged at her hair. The sensation jerked her into a drowsy, disoriented haze. Then, the sudden feeling of her hands being squeezed and pinned to a cold, hard surface shocked her into full consciousness.

"What the—?"

She looked up from the gnarled, veiny hand shackling her to the table. Charles was looming over her with the veil draped over his wrist – his stare close enough for her to see every tiny burst blood vessel in the yellowy whites of his eyes.

Fury boiled inside her and she shoved his hands away, forcing him backwards to land with a thud on the marble floor. He winced as he propped himself up on his elbows; each cagey, awkward movement prompting a gasp of pain.

"I don't know what you think you're playing at—" She stood to confront him, nudging the chair with the back of her legs. It shot across the smooth marble and crashed into the back wall. Seconds later, a framed picture fell to the floor, scattering shattered glass across the floor.

"Well, I'd say you've certainly got your powers back, Alice."

All she could do was stare at the broken picture lying on the floor.

What the hell is happening to me?

"You know, I was only trying to help you. You were almost ripping your skin off back there." He struggled to his feet with a long, drawn-out groan. Alice flinched as her fingertips dabbed the raw, sticky dampness on her chest. She held her bloodstained hands up in front of her and winced at the redness seeping out from underneath her nails.

The familiar scent of woody incense drifted under her nose. The temperature in the room dropped, just enough for her to shiver.

"Why the hell didn't you tell me I was a witch, Charles? Pretty crucial information, don't you think?"

He narrowed his eyes as he brushed past her shoulder. "And, to what end do you think that would have been helpful, my dear? What in God's name's difference would it have made – other than to upset you from the very start? No..." he shook his head, "... you had to relive it. Self-discovery is how this whole karma thing works, I'm afraid."

She watched him snatch a large book from a table in the corner. He limped back towards her, holding it out like a sacred offering. "This is what it's all been about, Alice. Why you're here in this very castle on this very night – in *this* lifetime."

He glanced at the clock on the mantelpiece as a blinding beam of moonlight streamed in through the window, landing in a halo at her feet.

"The moon is at its fullest and most powerful for the next half hour or so. Everything is exactly how it should be." He was lost in thought, sweat glistening on his face as he stared into space.

"When's Victor coming back?" Alice felt her skin prickle as the moonlight crept slowly upwards to illuminate her ankles.

"Read it." Charles dropped the book on the table in front of her with a loud thud.

"But I thought Victor had to be with me? Surely we do this together?" She edged herself towards the green leather tome; her bloodied fingers hovering over the large pentangular symbol dominating the cover. She trailed her fingertips across it before sliding them down across the worn, cracked leather to gently stroke the gold, embossed lettering – first O then B then V. She could almost taste the rich history as she held the thick frayed spine in her trembling hands. *The Order of the Black Veil – A Complete History.*

Euphoria surged through her, like a hit of drugs shooting through her veins as she read the ornately-scripted title.

"You'll never escape the Order, Alice. It's in your blood, in your soul."

"I feel like I could do anything," she whispered, every nerve in her body tingling.

"Your powers are back with you now, at the peak of this full moon." He thrust his hand towards the flawless light streaming through the window.

Mindlessly, she flung the book open. It landed at the middle pages – exactly where she knew it would fall. At breakneck speed, her eyes devoured the bold italic script; instantly absorbing and processing the key words – ***prophecy, full moon, 27th August 2019, transference of power***.

Her eyes darted towards Charles as he paced the floor in front of the window.

"But there's nothing about repenting for past sins here. Only that the prophecy states if a cult member dies wearing the pendant, they must—"

Charles slammed his hand on the table, "—they must return to transfer their soul and any associated powers in the next incarnation. Exactly. And that would be your remit now, wouldn't it, Alice?" His twisted grin made him look almost demon-like in the harsh glare of the moonlight.

"But we don't have time for any sin repenting now because of Eva. Her interference has only accelerated the timescale." His jaw was tightly clenched; the veins in his temples fit to burst.

"We must go straight to the transference ritual." He rubbed his hands, sneaking a look at the clock on the mantelpiece.

The hairs on Alice's arms began to prickle – something wasn't right. She'd never been more desperate for Victor to walk through the door and whisk her away. Her gut was screaming at her to defy Charles.

"But what if I don't want to..." She looked up at him, holding her breath.

His high-pitched, piercing laugh fell somewhere between disbelief and hysteria.

"What if you don't want to? Did you really just say that?" He banged his fist on the table, his incredulous eyes bulging with rage.

Alice winced as a blinding pain shot across the back of her head. Charles marched to the wall beside the mantelpiece and shifted a small painting to the side. By the time he walked back towards her, the pulsing tension had spread across the top of her skull, pushing down like a lead weight onto her forehead.

Charles perched himself on the table in front of her, swinging the pendant back and forth before her screwed-up, teary eyes.

"But why me?" She rubbed her temples to ease the headache. "I get all the witch stuff but what do I have to do with the Order? Why am I so important?"

He sighed. "You were always a good witch, Alice."

"But what I did to him…" She shook her head as the words fell away.

"I believe that the depth of love you had for Henri completely outweighed any logic concerning your marriage. Love skews all sense and reasoning." Charles rested his hand on her shoulder. "I know for a fact that Henri couldn't bear to live without you." He paused. "That's why he swallowed the same poison you did that very night."

The thought of her one true love taking his own life because of her broke Alice's heart.

"The very poison I supplied for him… as a favour."

Her breath caught like glass in her throat. She opened her eyes and looked up at Charles – the man who had aided both their deaths in the last life. He grinned at her sudden realisation.

"You're the chosen one, Alice. It's written in the book. You were the one with all the powers, the one everyone in the Order worshipped." He gently swept a loose curl over her shoulder. "You had everyone beguiled with your beauty and your power. Remember when I told you that you can't escape your destiny? This is your calling."

He was close enough for her to feel his rapid breathing on her cheek. She leaned back, eyeing him suspiciously as his lips quivered with anticipation.

CHAPTER THIRTY-TWO

"So, it looks like you're the only one here to transfer it to?"

"Well, yes I suppose it does, doesn't it?" He stared straight ahead, slowly stroking his beard.

"But it doesn't have to be you, though, does it? We could always wait on—"

He tutted, whipping off his tweed jacket and tossing it onto a chair. "You know, we're running out of time now."

Alice bristled. He was hiding something – she could feel it. "Maybe we should just wait. I'd rather be with—"

He grabbed her arm and dragged her to the window. Her shoes squeaked their way across the shiny marble. "Do you see that, Alice?" He pointed to the flawless full moon just brushing the tallest mountain peak. "There's no time left now. In a few minutes, the moon's optimum power will have passed. Now, just put the damn pendant on, open the book and recite the words to me – it's not difficult. Believe me, you won't like the consequences if you don't."

Charles' face was shimmering with sweat. He loosened his bow tie and yanked open the top button of his shirt. She snatched her arm away from his sweaty grip and stormed back towards the book. Just then her vision faltered and she swayed to the side, banging her hip against the table. As she fell dazed into the seat, she felt the coolness of the pendant being placed around her neck. She flicked through a few pages of the book before deciding where it should fall open.

"You're not at the right place." Charles' arm appeared from behind her to grab the page but she shoved it away.

"I want to find out what happens if I don't do this." Another dull ache spread across her forehead as the image of a body lying on a floor flashed into her mind.

"No, Alice, you really don't want to know." He pulled the

book towards him and tore through the pages until he was almost at the end.

"Incantation of the prophecy – here we are."

But Alice didn't hear him as another vision shot like lightning into her brain. It only took a few seconds for her to make out a bedroom and a blonde woman lying face down on dark wood. Alice knew straightaway who it was.

"Oh, Jesus," she whispered. "Something's wrong." As she stood up, all she could see was red liquid seeping out from underneath the body.

She stood up and ran towards the door. "It's Eva. She's on the floor."

"What are you talking about?" Charles stormed after her. "No, you can't leave now." He lunged to try and grab her arm as she fled into the corridor.

"Where is she?" Alice yelled behind her as she hurried down the hallway. But her feet were already whisking her down the stairs towards the door at the bottom.

"You don't know what you've done—" Charles' cry faded into the distance as she rushed though the swinging door before stopping dead at the first door on the left. Her gut told her it was Eva's room. She put her ear to the cold, hard wood. Nothing.

She held her breath and lowered the handle. The wooden floorboards groaned beneath her feet as the door opened with a sharp click. She nudged it just enough for it to swing open a bit by itself; her eyes scoured what she could see of the dark floor. With her heart hammering in her chest, she peered around the door into the still shadows. A large red chair sat facing the far wall in front of a fireplace. By the side was a small circular table, with a glass tumbler sitting perilously close to the edge.

As she crept across the threshold, she noticed a hand resting on one of the arms of the chair. Drawing closer, she saw the limp wrist was dangling over the soft, curved edge. She swallowed hard. It had to be Victor. With her eyes half-closed, she stepped forwards to touch the back of the velvet chair. Then she forced herself to look down.

"No—" Her eyes widened in fear as she stared at the head flopped lifelessly to the side. The thick, dark hair was unmistakable. She panicked and dashed around to the front. Victor's eyes were closed. He looked so peaceful – *too* peaceful. She grappled frantically to loosen the cufflink on his shirt then pressed her fingertips on the inside of his wrist.

She whimpered when at last she felt a slow, rhythmic pulse. "Jesus, what are you doing to me?" She shook his shoulder – partly to rouse him, partly to ease her own frustration.

But after a few seconds, he still wasn't wakening. She raised the half-empty glass to her nose and winced at the acidic aroma.

A creaking floorboard startled her in the deathly silence. She turned to see Charles' silhouette filling the narrow doorway. He tutted and placed his hands firmly on his hips.

"What the hell is in this?" She held the glass out in front of her, trying desperately to control her trembling hand.

"Looks like he's out for the count. Had a bit too much of the old whisky, I think?" His voice was calm and measured.

"It isn't just whisky, though, is it?" She sniffed it again. "You know, I just can't figure out what that other smell is? Maybe I should have a little sip…?" He stepped towards her as she slowly lifted the glass to her mouth. "Or maybe you'd like to try it yourself, Charles?"

He stared at her as she held it against her lips; the look on his face only fuelled her bravery. She tipped the liquid just enough to tease him before he snatched it from her and threw it across the room. She watched it smash against a tall glass cabinet; spraying countless shards of crystal across the floor.

"That's it. Enough of the games now," she said, eyeballing him. "Why did you drug him? Wasn't it enough helping to poison us both the last time?" As she nodded towards Victor, something bright caught her eye in the far corner of the room. She could just about make out another door lurking in the shadows. A tiny sliver of light seeped out through the gap at the bottom.

"I thought you said Victor came to check on Eva?" She couldn't take her eyes off the narrow strip of light.

Charles caught her gaze. Together, they stared in silence at the closed door; an unspoken dread hanging in the air between them. Every hair on Alice's body stood on end as she *saw* what lay behind it.

"Yes, he came to check on her then obviously decided to stay for a—"

Alice cut him off. "She's in there."

"Look, leave her be. She's probably sleeping anyway. We have to finish what we're – what *you're* – here to do or…" He made to grab her arm as a sharp chime from the clock on the mantelpiece echoed in the stillness. By the twelfth and last chime, she was already standing in the shadows facing the door. "God, I hope it's not real."

"This is your last chance to do as I say." Charles' threatening tone didn't deter her.

She squeezed the handle down and gave the door a gentle nudge. "Or what, Charles? I think we both know who's in control now. In case you'd forgotten, I'm the one with the power here so, I'm afraid, your empty threats are just that – empty..."

She flinched as a dull ache spread through her forearm then shot down to her wrist. She rested her palm against the cold panel of the door, doubling over as the excruciating pain flexed and contorted her hand into a gnarled, claw-like fist. The hideous feeling of her skin tightening and shrinking against her body made her stomach heave. She stared in disbelief as her hand started to age before her eyes.

"I'm sorry – you were saying, Alice?" She looked up at Charles, her eyelashes heavy with tears as another intense muscular contraction tore through her arm.

"You really shouldn't be so arrogant, you know." He laughed as she struggled to raise her head.

"What's... happening...?"

"Exactly what I told you would happen, Alice. Exactly what I warned you about. But you wouldn't listen, would you?" His warm spittle sprayed onto her cheek.

"It's too late now – time's run out for us, I'm afraid. Although I think *you're* the one who should be the most afraid..." She winced as he prodded the parched, wrinkled skin on the back of her hand.

It took every ounce of strength she had to lean in and push the door open with her feeble fingers. She grimaced as another bolt of pain shot up her arm, contracting every muscle into a tortuous spasm. Wizened, crepe-like skin covered her arm all the way up to her elbow now. She watched in horror as it slithered further up towards her shoulder.

"You're dying now, Alice. Ageing before your very eyes. The book prophesied this punishment." He pushed her to the side and stormed into the room in front of her. When he fell to his knees seconds later, she knew that her vision had been right.

Her hand shot to her mouth as she peered over his head. The grim scene was far worse than she'd visualised. A figure lay chest down on the floor by the side of the bed, with the head facing away from them. Alice stepped over the splayed legs to the other side, avoiding the pools of blood seeping out from underneath the thin, crooked arms. She knelt down to look into Eva's open, lifeless eyes. Her ashen skin strained more than normal against her cheekbones yet all the muscles in her face were completely relaxed. Her pale, dry lips were solemnly closed. Alice touched her cool forehead and checked for a pulse in her neck. She shook her head. "She's gone."

Charles shook his granddaughter's shoulders; rocking her frail, limp body back and forth on the cold, hard wood.

Alice shoved his hands away and shot him a look. "I think I can help her," she whispered, as a tingling spread from the tips of her fingers down to the palm of her normal hand.

"You won't live to do it, my dear." He pushed himself up off his knees and glared down at her. "You'll be dead soon – just like *her.*"

Alice was too caught up in the moment to notice Charles disappearing into the next room. She lifted one of Eva's arms to look underneath and gasped at the deep incision running along the inside of her wrist. She knew without looking that the other one would be exactly the same.

Willing herself not to pass out, she placed her normal hand on the seeping redness of the first arm. A buzz of energy surged through it and tiny vibrations began to ripple below the surface of her skin as her eye caught a bloodied shard of glass just beyond Eva's fingertips. She struggled to keep her hand steady over the cut as the pulsing intensified, like a burgeoning, pent-up energy desperate for release.

Her eyes slid to her wrinkled, contorted hand as a bolt of pain shot from her shoulder straight up to her neck. Gasping in agony, she screwed her eyes shut and focused all her strength on the hand covering Eva's wound. Then, she opened her mouth to speak in the lowest of tones:

"Mother of Mercy and Healing,
Send the energy of Hygeia to nourish from her Sacred Bowl,
Send the energy of Brigid to heal with waters of Her Sacred Well,
Send the energy of Demeter to restore life to withering cells,
Send the energy of Quan Yin to bless the healing with peace,
Send your healing wisdom to the body to restore its sacred balance,
Thank you Great Goddess, Mother of All Life."

The chant she wasn't even aware she knew, flowed naturally from her lips. But it was only a few seconds after uttering the last word, that Alice realised she hadn't taken a single breath throughout the entire monologue.

Suddenly, every inch of her felt like it was being drained of life as a raging heat blasted from her palm. She lifted Eva's wrist up to see the bloody wound vanishing before her eyes. She stared in disbelief as the severed tendons and cartilage began to knit and fuse together and the hacked, bloody flesh seamlessly faded away.

Frantically, she transferred her grip to the other wrist. With almost nothing left to give, Alice screamed in despair as another surge of heat blasted out to smother the deep, raw gash beneath. Seconds later, perfect, flawless skin bonded effortlessly over the cut – as though it had never even existed.

She lifted Eva's head off the bloodied floor and cradled it in her arms. As she pulled her close, Eva's eyes rolled back in her head and she choked out an urgent, lung-busting cough. Weeping with relief and tiredness, Alice collapsed on the floor with Eva still resting on her chest. Deep, mournful sobs heaved inside her but she didn't have the energy to let them out.

She wasn't sure she'd be able to get up again as Eva's slow, rhythmic breathing lulled her towards sleep. As her damp eyelashes finally fell together, a sharp creak jerked her awake. She strained her eyes as far to the side as she could.

She managed a weak smile as Victor rushed towards her, dropping to his knees.

"Alice… are you alright?" He stumbled as he leaned in towards her. She nodded, grappling for the arm he'd thrust out to catch himself.

"What's going on?" His voice was slow and slurred. "Was I asleep?" He stroked her face and looked down at Eva, confused. "Is she ok?"

He cradled her neck, lifting it off Alice's chest. "Oh my God—" His eyes caught the smeared blood that had spread underneath them.

Eva coughed and shifted towards Victor.

"I didn't give you all of it. I didn't want to give you any of it but he—" She coughed again and lifted up her wrists. She shook her head and looked up at Alice. "Where are they?"

"Where's what?" Victor cut in. "And what didn't you want to give me?"

Alice stayed silent, sensing that Eva was about to open up to them.

"It was Grandad – he told me I had to drug you." Her

breathing was fast and shallow. "To keep you... out of the way."

Victor's body tensed.

"But I didn't even put a third of it in your drink, I promise." Alice didn't have to look at her to know she was about to start crying. "I couldn't live with myself—" Eva broke down and buried her head into Victor's chest.

Alice propped herself up onto her normal elbow, keeping the withered arm out of sight. She shuddered when she noticed the fingers on her other hand were wrinkling as well.

"All I've done is lie to you both – I don't deserve to live." The muffled words came slowly through heaving sobs. "But I only lied because *he* told me to." She turned towards Alice. "The abuse story in the pub, working as a chambermaid. He said you needed to touch the pendant, that way he'd know it was you for sure."

"It's not your fault, Eva." Alice caught her breath as the pain of a thousand hot needles piercing her skin shot through her hand. Her eyes brimmed with tears as the tightness in her chest increased until all she could do was take shallow sips of air.

"But I slashed my wrists, Alice. I wanted to die. Why didn't I?"

"I can't listen to this anymore." Victor struggled to his feet with Eva in his arms. He swayed slightly as he found his balance before laying her down on the bed. "I'm going to find him." His voice was firm and clear as he bent down to help Alice off the floor.

She gasped as the pain in her arms almost stopped her heart. "No, it's fine." She thrust her hands behind her back and fell against the bed. "I'll stay with Eva for a bit."

Victor would find out about the ageing soon enough, she just couldn't deal with it right now.

"He's in the altar room, by the way." In her mind's eye, she could see Charles standing beneath the portrait, clutching the book in both hands.

He nodded. "Are you sure you'll be alright here on your own?" He glanced at Eva as she clutched a pillow to her chest.

"Please don't hurt him, Victor."

He gave her cheek a reassuring stroke. "I'll only do what needs to be done."

And, with that, Victor left the room to seek out the man – the friend – who'd deceived him for far too long…

CHAPTER THIRTY-THREE

Alice stared in horror at the drying pool of blood on the floor just inches from her toes; a hellish reminder of the awful scene that had played out like a living nightmare in front of her just moments before.

She forced herself to look down at her arms. Saliva pooled in the back of her mouth as small bones protruded sharply through the sallow, withered skin. If it hadn't been for Eva lying behind her, she knew she would have screamed until she had no breath left.

Then, she thought about Victor – and her mum. Sitting on the cold, hard floor in the god-awful silence of the remote chateau, she tried everything not to contemplate her impending mortality; the imminent fate she alone had brought about. She dropped her head into her hands as a glorious image of her and Victor kissing on their wedding day drifted into her mind. There wasn't a cloud in the sky as a flock of tiny chirping birds wheeled and swooped around them before rising up into the perfect azure blue.

In the background, three beautiful infants ran carefree under a canopy of endless apple trees, weaving this way and that through a blissfully lush, landscaped garden. The dappled sunlight caressed their innocent, beaming faces as helpless giggles echoed in the still, balmy air.

The scene was so perfect, so utterly idyllic that Alice knew she must be close to death. Perhaps this was her last vision of happiness? Of what could have been...?

But she couldn't do it alone again. This time, she had to be with Victor at the end. Taking a deep breath, she pushed herself off the floor with both hands. Something snapped in her wrist and she fell heavily onto her elbow. She was on the edge of passing out with the pain when something nudged her shoulder.

"What's wrong with your skin?" The voice was low and husky.

It took a few seconds for Alice to come to. Then the realisation that her skin had been seen forced her awake.

"I'm being punished, Eva." It was all she could think of to say.

"What, for saving me?" Eva sat upright and swung her legs over the edge of the bed. As she dangled them playfully in front of her, Alice couldn't believe this was the same girl who'd been dead less than half an hour earlier. "I know it was you. No-one else could have helped me."

"It's complicated," she began. "There's too much to—"

"Please don't hate, me, Alice," Eva said, hurriedly. Alice looked up into her pleading eyes. She seemed desperate to continue.

"In the beginning, I just wanted to please Grandad. He did so much for me after mum died..." She bit her lip. "But I had these feelings for Victor – and they just got stronger and stronger. They sort of crept up on me and nothing could make them go away." She took a deep breath. "Then, one evening in the restaurant, I saw him looking at you in a different way.

It was just different – a way he'd never looked at you before." She paused, her mouth trembling. "After that, I noticed it every week. Every time you walked past, he couldn't take his eyes off you." She huffed under her breath. "Of course, you never noticed – he always hid it perfectly. But not from me..."

Alice forgot all about her pain and exhaustion as she listened to Eva.

"I know I've got my problems, but I'm not blind – or stupid. That's why I was so glad when Grandad came up with the whole abuse story. He knew it would lure you in to help me but I secretly hoped you'd hate Victor for it. You see, I was terrified that my worst fear would come true, just like it has – that you'd fall in love and I'd mean nothing to him..."

In that moment, a deep sadness and pity crashed over Alice; an innate empathy and understanding for the troubled young woman that defied all the hurt and bitterness she'd ever caused her.

Now, she finally understood Eva's story.

"I've always known it was you in the painting. So, I read up as much as I could about the Order and what was going to happen here." She dropped her head. "But I didn't figure I'd be so jealous of you. I'm truly sorry for hating you. I just can't believe you saved me – after all I've put you through..."

Alice sighed. "It's the least I could do." She paused, staring straight ahead. "But I have to go after Victor now. You'll be alright here on your own for a bit?"

She noticed Eva frowning at her sharp gasps of breath as she struggled to stand.

"Maybe I should come with you...?"

Alice shook her head and pulled her sleeves down past her wrists. "Thanks, but I have to do this myself. Just get some rest – Victor should be back soon."

Eva nodded, her eyes narrow with concern.

As she stood in the doorway, Alice turned to say what would probably be her last words to the girl. She could feel her heart slowly breaking as she wiped away the hot tears before they spilled down her cheek.

"Take care, Eva."

CHAPTER THIRTY-FOUR

Alice fell against the wall as another swift and brutal palpitation took her breath away.

Freezing cold air billowed up around her as she stumbled towards the bannister. Her frail fingers gathered her cardie into a loose scrunch around her neck as the insidious chill seeped deep into her bones, slowly numbing her senses. The tears were flowing fast now, blurring each step in front of her as her withered fingers felt the same wrinkled, paper-thin skin creeping further up her body.

Each feeble, trembling step up the staircase was an agonising strain on her heart. Her legs were close to buckling as she finally placed her aching feet on the top landing. It took all her energy to even think about crossing the last stretch of wooden floor. In the all-consuming silence, her slow, laboured breathing was deafening as each rasping wheeze ended as a brief, ghostly cloud in front of her. Yet, no floorboards creaked or groaned as she moved this time – it was almost as if she wasn't even there.

She let her palm glide over the smooth handrail as she shuffled slowly but determinedly down the corridor. Huge portraits loomed from the sage green walls; the dull, lifeless eyes almost mocking her as her shaking legs struggled to carry her forwards. The welcome smell of incense wafted under her nose as her eyes caught a panel of glass in a nearby cabinet. Just a second or two of her hideous, haggard face was all Alice could bear. How could the wizened, crevice-ridden, sagging reflection possibly belong to her?

She stifled the retching in her throat and crept closer to the altar room. The door was closed over but not shut; a sliver of light seeped through the tiny vertical gap. As she drew nearer, she heard raised voices then a single, dull thud. She nudged the door open to see Victor and Charles in silhouette before the altar. In the dark shadows of the vaulted corner, she could see Victor's hands around the old man's throat.

"How could you?" he snarled, "I trusted you..."

Her eyes slid to the book lying open inside the pentangular symbol on the floor, as though it had been dropped or thrown.

Charles let out a guttural, choking sound as he grappled to loosen the grip around his neck.

Everything in front of Alice began to blur as she stumbled backwards; her shaky legs finally giving way beneath her failing, fragile body.

Just then, Victor's eyes darted towards the door. All the tension drained from his body when he saw her stooped in the doorway. Her heart pounded painfully in her chest as he rushed towards her. Every muscle stiffened as he drew closer in the fading firelight. Any second now he'd see her face... her hideous, haggard face.

She lifted her hands to try to hide it but he pulled them away.

"What... what is this?" He rubbed the thin, crepey dryness on the back of her hands and looked into her eyes.

"Victor, don't. Please... don't look at me—" She snatched

her hands away and covered her face. But she couldn't hold it back any longer; the frantic, heaving breaths forcing hot tears to spill into her cradling palms.

"Alice, please…" He prised her hands from her cheeks and replaced them with his own.

She turned away, both embarrassed and disgusted by his sympathy. Her heart sank as he frantically scanned her from head to toe. Then he pulled her close, hugging her to his chest as though his life depended on it. Only then did she let herself collapse into his arms.

"This wasn't meant to happen. How could you let—" Victor's voice cracked as he bellowed behind him.

"Oh, but I didn't let anything happen." Charles' arrogance echoed around the room. "Alice chose not to play by the rules, I'm afraid." He strutted towards them, pausing to snatch the open book from the floor. He lifted his head, disdain etched all over his face. "All she had to do was transfer her powers and everything would've been fine." He tutted, caressing the cover with his fingertips. "But, oh no, young Alice here decides she'd rather waste whatever power she has left on saving Eva. But, what are you left with now?"

Victor stiffened as Charles brushed past them.

"Ah, yes… that's right. A serious case of rapid ageing – oh, and a rather unsavoury dose of imminent death."

"Right, that's it," Victor seethed as he scooped Alice into his arms before laying her down onto the padded bench by the fire.

"What are you—?" she whispered.

He nodded at her and walked back towards Charles.

The two men stood just inches from one another beneath the portrait, now so faded it looked like nothing more than a ghostly apparition.

Victor leaned in to glare down at the old man. "You've got one last chance to tell the truth about why you *really* wanted Alice to come here."

A beat or two of silence. "Or what, Victor?"

"Oh, you don't want to know what I'd like to do to you right now... old friend." His hands were clenched tightly by his side; so tightly, Alice imagined the knuckles bursting through the skin.

"You told me it was purely to repent for her sins. Or *this* would happen."

He thrust a hand out towards Alice slouched on the bench. "But you deliberately kept me away so she'd transfer her powers to you. It had nothing to do with repenting, did it?" He leaned in closer, his eyes bulging with rage. "Well, did it, you deceitful son of a bitch?"

He jabbed his finger into Charles' chest, forcing him backwards onto his heels. "It was all about you, wasn't it?"

As the old man struggled to keep his balance, he snatched the book from his grasp, marched over to the fire and paused – holding it just a hair's breadth above the tallest flame. Victor shot Alice a look. She held his gaze and shook her head.

Charles laughed but it caught in his throat. "You wouldn't dare."

Just then, a strange bubbling sensation began to spread inside Alice's stomach; like tiny fluttering butterflies trying to escape. As she felt the gentle pulsing with her palm, a wave of dizziness washed over her. Then everything went black. She fainted and slumped forwards, falling like a limp rag onto the floor. The impact as she dropped onto the marble jolted her back to the brink of consciousness. In the disoriented haze, she could feel her head being lifted.

"Alice…" The distant voice made her eyes roll forwards. Now her head was resting on something warm and firm as an orange glow slowly seeped through her eyelids.

"I'm so sorry." She was just about aware of Victor's head gently resting on hers. A few sharp, shallow breaths later and he was sobbing as he nestled into her neck.

"This is all my fault. I should never have brought you here." Warm tears dripped onto her skin, trickling down into her collarbone. It took all her strength to lift her hand and stroke his head. If this was to be their last moment together; their last embrace, she wanted it to be special. His thick hair felt so comforting between her fingers; so wonderfully soft and smooth that she couldn't bear to let it go.

"I love you so much – please don't leave me again." He hugged her close and kissed her neck. She tried to smile but as she prised her eyes open, she saw Charles glaring down at them. Anger swelled inside her as she watched him standing, arms folded, emotionless to the scene in front of him. She squeezed a handful of Victor's hair in frustration. But it was only when her fingers slid effortlessly through it seconds later, that she realised how easy it was to move them again. She tilted her head to look at the hand resting on his hair and gasped at the perfectly normal, flawless skin.

Victor flinched at the sound and craned his neck to look up; his eyes red and swollen with tears. As he moved, she caught sight of the skin on her arm healing all by itself. She held her breath as each fine line and deep crevice appeared to regenerate; spreading and flattening out before her eyes. By the time she felt able to breathe again, the parched, crepey texture had returned to its normal, smooth surface.

Charles' eyes swooped on the transformation.

"So, you *did* transfer your powers, after all, Miss Alice? Well, aren't you a sly little minx?" he smirked. "You're a damn good liar as well, I'll give you that."

Alice propped herself up onto her elbows, with not an ache or pain to be felt.

"No, no... I didn't do anything—" She effortlessly twirled the stud in her earlobe. "How is this happening?" She looked at Victor, searching for an answer – for anything that might make the slightest bit of sense. He pulled her close.

"So, when did you do it?" Charles shook his head. "It had to be before we found Eva..." His eyes darted towards Victor. "But it hasn't been transferred to him, though."

Alice sprang to her feet in front of him. "Look, I know I used the last of my power to save Eva but..."

He raised an eyebrow at her.

"But I haven't transferred anything to anybody, you have to believe—"

"Christ, Charles, just let it go now," Victor cut in. "Accept you've lost the battle and be done with it."

The old man huffed, looking down at his feet. "That's pretty harsh." He paused. "Especially to someone in my condition."

"What're you talking about?" Victor snapped.

"No time for that," he said, forcing a smile. "Anyway, you've far more important things to worry about now."

Alice narrowed her eyes. "What do you—"

"Oh, come on, Alice..." He grinned as he pushed his specs further up his nose. "There's only one other way to transfer the power; only one other person it can be transferred *to*..."

His gaze dropped to her stomach.

"Surely you've figured it out by now?"

She shook her head as the realisation impacted in her brain. In that moment, all she could feel was Victor's eyes boring into her. She swallowed hard and placed a protective palm across her stomach. "No, no, I don't think so—" Both her mind and pulse were racing. Victor grabbed her shoulders.

"You're pregnant?" he whispered, staring at her.

"No. Maybe...Jesus, I don't know." She turned away, unable to look at him.

"Maybe *you* don't know – but the prophecy certainly does." Charles' shoes clipped sharply across the marble towards her. "There's no other explanation, Alice. You've negated the punishment by bringing new life into the world. That very caveat is scripted in the book."

She looked up at Victor. Her throat tightened as she watched his clenched jaw and distant eyes. It was only when he grabbed her hand and squeezed it that she felt she could breathe again.

"Well, then, I suppose congratulations are in order?" Charles offered his hand.

Victor looked down at it then shook his head. "So, what's this about your condition?"

Charles dropped his hand and fiddled with the ring on his finger. "I'm afraid I'm not very well, Victor." His eyes were firmly focused on the gold band as he struggled to drag the words from inside.

Victor frowned. "Why haven't you mentioned it before?"

He huffed under his breath as he looked up at Genevieve's portrait. "No point. It's terminal, you see. Stage four pancreatic cancer."

"Oh my god..." Alice let out a slow, deep breath. "How long have you known?"

"The start of the year. Anyway, I didn't want to burden you—" Charles paced the floor in the fading firelight.

"You should've told me," Victor snapped. "I have friends who could've helped you. Jesus, you of all people should know I would've paid—"

Charles waved his hand. "It's too late for that now. By the time I was diagnosed, it was already terminal."

Alice shook her head. "So, that's why you wanted my powers."

"Bit more to it than that." He held his hand out. "Please?"

Victor tutted. "Really? After everything you've done, you expect—"

"No." Alice turned towards him. "Maybe we give him one last chance to explain?"

He shoved his fingers through his hair then bumped down onto the bench by the fire. Charles had already disappeared into the darkness beneath the vaulted ceiling. "There's something that belongs to you now—" His low, controlled voice seemed a lifetime away as it echoed in the gloomy shadows.

Her pulse raced as he stepped back into the firelight cradling the veil in his palms, as though it were some kind of sacred offering. She couldn't take her eyes off it as she edged towards him across the floor.

"It's always been yours, Alice," he whispered.

As her trembling fingers reached out to caress the soft black mesh once again, her eyes caught a flicker of light on the far wall. She turned to see the portrait bathed in a luminous amber glow; as though it were coming to life before her eyes.

"That's your energy, your power." Charles stood beside her in the shimmering radiance. "She's even more beautiful than

302

CHAPTER THIRTY-FOUR

I remember, if that's possible…"

Alice watched his enthralled face as he gazed adoringly at Genevieve.

"Of course, she never knew how much I loved her—" His voice tailed off as he grabbed Alice's hand and pulled it firmly to his side.

"What the hell are you playing at?" Victor's voice boomed across the room.

Charles flicked away the interruption and stepped closer to the painting. "You know, there's no pain quite like that of not being able to be with the one you love. I don't think there's a man on God's earth who'd dispute that." He took a deep breath. "Even worse is when they don't feel the same…"

His tired, grey eyes misted over. She couldn't be sure if it was the fading light or the defeated look on his face but, for the first time, Alice felt a deep and genuine pity for Charles. In that moment, right in front of her, he was just a hopelessly frail, vulnerable old man.

"So you see, Alice, what I'm trying to say is that I wanted to punish you. Both of you, in fact, for the unbearable pain and misery you caused me all those centuries ago – a worse pain than even this."

He winced as he took a sharp breath in, clutching his side. "The love you withhold is the pain you carry lifetime after lifetime. I know that now." His face softened as the pain passed. He glanced down at the veil.

"I took it before you went to the stake that night. I just needed a part of you I could keep after you were… gone."

He turned towards her, appraising the black mesh in his fingers as he held it out. "But I vowed to myself there and then that I'd return it to you – in the next life."

"But, Charles," she said, slowly easing herself towards it. "I had no idea you were... Christ, what am I saying – that wasn't even me."

He smiled, raising an eyebrow as she took it in her hand. "That's why I was more than happy to supply the poison for you both."

"So, if you couldn't have her then nobody could. She may as well be dead?" Victor shot him a look. "Pretty convenient, eh?"

"Aah... but was it not, to all intents and purposes, a mercy killing?" The old man's eyes flitted back to Alice. "I'd say you won, though, wouldn't you, Victor – got the prize at the end of the day?"

"She was married to the Comte, for Christ's sake. I'd say he well and truly got the prize."

"I think we both know that was anything *but* true love." Charles looked over his specs at him. "Not a patch on your clandestine, all-consuming," he sighed, "soul-destroying love."

Silence engulfed the room as the two men locked eyes; first steadfastly then waveringly – then reluctantly. The tension between them was slowly dissolving.

After a few seconds, Victor nodded then looked away; like an unspoken acceptance that what had gone before was finally being laid to rest. There was nothing more either of them could say now. It was over – all that had passed should remain there.

A chill shot through Alice at the realisation that she'd been the object of both their affections.

She didn't know what to say – or feel – as Charles caught her eye. In that instant, something flashed across his face. It was a look she couldn't place; neither shame, nor regret nor remorse. Yet, to Alice, it somehow signified that he knew his time was up; a resigned acceptance that *this lifetime* was perilously close to its end. And there was nothing he nor anyone else could do about it.

The silence hung like a dead weight in the air.

Then, just like that, the wise, avuncular old man returned, head held high. "You did the right thing, young lady. Be proud of that."

Alice shrugged, unsure if – or how – she should react.

"So, what now?" Victor said, squeezing Alice's hand.

"Well, that's entirely up to you. But, I warn you, there's a lot to learn. This is just the beginning. You know that?" Charles nodded at her stomach as he lifted the book off the marble. "Just promise me you'll take care of Eva." His voice wavered just enough for it to be convincing and no more.

"I think in the circumstances, it's the least we can do, don't you?" Victor looked him dead in the eye.

Alice thought about Eva all alone downstairs. "I'll go check on her." She held her stomach as she made for the door, still in disbelief that a child – Victor's child – might be growing inside of her. "I'll bring her straight back up."

"Actually, if you don't mind, I'd rather see her myself," Charles said, brushing some dust off the cover before gently placing the book on the wooden seat by the door. He slowly trailed his fingertips across the green embossed cover then gave it one last pat. "A bit of time together before—" His voice faded away as he strolled out into the corridor.

Alice poked her head through the door as he disappeared down the stairs. She looked back at Victor. "He isn't coming home with us, is he?"

He walked up behind her and slipped his arms around her

305

waist. "No, probably not." His hands dropped to her stomach. "We'll confirm this for sure when we get home." He was lost in thought as she looked up at him.

"Jesus, what just happened here?" She placed her head on his chest. "I can't believe Charles could be so... so—"

Victor tensed. "Like he said, we've more important things to worry about now."

She smiled as he stroked her cheek. "But if it *is* true, I need to know more. I mean, what's the future for our child? What in the hell powers is he or she going to have?" Her mind raced with endless questions and scenarios as she draped the veil over her arm and walked towards the book. As she picked it up, the gold lettering glinted in the flickering firelight, almost dancing, as though it were coming to life right there in her tingling hands. The effect was mesmerising as her eyes slid back towards Victor.

"Jesus, I was a witch – maybe I still am. How can you possibly love me?"

"Hey, come on." He tucked a fallen curl behind her ear. "I love you – I've *always* loved you. That will never change. We were meant to be together."

Alice fell into his arms, book and veil pressed hard between them. No sooner had she dropped her head than he tilted it back up to kiss her. "Please, trust me. This is our new beginning together—" He paused, "—again."

Alice looked up at the portrait as she clutched the worn green leather and black mesh to her chest. With the colours now fully restored, she couldn't help but notice the ever-so-subtle curl to Genevieve's lips; the gentle crinkling in the corners of her dark brown eyes. She was sure she'd never seen those things before.

306

Then, just like that, it struck Alice that finally she knew what trust actually was. What the concept of placing your life, your beliefs, your heart's desires into someone else's care actually involved.

And, it looked like this was the only option now – a fresh but uncertain new beginning offering nothing more than unfulfilled promises.

But promises – and trust, nonetheless...

CHAPTER THIRTY-FIVE

Alice shifted in her seat as the car pulled away from the pillared entrance.

The dry toast that had been lodged in her stomach since breakfast was now threatening the back of her throat. She took a deep breath and covered her mouth as they picked up speed down the gravelled driveway.

She felt Eva's eyes on her as she stared out at the distant mountain peaks basking in the pale pink glow of the early-morning sun.

"When's Grandad coming home?" Eva whispered, leaning on her arm. "He wouldn't tell me when I asked him last night."

Alice watched the back of Victor's head, sitting motionless in the driver's seat.

"I don't know." She bit her lip, recalling the men's tense exchange before they left. Victor was clearly struggling with Charles' betrayal. But, to inveigle his own flesh and blood into his lies and deception, well, that was unforgivable. It was no wonder Eva was as troubled as she was.

"He seemed a bit strange – not his usual chatty self…" Her voice wavered. "I'll miss him so much."

Alice pulled her close and swept some strands of hair from her face. She wasn't sure how much Eva knew about her grandad's illness. She budged awkwardly on the leather seat, trying to loosen the usually comfy waistband that was now digging into her midriff.

"Eva, you know he's not well, don't you?" The grip tightened on her arm.

"Yes, but that's all I know." Eva's head fell into her lap. Her body shuddered in time to her soft whimpers. Alice knew she had to choose her words carefully.

"He's just going to stay here for a bit. His cousin's coming home tomorrow so he'll look after him." She caught Victor's eyes in the rear-view mirror. "He won't be on his own, okay?"

Eva nodded into her lap. "But he is coming home, right?"

Alice twirled her earring and snatched a glance at the mountains disappearing behind a row of trees. "Eventually... he'll be home eventually." It was all she could think of to say.

When the car came to a halt at the bottom of the winding driveway, Alice had an overwhelming urge to look back. She stared at the chateau for as long as she could before unexpected tears blurred her vision. She faced the front and swallowed hard to ease the lump in her throat.

As the car pulled out onto the deserted, single-track road she glanced behind her again and caught a faint green halo illuminating the perimeter of the chateau. For a second, she thought she was imagining it – then, as the familiar light flickered and faded away, she knew she really had seen it after all.

She rubbed her eyes as Victor accelerated towards the glorious sunrise up ahead. Then something made her look back one last time. Her eyes searched for it after they'd sped past the trees that had blocked her view but, after a few seconds of scanning the surrounding countryside, she still couldn't see it. Despite being sure of its exact location on the hillside, the chateau was nowhere to be seen; completely invisible – like it had simply vanished into thin air.

Alice swivelled to face the front and caught Victor's eyes in the rear-view mirror; this time, gentle crinkles appeared at the corners.

"Where—?"

He shot her a wink. She shook her head and smiled as Eva fell asleep against her shoulder.

"Not long to the airport now," he said, his profile in perfect silhouette against the most beautiful sky Alice had ever seen. She sat lost in thought for a moment, drinking in the stunning vignette of pink hues rising up to blend seamlessly with a palette of vivid orange that seemed to set the whole sky on fire.

She yawned as a sudden tiredness washed over her. Gradually, the maelstrom of intense thoughts and emotions faded away; all worries and fears drifted into the far-off, hazy distance, and her eyes grew heavy.

After a few seconds, Alice couldn't fight it any longer – her eyelids began to close then finally fell shut.

* * *

More than anything, it was the smell that reminded Alice exactly where she was.

That sublime and unmistakable fusion of sweet, savoury and spice she'd never experienced anywhere else; all gloriously mixed with a heady top note of fine wine mingling with the overriding aroma of freshly-brewed coffee.

It had been three whole months since she'd handed in her

notice at Amo Mangiare, yet the second she'd walked through the door, every sense was stirred and every memory came flooding back.

The only difference now was the perspective – she couldn't recall ever sitting at a table as a waitress, so to be dining at the most exclusive one in the highly sought-after alcove, was more than a little surreal.

She smiled at the young pianist working his magic at the gleaming grand piano just below them. He acknowledged her with a wink before closing his eyes and losing himself in another hauntingly beautiful, intricate melody.

"You okay?" Victor reached for the half-empty jug of water by his wine glass. "Think you could do with a top-up."

She smiled as some ice cubes and a slice of lemon plopped into her glass at the last second. "Yeah, fine. Some more ice to crunch and it should pass again." She took a deep breath and raised her tumbler. "Here's to the three of us, then." She adjusted her loose-fitting red blouse, making sure it draped perfectly over the waistband of the stretchy skirt she now had to wear slightly lower under her swelling stomach.

He clinked his glass against hers and leaned over to kiss her, just as her mum and Gordon appeared in the doorway.

"So, do we tell them now or not?"

Victor patted her hand. "Think I'll leave that one up to you."

As she stood up to wave, Gordon caught her eye and smiled over. She couldn't help but notice the quick cool glance towards Victor as they wriggled out of their coats and passed them to the maitre d'.

"Here we go then," she whispered under her breath.

Victor stood to pull out the two empty chairs across from them as her mum hurried across the wooden floor towards them.

"Sweetheart—" she said, her grin as wide as Alice had ever seen it.

"Mrs Webster, it's a pleasure to meet you." Victor offered his hand as Gordon appeared by her mum's side. Judging by their contrasting expressions, Alice knew it wasn't going to be easy changing the old man's opinion about him. He snuck behind Victor to give her a hug. "Hey, you." He took a step back to admire her. "You look good – *really* good."

"Well, high praise indeed, I guess." Alice caught her mum giving her the once over from across the table. Just then, a familiar face appeared beside them.

"Hey, how's it going?" Victor rubbed Eva's arm as she handed the menus out to them.

"So, this is Eva. I think I've mentioned her before…" Alice paused, catching the look of confusion on Gordon's face.

"She's not long started here—" She smiled up at her. "But I think you look like a seasoned pro already. Much better than working for him as well, I'd imagine," Alice joked, nudging Victor.

"Thanks. I'm getting there, I think." She laughed, nervously smoothing the stiff white apron over her black skirt.

Victor smiled up at her. "You're doing great, don't worry."

"Yes, she is." Ben's beaming face popped up over her shoulder. "Good to see you again, Alice."

She waved at him and laughed under her breath as Eva's coy smile and sudden flush suggested it wasn't just the waitressing, new apartment and weekly therapy sessions that were going well. She took their drinks' order then disappeared down the short wooden staircase, followed closely by Ben.

"What a lovely girl," her mum trilled, pulling her reading

glasses from her bag.

Alice watched Gordon's sombre look over the top of the menu.

"So, breaking news – the missing girl's been found." He nodded to thank Victor for pouring his water.

"They've found Kelly?" Alice's heart raced as she looked up from her menu. "Jesus. That's been, what… almost two and a half years now?" She reached for her glass as her breath caught in her throat. She couldn't bring herself to look at her mum. "So, she's okay, then?"

"Perfectly well, it would seem," he said, matter-of-factly. "Her dad phoned me yesterday to tell me the good news before it got to the press. Such a relief for them. They honestly thought they'd never see her again…"

Alice twirled her earring between her fingers.

"Where? I mean, where was she found?" She gulped the ice-cold water and focused on a passing waiter.

"America of all places. Would you credit it?" He humphed. "Ran away to be with some long-lost exchange friend in deepest, darkest Texas or thereabouts. God only knows how the authorities didn't find her." He shook his head. "Hey, maybe that boyband appeal did the trick?"

Alice let out a nervous laugh as Gordon winked at her. At long last, she knew that her dad hadn't been involved after all. She glanced at her mum, who was lost in thought pointing at random dishes on the menu, blissfully unaware of the relevance of the conversation and her daughter's inner turmoil.

Victor stroked her thigh under the table as Eva returned with a trayful of drinks.

"I can't believe you're on orange juice, by the way?" Gordon laughed as he stood to excuse himself. Just as she'd anticipated, his comment didn't go unnoticed by her mum whose knowing look was becoming increasingly hard to ignore. As she fidgeted with the clip in her hair, Victor broke the silence.

"Yeah, you've not been feeling that great for a few days now, have you?" He reached for her hand on the linen tablecloth. "No days off working for me yet, though. A real trooper, this one."

Alice caught the softness in her mum's eyes as she glanced at their hands.

"So, how was your trip to France then? You didn't say much about it at the house—" Eva caught Alice's eye as she placed the last drink carefully onto the table.

"On the whole, I'd say it was pretty productive. Wouldn't you?" She turned towards Victor. He ran his fingers through his hair then loosened his tie.

"Yeah, certainly productive. And never a dull moment, that's for sure. It's certainly given us plenty to be getting on with back here."

Alice smiled to herself as he shifted his cutlery to make sure it was perfectly aligned.

"So, you ready to order now?" Eva had pen and notepad at the ready as Gordon reappeared.

Alice couldn't help but watch his hands as he held the menu up in front of him. That was when it struck her that she hadn't noticed any tremors or shaking since he'd come in. He passed the menu back to Eva and turned his attention to Victor. "So, I hear you're quite the successful businessman."

Alice grimaced at the sarcasm but Victor was unfazed.

"Yeah. I've a few companies on the go at the minute, mainly—"

Gordon cut across him. "And I believe Alice is working for you now?"

She shifted in her seat as his eyes darted back to her.

Victor patted her hand. "Indeed she is. Only just started, but it's all good so far."

"Mixing business with pleasure then, eh?" Gordon half-laughed as he turned to her mum, who promptly tutted her displeasure.

"Seriously, though, you couldn't do better than this one. Pain in the backside to work with sometimes—" he winked at her, "—but I guess you already know that?"

Alice felt a surge of relief when Gordon's barbed comment resulted in the first shared laugh of the evening, just as the main courses arrived. The veritable smorgasbord of tender fillet steak, seafood risotto, the restaurant's succulent signature veal dish and aromatic vegetarian curry were met with hungry eyes and coos of delight.

By the time everyone's plates had been cleared, both wine and chat were flowing freely and the initial tension between the two men had all but gone. As she watched them all around the table; the three people who meant the most in the world to her, a warm contentment spread through Alice – a feeling that, only six months ago, she'd given up hope of ever experiencing. She secretly hoped this was a sign of things to come as dessert moved onto coffee and home time finally beckoned.

As Victor snuck away to pay the bill, Alice knew the moment had passed to announce their news. She was lost in thought when Gordon put his arm around her shoulder as they left the table. Seconds later, standing by the entrance, she folded her arms in amazement. "Well, would you look at that...?" She looked on in disbelief as her mum slipped her arms effortlessly into her long coat.

"I know, wonderful, isn't it?" she chuckled. "Started to get better not long after you dropped my pills off the last time – remember, just after your and Vincent's trip to France?"

"That's brilliant. The pills are kicking in now, then...?" Alice said, stunned at the sudden improvement. She leaned in towards Gordon who was still rolling his eyes at her mum's misnomer. "So, how're *you* doing these days? Didn't want to ask earlier—"

"You know, I'm not too bad, not too bad at all. The shaking's actually got a lot better – even today. Must be seeing you again, eh?" As he rubbed her hands between his, something began to stir in Alice's mind; a tiny, bubbling subconscious realisation that she couldn't – or rather – didn't, want to deny.

"So, everything's alright, is it? I mean with..." Gordon watched Victor chatting to her mum by the door.

"Yes. Everything's perfectly fine. Just like I said it would be." She playfully rubbed his arm. "We've plenty to catch up on, though, that's for sure."

"Oh, don't worry – I've plenty of questions I want answers to, young lady," he said, raising an eyebrow.

"So..." her mum held her back as they made for the door. "You have to look after yourself properly now. Plenty of rest and lots of good, home-made food, you hear?" She winked and leaned in towards her. "Congratulations, sweetheart. You both look so happy together."

Alice laughed as she squeezed her arm. "Jesus, you don't miss a thing, do you?"

"I'm your mother, it's my job not to miss anything. You'll understand that soon enough." She grinned as she fastened the last button on her long, navy coat.

"Can we pop round to yours tomorrow, then? Tell you both properly."

Victor narrowed his eyes at her as he stood by the door.

Alice turned towards her mum. "I'm sorry – I just couldn't get it out earlier. It was Gordon's face…"

"Look, don't worry, I'll deal with him tomorrow. Besides, he's got eyes – he can see for himself how happy you are. Isn't that all that matters?"

Alice smiled across at the man who was soon to be the father of her child. "Yeah, guess it is."

"And I'll make your favourite veggie lasagne." Her mum paused as she linked arms with her in the doorway. "But only if you tell me everything I want to know."

As they stepped outside, a blast of cool, night air was perfect for relieving the dull, throbbing headache that had been building behind her left eye ever since they'd started their desserts.

Yet, oddly, it hadn't registered until now.

Shoving her hands into her pockets, she felt first her long-neglected crystal, then the note from Charles that had been slipped inside the book, marking the section *Post-Transference for Subsequent Generations*.

She'd kept it close ever since, reading it over and over – just like the first note she'd been given all those months ago.

But apart from begging for forgiveness, this note revealed something she'd long suspected. Yes, she'd always felt there was something strange about the chateau – something unto-ward; a feeling that somehow everything wasn't quite as it seemed. That's why, when she'd searched the internet, she'd found pictures of a chateau that had stood in ruins for well over a century.

317

Yet, it still took her breath away to see the truth with her own eyes that it was actually a sacred and mystical building – a portal between past and present – reserved only for those precious few who'd worshipped the Order in a previous life.

And, that's when she finally read the book properly – twice through, from cover to cover, prophecy and all.

That's when she finally understood that everything she'd experienced had led her to this moment – to be exactly where she was meant to be – in the right place, at the right time. Destiny and fate had once again prevailed as Charles had predicted.

The Order was in her blood now and nothing could change that.

But this was just the beginning. According to the prophecy, another journey into the past was beckoning; this time with her unborn child.

Alice loosely belted her coat and took a last look around the restaurant where it had all began. She caught Eva's eye as she glanced at the clock; 10:05pm.

She smiled.

This time, Eva smiled back…

About the Author

Gillian Charnock was born in 1975 and grew up in a village on the banks of the River Tay in North East Fife.

From the age of 8, tennis was her life – resulting in various caps for representing Scotland and Britain until the age of 17. However, Higher exams and a persistent future husband conspired to stall her lofty ambitions of becoming Wimbledon champion, and a career in journalism working for D.C. Thomson soon beckoned.

Three children and a thriving family business later, the urge to write her first novel came calling thanks to a creative-writing course. 'Veil of Secrets' is the end result of Assignment 3: 'Draft a synopsis and complete the first chapter of a novel'.

Now she has the writing bit between her teeth and is currently working on the next book in the 'Secrets of the Veil' series.

If you've enjoyed reading this book and would like to know how Alice's story continues, you can keep in touch at www.gacharnock.co.uk where you can sign up for a newsletter with news and updates on the sequel plus lots more.

Gillian would love to hear any feedback on the novel or see your photos of the book in far-flung places! If you could spare a few minutes of your time to leave a review on Amazon, it would be greatly appreciated!

You can connect with me on:

🌐 https://www.gacharnock.co.uk

📘 https://www.facebook.com/gacharnock

Printed in Great Britain
by Amazon